THE WAY TO REDEMPTION

Henry Fitroy found the priests in a small study, sitting at ease in a pair of cushioned chairs on either side of a marble hearth, slippered feet stretched out toward the fire, gold rings glittering on pale fingers. Cleaned and fed, they still stank of her death.

". . . confessed to having relations with the devil, was forgiven, and gave her soul up to God. Very satisfactory all around. Shall we return the body to the Sisters or to her family?"

The older Dominican shrugged. "I cannot see that it makes any difference, she . . . Who are you?"

Henry lifted his lip off his teeth in a parody of a smile. "I am vengeance," he said, closing and bolting the heavy oak door behind him. When he turned, he saw that the younger priest, secure in the power he wielded, blinded by that security, had moved toward him.

Their eyes met. The priest, who had stood calmly by while countless *heretics* found their way to redemption on paths of pain, visibly paled.

Henry stopped pretending to smile. "And I am the devil Ginevra Treschi had relations with."

He released the Hunger her blood had called.

They died begging for their lives as Ginevra had died.

It wasn't enough.

From "Sceleratus" by Tanya Huff

THE REPENTANT

Edited by
Brian Thomsen
and
Martin H. Greenberg

DAW BOOKS, INC.
DONALD A. WOLLHEIM, FOUNDER
375 Hudson Street, New York, NY 10014
ELIZABETH R. WOLLHEIM
SHEILA E. GILBERT
PUBLISHERS
www.dawbooks.com

First Printing, October 2003
1 2 3 4 5 6 7 8 9

ACKNOWLEDGMENTS

"Introduction" by Brian Thomsen. Copyright © 2003 by Brian Thomsen

"Lycanthrope Summer" by Jeff Grubb. Copyright © 2003 by Jeff Grubb.

"The Salem Trial" by Jody Lynn Nye. Copyright © 2003 by Jody Lynn Nye.

"The Den Mother" by Edo van Belkom. Copyright © 2003 by Edo van Belkom.

"Brothers in the Flesh" by Fiona Patton. Copyright © 2003 by Fiona Patton.

"Heat" by Jean Rabe. Copyright © 2003 by Jean Rabe.

"She Dwelleth in the Cold of the Moon" by James Lowder. Copyright © 2003 by James Lowder.

"Sceleratus" by Tanya Huff. Copyright © 2003 by Tanya Huff.

"Slaughter" by P.N. Elrod. Copyright © 2003 by P.N. Elrod.

"A Hollywood Tradition" by Brian M. Thomsen. Copyright © 2003 by Brian Thomsen.

"Intercession" by Chelsea Quinn Yarbro. Copyright © 2003 by Chelsea Quinn Yarbro.

"The Devil You Know" by Nina Kiriki Hoffman. Copyright © 2003 by Nina Kiriki Hoffman.

"The Recall of Cthulhu" by Tom Dupree. Copyright © 2003 by Tom Dupree.

"Redeemed" by Allen C. Kupfer. Copyright © 2003 by Allen C. Kupfer.

CONTENTS

vii

INTRODUCTION

by Brian M. Thomsen

REMEMBER the days when the monsters were the bad guys?

What happened?

From Sam, the sexy witch housewife of *Bewitched*, to Angel, the vampire cursed with a soul, once stereotypical villains have crossed over to the side of the heroes.

Maybe it was Lon Chaney, Jr.'s self-loathing Larry Talbot (aka "the Wolfman") that engendered our sympathies, or perhaps the dark sexiness of Frank Langella (Broadway's Dracula) or *Dark Shadows'* Barnabas Collins that tipped the scales.

No matter what it was, the public has spoken and the creative community has responded.

Now even the lowest of the bad guys, soulless or bestial as they may be, can embrace the side normally relegated to the white-bread good guys of yesteryear.

Vegan werewolves, regretful demons, altruistic vampires, and even life-affirming zombies—nothing can be ruled out.

Even when you are damned, it is never too late to repent.

Who knew that Glinda's question ("Are you a good witch or a bad witch?") could be as pertinent to today's Los Angeles or New York as it was to Oz so many years ago?

Give the Repentants their second chance to make it up to humanity.

After all, there but for the grace of God and the devil's damnation may all of us soon tread.

WEREWOLVES & WITCHES

WEREWOLVES and witches have always suffered from a bad rep. From medieval times and earlier to the Bible Belt today (even when they were victims of persecution as in the days of the Inquisition or the Salem trials) the assumption is made that neither group is meant to be trusted.

Who wants to be around someone who is sleeping with the devil or bestial in actions and appetites? (Assumptions misinformed at best.)

Among our repentants today are a lycanthrope more akin to our loyal canine companions and a witch more reminiscent of the Charmed Ones than the foil of Hansel and Gretel.

True, there may be dark maidens in league with the devil out there, and ravenous wolves in accountant's clothing . . . but next time you come across a furry friend in a woolly coat, give him the benefit of the doubt.

Maybe you'll be asked home for supper?

LYCANTHROPE SUMMER

by Jeff Grubb

Jeff Grubb is the bestselling author of numerous novels in the *Dragonlance, Forgotten Realms*, and *Magic: The Gathering* lines of game-related novels, as well as an award-winning game designer. In addition to numerous short stories, Jeff has also authored several comic books. He currently resides in the Pacific Northwest.

THE farms were the best for running. During the day heavy hooves pounded the earth flat and peglike teeth kept the grass cut low. The wolf could make great speed here, and let itself loose, running for the mere sake of running. Not toward anything. Not away from anything. Just running.

It reached the end of the field and jumped the low cross-tied fence. The next field was fallow, uneven from the passage of a plow earlier in the season, with weeds growing up in the ridges. The field beyond that was coming in with corn, higher than the wolf's shoulders, already tasseling. A place to lose things. A place to hide, but not a place to run. So the wolf arched away from this cluttered field.

Another fence and onto the road. This one led down to the lake, a distant black pool that shimmered with its own sleeping evil. The wolf sat down and raised its head to howl, to keep the evil contained.

The wolf did not see the truck until the machine was almost on top of it. The truck crested a low rise, and its single working headlight skewered him like a lance.

The wolf was stunned, but only for a moment. The truck honked. Then another part of its brain took over, and it rose on its hind legs, and ran clear of the road. It gripped the top rail of the fence and dived over, curling up in the darkness of the other side. Its wolf brain said it should keep running. Its other brain said no.

There was a squeal of ancient brakes. The truck slowed. There were voices, but no one got out. Then, slowly, it picked its way up again, and the humans were gone once more.

Now the wolf let go of its other brain and let itself run again, back the way it came. Over the earthen waves of the fallow field. Over the second fence. Back to the horse-cropped field. Far from the roads.

Only then, alone in the field, did the wolf let out a prideful howl

They had rules. He had rules for her. Schoolwork before TV. Be home before curfew. And most of all, don't do something illegal or stupid, because he would have to come down on her twice as hard as he would have to for one of her friends.

She had rules for him. Call her Eleanor, not Ellen or Ellie or Red or—Good Lord—not Pumpkin. Don't try to cook something from a recipe in the newspaper, no matter how good an idea it seems at the time. And most of all, don't embarrass her to death in front of her friends.

So when Jim Summers came into Talbot's and saw her in a booth at the far end of the diner with Peggy Munroe and a young woman he didn't recognize, he didn't go up to her right away. Instead, he seated himself at one of the stools, near the door. The old mongrel dog Igor, sprawled nearby, raised a saliva-roped muzzle and whined at him until he rubbed it behind the ears.

Igor gave Jim more notice than his own daughter in public. But that was one of the rules.

He was seated near the door, and could still hear the old cruiser ticking softly in the summer night as its engine cooled. He took off his hat and ran a hand up over his balding pate. He used to do it when he had hair, to straighten it. Now the motion was just a relic of the past.

Old Marie behind the counter knew the routine, knew the rules. She came up with a double-wide slab of pie crowned with a thin crescent of vanilla ice cream—just enough to make him feel good, not enough to make Eleanor worry about his weight. Marie served the pie, stepped back two paces, and folded her pipestem-thin arms in front of her prim apron. This was one of the rules they had, him and Marie. She wouldn't reengage again until he said something. Instead, she'd just wait like a vulture.

"Good pie," he ventured after a forkful.

"You deserve pie," said Marie, her thick accent still clinging to her after twenty years in Lake Bern. She was originally from some part of Chicago, an hour's drive south of Lake County, but her voice always made him think of old cartoons. In another life she would be chasing Moose and Squirrel. "Hear you bring down Olsen boy this afternoon."

Summers shrugged, "Everyone knew he was

breaking into people's houses. He just got careless this time."

"Hear you chase him three blocks. Through back-yards. Down alleys. He outrun three deputies. But not you." She pointed a chin at him for emphasis.

He shrugged again, "Where did you hear that?"

"Perry in earlier. You outrun him, too," she said.

"Perry talks too much," he said. "Good pie. So what's *their* story?"

Marie didn't even turn around—she knew that would spook Eleanor. "Big shot. From the coast."

"Which one?" he asked, forking another morsel into his mouth.

"West," said Marie. "TV folk. Girl looks like she fell asleep in tackle box. Rings on face. Earring on tongue. Bah!"

Jim used the last of the ice cream to pick up the crumbs around the perimeter of the plate. "Why is she here?" The unspoken question was *why is she talking to my little girl?*

"Some kind TV show. Ghosts and monsters. They shut up real good when I come by, but Old Marie hear real good, even now." She managed a lean grin.

He sighed. Eleanor hadn't said anything about it at breakfast, their normal time for cross-checking and rumors. Was this something that she had not mentioned, or something that just happened? There had been a lot of things that "just happened" this summer already.

He allowed himself a glance at the group in the far booth. Always a bit of a risk, making Eleanor flustered, but he still worried about her. If Eleanor didn't do anything, he would take his hat, pay the tab, and head back to the cruiser.

She been staring at him the entire time while he

was talking with Marie. When he looked up, she raised both eyebrows and ratcheted her head backward.

Okay. This was different. She was at the age when even the shadow of her old man was enough to send her into a teenaged slouch. Now he got the come-ahead.

He took his time paying the bill anyway.

She half rose from the booth and pecked him on the cheek, then brushed a strand of her flame-red hair out of her face. That was new as well, something she would do leaving the house, but never in public. Never in front of friends.

"Wanda, this is my father," she said, "This is Wanda."

The dark-suited, dark-haired woman half rose, but the table kept her mostly to her seat. "Sheriff Summers," he said, and offered a strong grip. This was someone who was used to shaking hands as daily business. Despite that, the silver rings on her fingers were all angles, and Summers fought the urge to wince.

"I'm Wanda Oland. NewReal Productions," she said. Her smile was cautious, but her eyes were alive. Predatory. Almost feral.

Old Marie was right. This Oland looked like she would jingle if she shook her head. She had at least a half-dozen rings in one ear, more in the other, a pair of slender hoops in one nostril, and another pair at the corner of her eyebrow. A flash of silver danced on her tongue as she talked. The reek of spiced tobacco hung on her jacket. She looked too young to be trusted with anything like real responsibility, and too old to be hanging around with a pair of teen-aged girls.

Jim Summers was prepared to start hating her right then and there.

What had Eleanor gotten into this time? he wondered, pulling up a chrome chair to the end of the booth and settling himself on it. The chair complained only mildly.

Eleanor filled in the details, "Wanda is part of the *New Reality* show." She paused as if that meant something.

"I'm afraid I'm not familiar with it," Jim said. Eleanor gave him one of the "my-father-is-the-most-primitive-man-on-the-planet" looks.

"Syndication," oozed Wanda. "Fastest growing new show in its genre." She paused for the factoid to sink in for a moment, then continued, "In addition to the show, we run a Web site for paranormal activity. Got a message about your werewolf. I'm here to do some scouting."

She was looking for a reaction from the sheriff. Jim considered several, then settled on a rather perturbed look at his daughter. "You saw a wolf and didn't tell me?"

"I didn't." said Eleanor, "Peggy did."

Jim Summers turned his baleful eye on Peggy Munroe. Without the years of resistance built up from being his blood relative, the girl was unprepared. She seemed to pull back in on herself, edging along the booth toward the window. "I didn't think it was important at the time. I mean, it was weird and all."

Jim Summers let out a chuckle and shook his head. He tipped his hat back, exposing a forehead that would best be called a five-head. "So why don't you tell me and the nice person from syndicated television what you saw."

Peggy Munroe looked at Eleanor, and Eleanor nodded. Eleanor was the pack leader of her little clique, and Peggy, usually one of the peripheral hangers-on, was a part of it this summer. Joyce was at horse camp and Cindy at cheer camp and Becky was seeing the Grand Canyon with family and Amanda was spending some time with her father in Orlando, which was just as well, because Amanda was known to be sneaking smokes between classes. That left Peggy and Eleanor, and Peggy could be talked into anything.

Peggy took a deep breath, looked at Wanda and at the sheriff, then said, "So I was driving down Bonard Road, late Saturday night, about four weeks back," she started.

Jim almost pointed out that Peggy had a Cinderella license and wasn't old enough to drive past ten yet, but restrained himself. Making the girl confront her crime would shut her up, and he wanted to hear what she had to say. Instead, he looked at Eleanor, but his daughter was watching Wanda Oland.

"I was right near where the old Drive-In Road comes in at the angle, when I saw what I thought was a large dog. There in the intersection. I slowed and honked at it, thinking it was just a farm dog. Then it stood up."

"It was sitting on the ground in the intersection?" asked Summers.

Peggy Munroe shook her blonde head. "No, it was standing up on four legs in the intersection, like it was watching for something. Looking down toward the old drive-in by the lake. Then it stood up on two legs. Like a man."

"Sure it wasn't a man?" said Summers. "Maybe some transient, or some kid who was out checking out the new highway extension?" Inside his head, he added *or someone who was partying in the woods too late*?

Again with the head shake, "I mean I saw it stand up like a man, then bound over the fence."

"Like a man, or like a wolf?" asked Summers.

"Do you believe her?" asked Wanda, her own face smiling with a lupine interest. This was a predator as well.

"I believe she believes," said Summers curtly. "And I want to know what she thinks she saw,"

Peggy looked confused, "What do you mean?"

"He jumped over the fence," repeated Summers. "Like a man jumps a hurdle, or like a hound jumps, head first?"

Peggy thought for a moment, and Summers knew she was trying to create an answer. "Like a wolf," she said at last.

Jim Summers made the grunting noise he always made when he wanted people to think he had discovered something. "And then?"

"And then, what?" said Eleanor, rushing to Peggy's defense like a good attorney.

"What did you do then, Peggy Munroe?" Summers wanted to make sure that it was Peggy that answered.

A long moment, then Peggy put in, "I went home. It was late."

"She didn't do anything wrong," put in Eleanor.

"I don't see any crime here at all," said Jim, putting aside the curfew violation, "You saw a large animal in the road. It left. You left."

Peggy paused for a moment. There was something else here, but it was a small thing. Peggy probably wasn't alone, Jim realized. At last, she said, "Yes, sir."

"And you didn't tell anyone," said Jim Summers.

Peggy shot a look at Eleanor and Jim was sure that if Peggy was ever part of a criminal group she would not last out a week. "Nosir," she ventured.

"You didn't tell your folks or call the police?" asked Summers.

"Nosir."

"Weren't you frightened?" His eyebrows shot up again, furry lines against the front of his brow.

"Yeah, but . . ." she paused. "I mean, when it stood up, I thought it was a dog, and it wasn't. I was frightened. A little."

"But you didn't tell anyone."

"No," said Peggy, then shook her head and let the teenage logic leak out. "I mean, people would laugh at me if I told wild stories."

"Right," said Jim Summers, very aware of Wanda's eyes upon him. "So you called these TV people in instead."

"She used the Internet," volunteered Wanda, her eyes never leaving Jim Summers' face.

The prey had been through here—its scent was heavy on the grass. It had dodged into the brambles, sure the wolf would not follow. Indeed, a lesser hunter would either give up the chase, or, if hungry enough, pursue it through the tangles, snarling its fur on the raspberry thorns.

Instead, the wolf circled the patch of briars. The tangle was small enough that the prey would dash through it. The wolf picked up the scent on the far side and was off again, through the woods and heavy ferns of the underbrush. Overhead a flock of some-things chattered in the darkness, their bat-shrieks just gracing the top range of the wolf's hearing.

At last the prey went to ground, huddled beneath the granite tangle of a glacial moraine. A green-eyed cat, abandoned by some summer tourists and gone feral. It was backed into a corner, its eyes wide, its fur puffed up to make it appear larger, its feline mouth gaping in short fangs that could not cut through the fur, much less the flesh.

The wolf regarded its prey for the moment, then, content with the hunt, turned back for its lair. It had been a good chase, but the sun was already blooding the eastern horizon.

It was time for breakfast.

Breakfast together. Another rule, though neither one seemed to remember whose it was. Sometimes Summers would be coming in when Eleanor was going out.

"You put her up to it," he said simply as she laid out the griddle cakes.

"Daaad," said Eleanor. "She saw what she saw."

"I didn't say she didn't," said Jim

"She sent the message," said Eleanor, and a bit of teenage whine crawled into her voice.

"The Munroes don't have Internet access," said Jim calmly, "ever since her brother got caught with all those pinup pictures on his hard drive."

"She could still have Internet access," said Eleanor.

"But she doesn't," said Jim, trying hard to not let his voice fall into police mode. "You do, though."

"She wrote the message herself," said Eleanor, not answering the question, and of course answering it at the same time.

Jim nodded; he had gotten the answer he needed. The rest of the meal was relatively cordial—small talk about chores. As she headed out the door, she pecked him on the cheek. No offense taken for the cross-examination.

"One more thing. Ms. Oland wants to talk to you if you get a chance," she said on her way out. "She's staying at the Motel 6 out by the Interchange."

Just before noon he had a chance to check out Ms. Oland.

She had a room at the Six, but wasn't in. Old Nowlan behind the desk was more than willing to let Summers have a look-see at the room, and watched as the sheriff moved around. One suitcase, open, with some badly rumpled shirts and jackets jammed into it. Basic toiletries in the sink. The desk was piled with books from the Lake Bern public library. Local lore and legends. Community history. A pamphlet on the old Indian mounds found down by the lake.

Other than that, nothing out of the ordinary.

"If she's a reporter," said Summers, "where are her notes?"

"She had a second bag," volunteered Nowlan from the door. "Heavy thing. Left with it this morning."

Summers nodded and made a guttural noise. Then he let Nowlan lock up again.

Summers shoved the problem to the back of his mind and took care of basic business. A domestic dispute over a lawnmower. A report of a broken window. Some beer cans found behind a garage that the eldest son swore, just swore, had to belong to someone else.

He found Wanda Oland at the intersection where old Drive-In Road met Bonard. The drive-in had been abandoned for the better part of twenty years, but the broad concrete slab of its screen rose over the low trees in the distance. The screen backed Lake Bern itself, and there was a dustup in the '50s when they put it up, replacing old Indian mounds with a pale monolith. There was another dustup in the '80s when they abandoned it because everyone in town was getting cable and VCRs.

Daylight did not improve Ms. Oland's complexion, and Summers wondered what would happen if the rings heated up in the sun. She was squatting, the back of her black jacket hanging inches above the dirt road, like she was sniffing for something. Her rental, a silver-tan vehicle of anonymous heritage, was pulled over to the side.

"It could have happened," said Wanda. "There was a fence over here. That could be the one he dived over."

Summers nodded, and said "Yep. You definitely have a fence. Pretty suspicious, I would say."

Oland let out a lupine grin, and said, "You don't believe her story."

Summers shrugged and repeated what he had said the night before, "I believe that she believes. She saw something then. Maybe a prowler. Maybe a woodchuck. Since then . . ." He let his words trail off.

"Pretty big woodchuck," said Oland, pacing off the distance between the center of the intersection and the suspect fence. "Where does this lead?"

"Fields," said Summers, "Johnson's farm, followed by the Weis place. Then my family's farm."

"You have a farm?"

"I just rent out the fields now," said Jim, removing his hat and spreading the sweat back over his bald spot.

Oland rested both hands on the fence. "You don't seem too surprised by all this."

Summers shrugged, "Things like this have happened before around here. UFOs in the '50s. Lake Bern was supposed to have its own sea monster back at the turn of the century. We had one feller in the '70s that set up shark fins in the snow one winter, trying to start a snow shark craze."

Oland managed another lean smile, "You think this is a hoax, then."

"Wouldn't say that," said Summers. "I would say that a young girl saw something and has convinced herself it's what you think it is. And as a result you're out here and giving her and her friends a lot more attention than they would otherwise get during a sleepy summer. Long as you don't rile up a lot of people too much, I don't see the harm. There is one thing you should know."

"Yeah?"

"The Munroe truck is a padiddle."

"Pah-what?"

"Padiddle. It has a bum headlight. If Peggy was driving that night, and she shouldn't have been, she wouldn't have been able to see too well. Without two headlights, shadows would look deeper, and things bigger than they should be."

"How do you know that? About the headlight?"

"In a county this small you get to know everything."

Oland turned to face Summers. "Sheriff, I like your attitude. I've had problems with small-town law before."

Summers allowed another shrug, "I'm county patrol. We take the larger view. But I'm still not going to stock up on silver bullets yet."

Oland smiled. "Silver affects some werewolves. There are Native American wolf-men, called skinwalkers, that are not affected at all."

"If you say so," said Summers calmly.

Oland said, "I'm going to hang around a bit, you know."

"Figured as much," said Summers, "Full moon's coming. That applies to both types of werewolves, I assume."

Behind him, Perry on the squad radio blurgled something. The tone was urgent, frustrated. Summers headed for the cruiser.

"Sheriff!" shouted Oland. "What happened to that snow shark fellow?"

"The fad didn't catch on. He ended up with a warehouse full of plywood fins," said Summers, and dodged back inside the cruiser.

As Jim pulled away, he watched Oland watching him. Then he switched on the mike for Julie at the station, and asked her to make a few phone calls.

Perry met him at the highway extension, where a new Route 50 was coming in to join the Interchange at the far side of the city. Many of the real small towns along old Route 50—Gorton's Corners, Rateliff, and Donovan—were being bypassed, but the new route was going to eventually spill out in the heart of Lake Bern, a concrete river bringing in a tide of summer tourists.

Summers could tell there were problems before he got there. There was even less activity than normal for a state crew, except right at the center of a tight knot of suntanned road workers was a bearded man. And Perry, of course, a beanpole among the rest.

Most of the crew were Native American, and looked more amused than insulted as the bearded man waved around a handful of rocks.

"This was obviously a Neolithic hunting camp!" shouted the bearded man at the foreman, who was apparently unimpressed with the revelation.

"What seems to be the problem?" said Summers, more to Perry than anyone else.

"Professor Maxim here has found some Indian . . ." Perry hesitated for a moment, "Native American relics, and wants the men to stop."

"As is my right," said the professor. "The law clearly states that if Native American artifacts are found, it is necessary to immediately ascertain their value."

The foreman, Bill Makepeace, seemed less than impressed with their value. "Those are old arrowheads. You find them in any field around here."

"*In situ!*" shouted the professor, as if the words were an incantation. "*In situ!* Take a look at the location and you'll see that there are obvious signs of a hunting camp. And the flaking!" He held up one of the flint tips for Summers to see, briefly. "This is late Neolithic pattern, if anything! You normally don't see this east of Madison!"

Summers made a low, decision-making grunt and said, "Perry, you go take a look at the *situ*, will you?"

"Sheriff, I . . ."

"Go take a look, I want to talk about this to Billy Makepeace."

Perry shuffled off, the professor haranguing him every step of the way, a small dog struggling to keep up with Perry's long strides.

Makepeace started in immediately. "It's a Saturday, Jim. I'm working double shifts already to get this done before the frost, and the project manager is climbing my back. Now this. He'll hold us up for weeks, maybe even until fall."

"So you're usually better at keeping the professor away from these things. What happened here?"

Makepeace gave him a long look, then said, "We found something else. Nastier than a few arrowheads."

"Something else" was under a heavy tarp. Makepeace gave an aggrieved look at where Maxim was lecturing Perry on stoneworking technology. Beneath the canvas was a gaping hole.

"Almost lost a grader to it," said Makepeace. "And while we were checking it out, the professor wandered up and found his arrowheads."

Summers pulled out his belt flashlight and shone

it into the cave. Inside was flat-bottomed, with a slash of colored chalk within. The sheriff put his hat aside, straightened hair that was no longer there, and let himself down into the room.

The room was low-ceilinged and rough-walled. This had been dug here and abandoned. There were human bones along one wall.

But it was the chalk inscription on the cell's floor that caught Summer's eyes. He walked around it, hunching his shoulders.

It was a circle of wolves, each wolf chasing the next wolf's tail. In the center was a black pool, from which a serpentine head and neck rose. The wolves had surrounded the thing in the pool. After a moment, he realized the wolves had human hands, and were carrying weapons.

"Ever see anything like it?" said Summers.

Makepeace had to admit that he had not.

"Here's a story. There were monsters in those days, so the Creator Spirit charged the wolves to protect people from them. Some of the wolves liked protecting the people too well, and became dogs. Some liked it even more, and were able to wear human skins. Never hear of it?"

Makepeace said, "Not my tribe. The stories I always heard as a kid referred to wolves in terms of evil men who could take wolf form."

"Skinwalkers," said Summers, thinking of his earlier conversation.

"Whatever," said Billy Makepeace. "Nasty magicians, they could turn into wolves or other animals. Big-time wizards. Scared me when I was a kid." He paused for a moment, then said, "I didn't know you were one of the People."

"Grandmother's side." Summers shrugged. "But I got the story from a book in the library. You get to know all the history of these small towns, you hang around long enough. But you're right. Some tribes say the wolf is an evil man's spirit. Some say that it is a spirit that has forgotten its true purpose. And it remembers its purpose when the monsters stir."

"I don't know about that," said Makepeace, looking at the altar in the center. "I do know that it gives me the creeps. I think we're better off burying it again."

"You don't mind the loss of your people's heritage?" asked Summers.

Makepeace chuckled. "My grandfather's people moved here in the 1600s, a hundred years before the whites got here. We moved in when the previous locals got horses and left for the plains. This place isn't part of *my* native heritage. But don't tell the project manager that—he trusts my native instinct."

"Then I suggest you pave over this part, and fast," said Summers, and went back to where the professor was still arguing with Perry. He had to tell him there wasn't anything he could do, and a few arrowheads weren't going to stop Route 50 from reaching Lake Bern.

Dinner, Saturday night. A rare evening meal when the two of them were home at the same time.

"I want you home by ten tonight," he said.

"Daaaad!" The cry of the wounded teenager.

"By ten. I don't want you breaking curfew."

"Daaaad!"

"No argument. I want you home."

Saturday night. Full moon brings out all the nutcases.

Two brawls, one at the Shack and one at the Old

Irish Inn, both over women. Perry had to deal with an overdose until the EMTs from county hospital arrived. Minor fender-bender made worse by short tempers and alcohol. Tourists up from Illinois got their travelers' checks stolen.

And then in the middle of it, Julie at the switchboard said Eleanor called. Said it was urgent. Call her.

"What's up?" said Jim.

"Peggy's gone," Eleanor's voice was husky, worried on the other end.

"What do you mean gone?" said Jim.

"We were supposed to meet at Talbot's, and she didn't show."

"Maybe something came up."

"I called her folks. She's supposed to be with me."

"Okay, I'll check around. You stay put."

"Daaad. I think something is wrong."

"Then you stay put," said Jim.

It was after eleven. Peggy should have been at home. Curfew. Jim drove by the Six. Ms. Oland's rental car was missing.

Checked in with Julie. She couldn't raise anyone at NewReality. It was Saturday, after all. Meanwhile, the EMTs had arrived. Perry was now handling a family disturbance.

Jim Summers drove out to Bonard Road. He killed the lights and drifted the last hundred yards.

The Munroes' truck, the one with the bum headlight, was off to the side, almost in the ditch. Summers flashed a light within. No one in there. He listened for a long moment, feeling nothing but the pull of the moon. Nothing.

Summers popped the trunk of the cruiser and carefully stripped. He pulled out the trunk key he kept on a chain and put it over his head. He looked up to the full moon, and slowly inhaled, and let the other brain take over.

At once he was aware of his location, not just as a point on the map, but as a part of the entire whole. The silent woods was now alive with prey—rabbits and mice and moles. The feral cat was out, but watchful and nervous. The scent of deer musk hung in the air, along with the silken pollen of tasseled corn carried on night moth wings.

And spiced tobacco. And the burned petrocarbons of a car exhaust, heading south toward the old drive-in.

Summers let the other brain take him, the brain that was part of the land. It was easiest during the full moon, easiest to change all the way. His body lowered and grew shaggier, his jaw elongated into a muzzle, his ears lengthened and grew more keen. It felt right, like throwing on a comfortable jacket, or kicking off an old blanket on a warm summer night.

Now, as the other brain took over, he could hear chanting in the distance. A single voice, female.

Summers ran, ran like he was chasing prey, not with freedom but with fear at what he would find at the other end.

The old screen was still there, its back to the lake. Summers ran through the parking lot, the empty rusted speaker supports like thin gravestones. Parked near the screen was a recent-model rental, its color indeterminate in the full moon.

On the other side was Oland, of course, dressed in heavy robes, a large bag open at her feet. Thick candles had been laid out around the ground, and in the center was the prostrate, unconscious form of Peggy Munroe.

Oland was smiling, and when she spoke, her face

seemed to distort and lengthen. Her chant became more of a howl. There was a soft jingle as her various piercings shifted along her ears and brows to take a more lupine appearance.

She paused, stopping the howl, and spoke. Summers could understand the words.

"Hello, Sheriff," said Oland. "Yes, I know who you are and what you are. There are those humans that became wolves, and those wolves that became human. You are one group. I am the other. We are natural enemies. The old werewolves of this area— the wolves that became men—were charged with keeping the creature beneath Lake Bern in its slumber. Now I will awaken it, and it will answer to me."

Summers crouched and leaped, his jaws wide to attack, to bowl over the skinwalker.

Oland smiled and dodged to one side, lashing out with a ring-bedecked, claw-slight hand.

Summers felt pain as the rings and claws sliced through his shoulders. His other brain, his human brain, called for discipline, but the part that was a wolf was enraged. He landed badly, sprawling, and wheeled to attack again.

Oland muttered something, her claws tracing a pattern in the air.

Summers tried to spring but could not. Tried to leap but could not. Tried to howl but found only a block of pain in his throat.

Oland laughed. "When I saw a note from Lake Bern on the BBS, I had to check it out. For where there are wolf-men, there are things the wolf-men must protect. And when I read about the lake monsters, and you mentioned them, I knew I had hit the jackpot."

Summers let out a snarl that ended up more of a whine.

"Don't worry, Sheriff. I'll get you a nice leash when all of this is done." With that, Oland turned back to her task.

The language of her chant was archaic now, inhuman, unheard since long before the Native Americans reached the shores of Lake Bern. She intoned a nearly unpronounceable string of syllables, and intoned again, pleading with the creature beneath to awaken, to respond, to accept her offering. To grant her power for her sacrifice.

Summers tried to move, but found he could not escape. His mind was bound by the skinwalker's spell. His other mind, his human mind, was functioning within the wolf form, but it was slamming against walls it could not detect. As long as the skinwalker chanted, he was held in place.

Oland's voice rose, and beneath the full moon the inky waters of the lake began to bubble. They started to coalesce into something ropy and sinuous, twining upon itself and gaining more power as it edged closer to the shore.

The creature of the drawing. The monster in the lake. The beast kept at bay by the howl of a wolf. Awakening now. And still Summers could not move.

Oland's voice rose again, and Peggy Munroe shifted, as if in an uneasy dream. The thing in the lake was near the shore now, and its spatulate tendrils now grasped at the soil and tried to clamber onto the dry land, for the first time in centuries.

Summers strained against the edges, and knew that should the beast within the lake emerge and be tamed, he would become a wolf forever. The other mind would go away, and he would always be a wolf. They would find his cruiser with the clothes in the trunk and write it off as one more mystery.

And Summers hated mysteries.

Summers pressed his mind forward, his other mind, and tested the mental restraints. Nothing. He pressed again, and again, and finally felt himself edge forward, just a little, his other mind pushing past the wolf form.

He would be too late. Like a horde of black serpents, the tendrils were weaving their way out of the lake and up to the pale screen. Up to the offered sacrifice.

He would be too late.

Then there was a blur of fiery reddish fur to Summers' right and Oland's chanting was suddenly cut off. The robed figure was toppled by a second wolf, this one much younger. It had Oland by the throat, and was batting her back and forth savagely.

With the chant's demise, Summers felt the restraints move. He looked at the tendrils coming ashore. They were almost at Peggy Munroe's feet.

He leaped for the young woman, grasped her gently at the shoulder, and pulled her up, toward the screen. Then he turned to Oland and the new wolf.

Oland was still alive, her arms flailing helplessly. There was blood down the front of her robes, and the new wolf straddled her weakened body, dodging her frail, silver-clad blows, her jaws locked around her throat.

Summers growled. The new wolf stopped, then growled back. Summers' growl grew louder, more menacing. The new wolf dropped its tail, and backed off two paces.

Summers looked at Oland. Throat crushed, but not dead. Bleeding, but not dead. If someone ran for the cruiser, they might be able to get help.

But what then? What would happen after that?

Summers looked at the tendrils snaking up, into the circle of candles now. He looked at the other wolf. He looked at Oland.

He sat down. The other wolf sat down. The tendrils reached Oland's foot, and snared it.

The skinwalker's eyes shot open in pain at the tendrils' first touch. She opened her mouth to scream, but only frothy, bloody bubbles emerged. The tendrils tightened around her foot, and slowly started to drag her down to the lake.

She tried to scream again, and brought up more blood. Her hands tried to gain purchase on the ground. She managed to roll over, but only succeeded in leaving a long, bloody smear along the grass and into the cattails of the lake.

As Oland was pulled down, Summers let out a howl. Not one of triumph, but of hope. One to lock the creature in again.

The new wolf howled as well, alongside him.

Then the red-furred wolf was gone, back through the woods, retracing its path. Summers padded back to the cruiser, transforming his shape with long practice, and pulled the key from around his neck. He dressed, reporting in that there seemed to be some activity down near the Old Drive-in and that he was going to check it out.

Peggy Munroe was still asleep when he got there.

Sunday morning breakfast. Sausage. Griddlecakes. Hot cereal. Juice. A thick stack of the *Chicago Tribune*. Not on duty until noon.

"How's the shoulder?" asked Eleanor.

"Sore, but well enough," said Jim sourly. "What did I say about you staying home?"

"If I didn't, she would have cooked your goose," said Eleanor.

"Nevertheless. You were out past curfew. Twice."

"Twice?"

"Once last night," said Jim Summers, "and once last month, with Peggy Munroe."

"That wasn't me on the road. I was in the truck with Peggy."

"Like I said, you broke curfew twice. This month and last."

Silence. The long silence of a teen unjustly punished, in her opinion. Finally the dam broke and the words came out in a torrent.

"Daaad. The wolf she saw had a big bald spot on its back. That was you she spotted on the road. It was all I could do to convince her to not make a bigger stink about it. I didn't really think they would send anyone. But it was you on that road. Not me."

"You're right," said Jim. "But that's completely different."

But despite further questioning, Eleanor could not find out why.

THE SALEM TRIAL

by Jody Lynn Nye

Jody Lynn Nye lists her main career activity as "spoiling cats." She lives northwest of Chicago with two of the above and her husband, author and packager Bill Fawcett. She has written twenty-two books, including four contemporary fantasies, three SF novels, four novels in collaboration with Anne McCaffrey, including *The Ship Who Won*, a humorous anthology about mothers, *Don't Forget Your Spacesuit, Dear*, and over sixty short stories. Her latest books are *The Grand Tour*, third in her new fantasy epic series, *The Dreamland*, and *Applied Mythology*, an omnibus of the Mythology 101 series.

"**W**ITCH," a low voice muttered as Sara Fuller Brooke, clutching her briefcase, shouldered her way out of the courtroom. The lawyer, thirty, dark-haired, with attractive if sharp features, stylish but conservative in a dark red suit, stood in the white-painted corridor looking around at faces in the crowd near the door, trying to find the person who had spoken. Bad start, she thought. Her very first trial motions in her new home of Salem, Massachusetts, and already she had made someone angry. Good. It was her job to win. Her client, the plaintiff in an acrimonious employment contract dispute, was

36

going to get a goodly chunk of money. The nine-million-dollar settlement they were asking for wouldn't stand up on appeal, but in the end Carmichael Paper Products was going to end up paying out five figures, if not seven. Her client did not have the most sympathetic character. Sara could tell the jury hated him, but that missed the point: that ageism was illegal, and blatant ageism could be proved.

Once she stood in the street, looking around at the autumn afternoon watching other people hurrying busily past the Colonial-era buildings, she realized she really had nowhere to go, and nowhere she needed to be. Though she'd lived in Salem for more than a month, she hadn't made friends yet, and there was no cultural event of compelling interest she wished to attend. What a difference from Boston, where the social life was like the traffic: if you didn't move aside, it would run you over.

It didn't matter at present. She wanted to get back to her research project at the library. Peace and quiet would be welcome after a stimulating afternoon of outwitting opposing counsel. Sara started walking, enjoying the fresh air and the process of discovery.

The library smelled comfortably of old wood and old books. Sara settled herself at one end of a long walnut table in the reference room with her back to the door. She disliked being watched while she was reading, but the bad-tempered woman at the desk had pointed out that too many priceless pages had been abstracted from priceless records with razor blades when thieves had privacy. Sara didn't like being tarred with the same brush, but she couldn't dispute the purpose. She was the Brooke family historian. The quiet reference room was proving to be a very good source of information of genealogical records. Her line could be traced back to Salem on her mother's great-great-grandfather's side. She had started out with records dating from just before that grandfather had registered the birth of his first child in Boston, steadily moving back through history.

Everyone here was mad about genealogy, she mused, paging through a two hundred-year-old parish record under the watchful eye of the gorgonlike reference librarian, a woman in her fifties with short brown hair framing a virtually square face with narrow brown eyes and a pursed, lipless mouth. Several people, also with antique tomes in front of them, nodded approvingly at her as she made notes on a handy legal pad.

Most of what she was finding confirmed what the family knew already. By following the records of births, marriages, and deaths backward, she gleaned ages, maiden names of brides, numbers of children both alive and dead, and cadet branches of the family that had shot off over the decades into greater Massachusetts or another part of the world entirely. The same names appeared generation after generation. If there was a James, it popped up again, either as the son of the former or a nephew, and certainly a grandson. Women were often called after their mothers, too. Sara was used to it by now, but it once shocked her to see references to Mary, Jr., or Hannah, Jr. The great-grandfather was noted in the early records of Boston to have descended from a line of Jacobs, but it was the wives she was interested in, a host of Marys, Anns, Elizabeths, Bridgets, and Abigails. One distant grandfather had come from Salem with his wife in the early 1700s. Her father had sent them to Boston with money to set the young man up as his man of business in import and export. Beyond that Sara knew little about them, but hoped she could find out. A similar name caught her eye in the midst of birth records at the turn of the eighteenth century. Could this be a long-lost cousin? Sara grabbed her pencil and swiftly jotted down the details.

The crabbed writing in the ancient documents was often hard to read. By the time she looked up again, she realized it was late evening. She stretched her back, glad to move again. The gorgon at the desk glared at her until Sara returned the huge book to the desk, but her voice was civil when she spoke.

"Did you find what you were looking for?" the woman asked.

"Yes," Sara said, delighted to share her success so soon. "The records are so complete. This time I have really found something. It seems that one of my many-times-great-grandmothers was the daughter of Nathaniel Saltonstall."

"The Trials," the gorgon said, and Sara could hear the capital "T" in her voice.

"He was the judge who resigned because he was disgusted with the miscarriage of justice," Sara corrected her sharply.

"Know all about them, do you?"

"Certainly," Sara said, glaring back. "I suppose you were there?"

"I'm a Burroughs," the gorgon said, eying her with an expression that trumped anything Sara could have produced. The shock of hearing the name caused Sara to pause.

"I know who you are," Sara said.

"And I know *what* you are," the woman said, almost gloatingly. "But you don't."

Sara felt all eyes upon her. Most of the people who remained in the reading room were looking at her as she picked up her books and withdrew from the room. The librarian was a descendant of Burroughs,

the chief prosecutor of the notorious and unjust
Salem Witch Trials, and proud of it. Well, Sara was
proud to learn one of her ancestors had at least stood
up for his principles, if he couldn't do anything to
halt the travesty that went on.

Funny how that series of events, now more than
three hundred years in the past, continued to affect
those who lived in the present day. Salem had the
figure of a witch flying on a broomstick embossed
into the pavement where sidewalks crossed. It was
simultaneously proud and ashamed of a period that
in Sara's opinion was one of the darkest and most
horrifying times in American history. But the Salem
Trials were living history, and she had just found
confirmation that she was part of it.

Before she left the building, she hunted down the
library manager and told her what she thought of
the insolent woman at the reading room desk. Sara
informed her that it looked bad for Salem to allow
an employee to insult strangers. The manager, wearing an expression that said she'd heard the complaint
before, promised to look into it. Satisfied, Sara withdrew, and thought no more of the reference librarian.
It was well past her usual dinner time, and she
was hungry.

The morning sun hit the center of the empty book-
shelves set into the wall of Sara's office. Her professional building was so new she was still having to
look for books in boxes that lay on the floor. She'd
been able to afford a very nice place, thanks to the
timely arrival of a check representing a handsome
sum generated by her fee from handling a personal
injury settlement that had survived the appeal process. The grand white frame house in the middle of
town dated to 1730 or earlier. Most of the rooms

were small, but over the protests of the local historical commission she had knocked out the wall between two of the first-floor sitting rooms for her
personal office, pointing out that they were not part
of the original structure. In fact, she would be within
her rights to knock out more walls, since her research
told her this part of the house had once been a ball-
room. She had the survey to prove it, and the commission was forced to withdraw its objections only
days before the carpenters arrived.

Her secretary occupied a smaller chamber off the
main hall, formerly a cloakroom; luckily from the
days before plumbing. At the moment Sara lived in
the upstairs rooms, awaiting completion of the brand
new condominium building where she would be living. At the back of her mind was the letter to file
suit against the developers if they didn't pick up the
pace; the building should have been ready for occu-
pancy three months ago. She was sure she could get
several of the other disappointed owners in on a
class-action suit. If not, she meant to go ahead re-
gardless. She was in the right, and that was all that
mattered. She put a calf-bound volume of historical
opinions on the shelf. Her predecessors would certainly agree with her.

"Ms. Brooke?" a deep voice interrupted her thoughts.

Sara looked up, startled. A man stood framed in
the doorway. He had blond hair and vivid green
eyes. A good-looking man, Sara decided. She liked
high cheekbones. They went well with the man's
strong chin. Like most northeasterners, he had the
healthy complexion of someone who enjoyed out-
door sports. Sara guessed the shiny calluses on the
percussion side of his right hand suggested a keen
rider.

He pointed out toward the front of the house. "No

one was at the front desk," he said apologetically. "I'm Samuel Paxton. May I come in?"

Sara threw her hair out of her face, swiping at the stray strands that refused to go back behind her ear. "I'm sorry, but my office hours don't begin until eleven."

Paxton grinned, throwing his sharp cheekbones into relief. "Then we won't be interrupted by clients," he said. "I wanted to talk to you personally."

Where were you when I wanted someone to have a drink with last night? she wondered, but she gestured him to a chair. Then she noticed a wedding ring on his left hand. Not a prospect, she admonished herself. "What can I do for you?"

"I heard you were in the library last night," Paxton said.

Sara reddened. Was she already the subject of gossip in Salem? "May I ask why that interests you?"

"You were studying the genealogical records," Paxton said. "Were those for someone else, or for you?"

"I don't see that that's any of your business."

"You'd be surprised." Paxton smiled, his green eyes crinkling, but it was a watchful expression, not a cheerful one. "Do you believe in magic?

"I'm an attorney, Mr. Paxton!"

The man settled back in Sara's best red leather visitor's chair, tenting his hands over his knee. "That's got nothing to do with it. You were investigating your heritage. You're in Salem. You must know its history. In particular, what you said to Abigail Burroughs was overheard by fifteen or twenty people."

Sara eyed him uncomfortably. "I believe in the trials. They are historical fact. They took place over three hundred years ago, and resulted in the deaths of nineteen innocent people."

"Innocent, perhaps, of causing harm to others," Samuel Paxton said coolly, watching her for a reaction. "Not innocent of witchcraft, though. The accusers were correct about that, though few of them realized it."

"Absurd," Sara exclaimed. "Witchcraft is . . . well, unreal. I don't believe in the supernatural."

Paxton opened his green eyes wide as he leaned toward her. "They call it the supernatural, but it's as natural as plants growing. Here." He reached into his pocket and held out a folded black cloth. Sara took it from him, noticing a hard little weight at its center. "Open it."

Swaddled in the square of black velvet was a segment of rock crystal about half the length of her forefinger, terminating at both ends with faceted points. Its edges were sharp, proving it had not been cut from a larger piece or finished on a jeweler's wheel. "Pick it up."

When Sara did, the stone flared with a brilliant blue light. Paxton's eyes glittered. "Do you see? It recognizes you. It knows witches."

"But I'm not a witch."

"You are," Paxton said, very pleased with himself. "The stone proves it."

Sara kept all expression off her face. "I don't have to credit magic to understand microtechnology, Mr. Paxton."

"It's not a device, Ms. Brooke, it's a witchstone. It only glows when someone who has the gift touches it. This proves you inherited it. We assumed it. We've been watching you for some time. This confirms our guesses."

"But I'm not descended from any of the victims," Sara protested. "The ancestor I found was one of the judges."

"You are," Paxton repeated. "Abigail Burroughs knew it the moment you mentioned Mary Saltonstall. She wasn't his natural daughter. She was a Corey."

"Giles and Martha Corey were in their seventies and eighties when they died," Sara pointed out. "They couldn't have had a baby—that *would* have been witchcraft." Her encounter with Ms. Burroughs had reminded her of the facts she'd studied in law school about the trials. At that time she had known every detail by heart.

"She was the victims' granddaughter. Mary's parents died not long after her grandparents. It was believed," and Paxton's tone said he doubted it, "to be from natural causes. Judge Saltonstall kindly took the girl in. He raised her ignorant of her heritage—safer that way. Anyone who interprets the birth records, and there are many who can, would be able to associate the infant girl who vanished with the one who appeared in the home of a distinguished and irreproachable justice. But she was a hereditary witch. And so are you."

Sara couldn't speak for a moment. It was too much to absorb. Before last night she'd been missing a small part of her history. Now she felt overwhelmed by the enormity of the possibility that she had a heritage that far surpassed anything she might have imagined. Her throat was dry. "What do you want from me?"

"*From* you?" Paxton asked, with amusement. "I'm here to give something to you: the chance to meet others like yourself. The talent manifests itself in childhood. Can you honestly tell me that you've never made anything come true that seemed impossible at the time?"

Sara opened her mouth to protest again, but

strange things did occasionally happen around her,
such as the juvenile love spell she had done back in
high school that had worked far too well. But that
was just a joke, she thought, then realized that Rolf
Moluch had followed her around like a sheep for a
month. His unthinking devotion had become scary.
She never *thought* . . . When she looked up, she realized Paxton had been watching her face. He wore a
knowing smile. That irritated her.

He rose from the chair, deposited a business card
on her desk. "Tonight. Seven thirty."

The handsome redbrick house with its white pillars
situated in the midst of its own manicured gardens
didn't look in the least sinister. Witchcraft, bah. Not
believing she really was falling for a such a patent
charade, Sara rang the bell. A fortyish woman in a
chic black pantsuit opened the door to admit Sara
only after the attorney presented Paxton's card.

Conversation came to a halt as Sara entered the
gracious sitting room behind her hostess. She'd had
all day to wonder what a modern "coven" would
look like. The room ought to be bare wood and brick
festooned with cobwebs, with everybody dressed in
Spanish Inquisition robes and reeking of brimstone.
Instead it could have been an impromptu meeting of
the Junior League at the house of one of its richest
members. Men and women glanced up idly at her,
then resumed their chats in low murmurs. A young
woman with her hair combed neatly back passed
among the guests with a tray. The glasses on it were
filled with pale-gold wine, not a more sinister brew.
Sara was almost disappointed. Ashamed of her imagination she nearly turned and walked out of the door.
Before she could go, a hand caught her elbow.

"Glad you could make it," Paxton said, looming over her like a lion with its prey. "We were just getting ready to begin."

That made Sara back up a pace, but he held her firmly. "Begin what?"

"To educate you about your true past. Trust me?"

"No."

Paxton smiled. "But you have to know, don't you? Don't worry. It's all to your advantage, I promise you. We wouldn't harm one of our own. Have a drink. Relax."

Sara took a glass of wine, but she couldn't relax. No one introduced themselves, which made her more uncomfortable. People began to slip out of the room one by one. When they returned, they wore heavy black silk robes over their clothing. Sara grew uneasy. Had she appeared in a timely fashion to become someone's sacrifice? Paxton assured her she had nothing to fear, but was she really one of them? They smiled at her, but the expressions gave her no clue as to their purpose. Soon, the woman in the pantsuit came to get her, brought her back into another room, gave her a robe and told her to put it on.

Sara slipped it over her head. They must indeed have been observing her, because the hem brushed the tops of her shoes, not a quarter-inch too long or too short. The woman smiled and closed the door on her.

There was a candle burning in front of a mirror on one side of the windowless room. Sara's alarmed eyes looked back at her from the glass. She ought to leave now, while she still could. She noticed a yellowed scrap of paper in a frame, lovingly preserved. Sara knew from her studies that the style dated from at least two centuries back. Below was a bowl of water with rosemary leaves floating in it. The writing on the scrap told her to anoint her forehead and wrists with it to open the doors of memory. Curiosity kept her from bolting, made her read the paper again, and follow the instructions. The spicy fragrance made her think of bakeries and Italian restaurants, nothing more. But what did she expect? She had no reason to believe in magic. Would what she was doing help to protect her from what was to come? She still thought she was being made a fool. If she saw one camera when she came out of the room . . . !

Her thoughts were interrupted by a rap on the door. Sara opened it to the woman, who led her through to the back of the house and took her down a narrow flight of stone stairs leading to the cellar. Former servants' stairs, she noted. The room had a low ceiling and flickering oil lamps on the rough stone walls. She realized that she could no longer hear the noise of traffic from the street. The click of her heels died quickly away. Perhaps the chamber was soundproofed, to prevent whatever happened here from being casually overheard outside. So she couldn't scream, she decided. An escape route was the next most important consideration. Two athletic-looking men with folded arms flanked the only door. It was no use. If things turned nasty, Sara would have to rely upon her rusty karate and sheer force of will.

The focal point on the bare flagstone floor was a modest little antique wooden table. Probably once used as a writing desk, its warmly glowing polished top bore gleaming silver candlesticks of colonial design, each probably worth a fortune. White and red candles stood in them, only the white ones burning. More candlesticks, empty, stood underneath beside a small white cloth bag. A wooden sea chest, black with age, hulked in the corner of the room. Beyond that, there was nothing in this room but thirty or so people, standing quietly in the gloom, waiting. Sara wanted to ask for what.

A rustle from the top of the stairs made everyone turn to look. Paxton entered, hands folded, solemn, his gleaming blond head catching the firelight. Sara noticed he was wearing a red robe. So, too, was an elderly woman escorted into the room by the gentle hands of a couple of younger men.

The old woman, her long white hair loose around her shoulders, stood frail but erect with her hands resting upon the surface of the little table. The strong bones of her face were underlit by the candlelight, transforming her from an ordinary Salem matron to the chieftain of an ancient tribe. Paxton joined her, standing by her side but clearly in a lesser role. The group closed around them, the whisper of silk the only sound in the room. Unhurried, the woman struck a match on a silver box, then lit five red candles on her altar. She looked around the circle, solemnly meeting the eyes of each person in turn. Sara felt a chill as the unwinking blue gaze brushed her and passed on. When she spoke, the leader's voice was as cold as her eyes.

"Welcome, friends. We meet again as our ancestors have for over two hundred years, to remember our forefathers and foremothers who were cruelly murdered in the cause of falsehood and injustice. They were lost to us, but not forgotten. Martha Carrier!"

Paxton stood forth. "Samuel Wardwell."

The woman to his left cleared her throat. "Alice Parker."

The naming went on around the circle, naming the dead of Salem, 1692. As each name was recited, a white candle on the table was lit and passed around to the speaker. Sara found the recitation overwhelmingly moving. Some of the nineteen victims of the trials were recalled more than once. Sara realized that the participants were naming their own ancestors. When it was her turn, she didn't know what to say. Everyone was looking at her. She felt an upwelling of sympathy for the people around her, but honesty kept her silent. In that she was descended from the Coreys she had only Paxton's word and some convenient facts that did not corroborate but could have been interpreted in several different ways. Her neighbor, a handsome man about her own age with black hair and a thin mustache took up the chant for her.

"Giles and Martha Corey. Sara Wildes." A burning white candle was pressed into Sara's hand. She clutched it, feeling helpless.

"A moment of silence," the priestess intoned, "for the dead of 1692."

Her neighbors hung their heads. A couple even had tears running down their faces. The old woman's voice continued.

"Our heritage reaches back into the lost days. Two wives had Adam, Eve and Lilith. Of Eve was descended the one kind of people; of Lilith the others. Yet their offspring were still children of Adam and blessed by God. They lived side by side in harmony, each with its own talents, respecting one another. Then dark times came. The children of Eve became jealous of our gifts."

Sara shifted uneasily. Skipping over millennia of history for the sake of convenience did play fast and loose with the facts. The old woman went on. "Since the dawn of time our forefathers and foremothers used their power for beneficial purposes, keeping their fellows from starving, curing ailments, protecting them from curses, danger, and weather, and all the wrath of a vengeful God. The thanks they got was death! Through persecution and wrongful accusation we have been forced to practice and worship in secret, away from those who consider us different. For fear of our lives we may not reveal ourselves to our stepbrothers and stepsisters. Therefore our gifts are now lost to them. Therefore our talents will be used only for our own benefit. So shall it be!"

"So shall it be," murmured the group. Sara wondered if she should respond, too, but the moment had passed. Not a wink or a smile to be found anywhere suggested that this was all in fun. These people took themselves seriously.

"Tonight," said the old woman, "we of the Golden Circle will work for the prosperity of our brother Matthew and sister Elizabeth Cuddy."

That sounded all right with Sara. She had nothing against people using their talents to benefit themselves. The assembly knew what to do without being instructed. She watched curiously as two men brought the wooden table into the very center of the room. A couple of women picked up the holders on the floor and placed them on the altar, and pressing candles of purple and green into them. When light struck these, Sara observed that those holders were gold, not silver. Their rich yellow gleam caught the firelight, licking into a fundamental part of Sara's brain reserved for the saturation of color found in stained-glass windows beside cobalt, ruby, and emerald. The old woman's harsh voice brought her to attention.

"Matthew and Elizabeth, state your need."

A craggy-faced man with rusty-red hair three down from Sara cleared his throat. "Well, you know where the hotel on Boston Street is being renovated.

We want to open a restaurant nearby. We've invested a considerable amount of our available capital in the license and hiring the right chef and other key personnel. The building is all right, but the current owner won't sell at our price. You all know who she is. She's not one of us. We need help."

"So shall it be," intoned the priestess. "We will gather our strength together on your behalf."

The priestess took a new green candle and began to stroke her hands up and down it with intense, almost sensual motions. Sara felt her cheeks burning, feeling as though she was watching an X-rated video. The action struck her as faintly obscene.

"For the benefit of Matthew and Elizabeth," the old woman said. She closed her eyes for a moment, then opened them and offered the candle to Samuel Paxton, who accepted it with a bow. He made the same gestures, chanted the same words. The candle passed from hand to hand, each participant appearing to concentrate deeply. Sara found the ritual interesting. It seemed harmless enough, offering the power of positive thinking in support of their friends, but she set no credence in it. Soon, her turn came, and the candle was placed in her hands.

"Put your strength into it," the old woman instructed her. "Give of your power for the sake of your brother and sister."

Sara opened her mouth to say that Matthew and Elizabeth were not her brother and sister, but as soon as she touched the candle she felt a jolt. Not like an electrical shock—a long, sustained hum as though she was touching a live power source, one that did not drain her but made her giddy as standing on a height, or drinking champagne. Yes, power, she realized, that felt as if it welled up from the heart of the earth and soared up into the sky. The candle in her

hand still looked ordinary. Therefore, what she felt
must have come from the others in the group. They
were funneling some kind of force into it. Sara's native good sense suddenly reasserted itself, and she
felt resentful. Was this another attempt at trickery,
like the so-called "witchstone?" To what end?

She observed the chief witch looking at her.
"You're a natural magician, aren't you?" the old
woman asked, her blue eyes alight with an inner fire.
"You couldn't have faked that response. You didn't
know what to expect, but you felt it. Don't deny it—
I know you did."

Sara hated people who read minds. She said nothing. Paxton smiled at her, his green eyes crinkling
with satisfaction. Others around her began to whisper. In the sound-deadening basement Sara could
only hear the man nearest her.

"What an asset!" he said to the woman on his left.
"What will she be like when she's trained?"

Trained?

"Give of yourself to us," the old woman said, ges-
turing at Sara's hands. In her wonder and subsequent
distrust she had forgotten the candle she was holding. She looked down at it as the priestess's voice
continued. "Let a little of your power come to our
aid. We're strangers to you, that is true, but you
would help a stranger in need. Wouldn't you?"

Sara couldn't deny that. But why not? The practical
part of her was appalled that she was becoming involved in such charlatanism. Yet, a little corner of
her mind was becoming excited at the possibility.
What child had never wished to have magical powers, the ability to fly, the power to turn enemies into
toads? Adults learned to suppress the yearnings,
knowing that such things were not possible. If she
did have . . . something . . . what a fabulous gift!

What they were seeking to do here was benevolent. If she had any natural magic, as the priestess suggested, it would be appropriate to use it to assist others, as she would do with any of her other talents. She felt she owed the Golden Circle something for showing it to her. Could she do what they did?

"For the benefit of Matthew and Elizabeth," she said, and bent her head over the green taper vibrating between her hands.

When she finished, the candle didn't feel any different than when she had begun. Disappointed, she passed it to the man with the mustache. The smile on his face changed abruptly to shock.

"Ma'am, I don't know where you come from," he said, holding the candle gingerly between thumb and forefinger, "but I'm glad you're on our side."

The remaining participants seemed just as surprised and delighted as they took their turns. Sara observed them, feeling like a charlatan herself.

The priestess nodded her approval as she accepted the candle again at last. She whispered a few words over it and gave it to Paxton. Sara was surprised by the respect that appeared in Paxton's eyes.

While the priestess touched a match to a black disk she placed in a silver bowl in the center of the altar, the participants began to whisper among themselves. Sara leaned over to her neighbor, who regarded her with respect.

"I have never done anything like this before," she said in a low voice. "Are you permitted to explain the meaning of your rituals?"

"Sure," he said. He gestured toward the altar. "This one is pretty straightforward. First state your intention, then get rid of the obstacles. We place the intention in the candle—and thanks for your input. That ought to make it work better. Now Mrs. Ferryman is going to burn incense. The smoke will suffocate any opposition to our wishes."

"That sounds very organized," Sara said approvingly.

"Ayeah," the man said, warming to his topic. "With our power we'll throw bad luck at the owner of the property that Matt and Leese want. She'll start to feel compelled to sell. The longer she holds out, the worse things'll be for her."

"By the time we're finished, she'll be begging to sell to us," said Matthew, with a vicious smile.

"At emergency prices," added Elizabeth, a gaunt-faced blond.

"You . . . you force others to do your biddng?" Sara asked.

"All the time," another woman said cheerfully. "We've been screwed over for hundreds of years. We've decided we're just not going to be anyone's punching bags any longer. We're proactive for our own benefit."

"But that's not right," Sara said.

"Isn't that exactly what you do every day . . . counselor?" Paxton asked, his eyes glinting. Sara looked at him in shock. She was litigious, but never without reason.

"I thought you were only working to increase their luck, in hopes that the seller changes her mind. Shouldn't she want to make the deal out of her own free will?"

"You make your own luck," Matthew laughed.

The other woman's face set like a mule's. "You don't understand. You didn't grow up *knowing* you weren't normal. We're just getting back a little of our own."

"They can never give us back our ancestors," Paxton spoke up, his eyes serious for once. "Or the decades their descendants spent in hiding or lying to themselves that they are not different from other people. Why should they not pay for their intolerance?"

"Now that you've met Abigail Burroughs, you realize she's not worth anything. Help us," Elizabeth said, her eyes pleading.

"Join hands," said the priestess, in a voice that silenced them all. Sara wanted to protest further, but the others looked away. She must either leave or participate. Reluctantly, she reached out to those on either side of her. Once again she felt that connectedness to the core of the universe. She closed her eyes, feeling waves of power flow through her from every direction. She reveled in the headiness of it. It felt marvelous. She wanted more of it, over and over again. The priestess' actions no longer seemed so obscene. There was a sensualness about all this, touching every nerve in her body. Her scruples were subsumed by a force greater than she was. How could she question it? The fibers of her being caught fire, and her soul swirled in a maelstrom of silken glory, away from such mundane considerations of whether what she was doing was right.

All too soon the glorious feeling drained from Sara's body, leaving her with only her doubts. The young men helped the priestess up the stairs.

"That was amazing," Elizabeth said, as the group broke up. "Thanks for your help. I'm sure we'll succeed now."

"You really are one of us," said the man with the mustache, taking her hand. "When we read the parish records, we couldn't be completely sure, but you're the real thing. Welcome to the group."

"Thank you," Sara said absently. Suddenly she could not wait to get away. She handed her borrowed robe back to her hostess and hurried home.

*   *   *

Sara passed a miserably restless night. Three AM glared from the clock face. She turned over in bed, angrily throwing off her light coverlet and sitting up.

She felt as though she'd been tricked. For a moment she had enjoyed the notion that not only had she suddenly discovered a wonderful talent in herself, but people like her to teach her how to use it. And yet, they had perverted her good intention. She was angry at Paxton, who had attempted to compare what she did for a living to their obscene compulsion of a helpless victim. She would never force others to do her bidding without their knowledge. Her tools were the laws and statutes of the land, and such resources were available to anyone else who wanted to make use of them.

She had sympathy for the members of the Golden Circle. The others were chained to their past, the knowledge of their forebears' persecution coloring their every movement with anger and hatred. Out of fairness Sara had to admit they had reason, but wasn't it better to understand the past and move on? Instead, they reveled in their differences and their grievances, much as the librarian held pride for her descent from the vile judge. Her distant adoptive ancestor had given her a gift as great as the one of magic: three hundred years of ignorance.

She tried to put herself in their shoes, trying to feel that it served Abigail Burroughs right to be helpless against them, but she couldn't. They kept saying she was one of them, but she wasn't. Sara had a sense of detachment from everything but the exhilaration of making contact with that infinite, intimate power.

"You feel it, don't you?" Paxton had whispered.

She had. At that moment Sara knew that everything he had told her about her history was true. In her mind she saw a baby wrapped in white being handed from a woman in a black dress and white collar to a man in a somber gray coat, knew her to be Mary Corey, now Saltonstall. Then she had felt her spirit swept up, swirling with the others in a dance as ancient as the movements of the stars. This is what the children of Lilith had that the children of Eve hated. Magic. The feeling was more wonderful than anything she had ever experienced. Her own heartbeat had been light and nearly imperceptible in the midst of a rhythm that opened gates inside her she never knew were there, surged through the room, through the land, *everywhere*. That knowledge, that sensation, had come to her through the Golden Circle, but she must never help them again, not like that.

Despair made her get up from her bed to pace the cold wooden floor. Did that mean she would never feel the power again? That was unthinkable!

She went to put on a videotape to take her mind off the evening. Out of impulse she chose *The Wizard of Oz* and sat down with a glass of brandy to watch it.

After a few sips she set the balloon glass aside. The heat of the liqueur in her belly reminded her of the power, but it was a pale substitute. Instead, she went to make herself a cup of cocoa.

The soundtrack of the film was still audible in the kitchenette as she felt her way down the narrow stairs in the gloom. She'd always hated Miss Gulch because the nasty woman was so unfair about Toto.

She missed the entire tornado scene and the switch from black-and-white stock to color. By the time she stumped back up to her makeshift living room, she could hear Billie Burke's sweet voice piping, "Are you a good witch, or a bad witch?"

Dorothy replied, as puzzled as Sara herself, "But I'm not a witch at all."

Sara found herself staring at the screen, her cocoa and the movie forgotten. Dorothy wasn't a witch. She was just a girl who found herself in extraordinary circumstances. But Sara . . . ? She was plunged back into her memory of the evening. She *had* felt something. It was no trick. Was *she* a witch?

If it walks like a duck, and quacks like a duck . . .

She'd had a client in Boston once, a self-proclaimed witch who had been tossed out of an apartment because of her religion. Margaret had paid her bill over time, not without a comment on the size of it, but acknowledged the debt and gratitude for Sara's hard work. She was everything the Golden Circle was not: modest, circumspect, living a simple life, devout in her own way which Sara frankly didn't get but admired for its sincerity alone. She had been ordinary except for her stated faith. At the time Sara had assumed Margaret couldn't actually do any magic, but what if she was wrong? What if the creed had developed out of a need to deal with the reality of having power that could be used against one's fellows?

What had that phrase been that Margaret spouted off time and again? It had been very important to her, and moved Sara at the time. "If it hurt none, do what you will." Pretty esoteric sounding, and very broad as a precept, but those eight simple words opened life up rather than proscribing it, as the faith of Sara's birth had seemed to do. They spoke of responsibility and mindfulness. No action should be taken that would injure another person. Those would be good words to live by. If Sara had to to accept the notion that she was a witch, that was much more of the kind she meant to be.

Great heavens, Sara thought, wryly, taking a swig of cooling cocoa, she hoped she wasn't going to have to start wearing undyed hemp clothes! Good-bye, Prada; hello, Birkenstock?

She never wanted to give up the possibility of experiencing that oneness with the universe, but the justice in her soul told her that with power came responsibility. She had allowed her energy to be used for evil purposes. That left a stain on her soul. As an attorney she was automatically resented by some people, but she always felt that she was helping to redress wrongs. She fought hard for her clients, and tried not to accept any that she thought were bringing fraudulent claims. The Golden Circle selfishly sought to bring about their will, not out of need, but out of greed. That was wrong. Harm was being done. What could she do, short of starting an actual witch hunt? The problem was that exposing them would expose her, too. She sat facing the television screen, not really seeing it. Her mind was a million miles away and three hundred years in the past.

When day came, she went for a long walk to clear her mind.

The Salem Witch Museum looked like a great medieval keep. Its entranceway was flanked by twin red granite towers and topped by a huge Gothic window. Inside, an earnest young docent, pleased to have such an early visitor, escorted her around personally, explaning the exhibits. The year 1692 kept leaping out at her, but the past was not dead. Not here. Not for her.

"Do you realize," Sara interrupted her, as the girl was about to launch into an explanation of yet another of the maps on display, "that you are the same age as some of the accusers who were responsible for precipitating the cases that imprisoned hundreds and executed nineteen?"

"Yes," the girl said, with an odd look, "but I would never do such a thing. Just because I'm the same age doesn't mean I'd behave the same way. It sounds to me like they were very spoiled and their parents told them no for a change. They were getting even. It was wrong."

Sara nodded, feeling age old. "You're wise. Thank you."

She left the building, sending up a fervent thank you to her adoptive ancestor. He had done the right thing. Separating Mary Corey from her past had given perspective to her descendants.

She was not like them.

Abigail Burroughs looked uncomfortably at the orange candle burning in the small pewter holder on the attorney's desk.

"I don't know why I'm here," she said.

"I want to help you," Sara told her.

The square-faced woman frowned. "You don't have to push. I've already agreed to sell up. I have no choice. I need the money."

"You do not have to sell if you don't want to," Sara said firmly. "Let me protect your interests. I will work for you on this matter *pro bono*. It won't cost you a thing. Let me help."

"*You?*"

It took time to convince Ms. Burroughs that she was serious, but by the time she left, Sara knew she was doing the right thing. The librarian did not want to shake hands, but Sara insisted. The pent-up magic in Sara's touch caused Burroughs to recoil. When Sara released her, Abigail Burroughs's face changed.

The brusque Spartan had been replaced by an ordinary woman who hated to ask for help.

"You know, I don't want to sell," she said. "That house has been in my family a long time."

"Then you won't have to," Sara said. "Trust me."

"I won't accept charity. I'll pay."

"Then you will," Sara said. "But let me advise you. I'm new here, and I have a different perspective on things. That will be valuable to you."

Burroughs gave her a strange look. "It may be."

Matthew and Elizabeth looked upset when they saw Sara at the negotiating table beside their intended prey. When they heard Abigail Burroughs backing out of the deal they had proposed, they knew their charm on her had been broken. Sara was pleased. Late nights of trying to duplicate their rituals, hoping to reclaim that heady magic, had paid off already. She felt strong resistance coming from the Cuddys, but it had no effect on her. Not only did she have the protection of the law, but she had placed magical wards of her own around her and her client.

"We thought you were one of us," Elizabeth hissed as Sara and her client left. With a sense of accomplishment and a touch of smugness, Sara smiled but did not respond. Abigail Burroughs didn't say another word. Sara dropped her off at the library and returned to her office.

The Golden Circle had had it all their own way in Salem for a long time. Sara did not deny that they had been terribly wronged, but cheating people was not the correct way to seek redress. She owed them a debt. They had given her a gift: the key to her own inner strength and ability. She would find a way to repay that. But how to learn to be Glinda-good, instead of a Wicked Witch of the West, without their help?

She flipped through her Rolodex.

"Margaret," she said, after dialing the phone and hearing it answered. "Sara Brooke. May I come to Boston this weekend and see you? I need some advice."

THE DEN MOTHER

by Edo van Belkom

Edo van Belkom is the Bram Stoker and Aurora Award winning author of more than twenty books and two hundred short stories. His novels include *Scream Queen*, *Blood Road*, *Martyrs*, and *Teeth*, while many of his stories have been gathered into two collections, *Death Drives a Semi* and *Six-Inch Spikes*. He lives in Brampton, Ontario with his wife and son, but his website is located at www.vanbelkom.com.

IT was a cloudy day outside and the rain had been coming down for hours.

So why was she wearing dark glasses?

And inside?

The discolored cheek and swollen lip suggested an answer that she was all too familiar with.

"How often does your husband beat you?" Valma Odjick asked.

The woman's head tilted downward as her eyes, through the dark lenses, swept over the floor. "Not that often."

"Once a month?" Valma asked, feeling the hairs at the back of her neck starting to bristle. "Once a week? Every day?"

"Once in a while, is all."

"And how many times have you called the police on him?"

No answer.

She reached for the phone. "Well, there's always a first time for everything."

"No!"

Valma hesitated.

"I called the police once before. It didn't do anything but make him mad. He kept beating me, but he did it so it wouldn't show."

Valma put down the phone. "You could always leave him."

The suggestion put a look of terror on the woman's face that was obvious despite the smoky hue of her glasses. "I can't."

"Of course you can."

"But I don't want to."

Valma just looked at the woman, noticing that the skin on her cheek had already turned red and was well on its way to becoming a deep dark purple. "Why not?"

A shrug. "I still love him. He gets mean sometimes, but most of the time he's a good man."

"Except for that one little habit he has of beating on you."

She nodded.

"And when you see him again, he'll tell you how sorry he is, treat you like a queen, maybe even buy you flowers or a diamond, and then he'll promise you he'll never do it again, right?"

"Yes."

"And that'll last a month, maybe two if you're lucky, but then something will piss him off and he'll come looking for you because he's got all this rage that needs to be let out and you happen to be the one closest to him. You're an easy target, a punching bag that doesn't punch back. You bleed quietly and heal in silence, living a lie for him so he can—"

The woman was crying now, sobbing openly into the hands covering her face. Valma knew she had pushed it too far, but the woman's situation and her refusal to do anything meaningful to stop the cycle of abuse was too frustrating for her to keep under wraps.

Valma took a deep breath and let out a long, calming sigh. This one was no different than most. They all wanted help, but they didn't want to help themselves. They wanted their men to suddenly be good and loving and gentle and caring, as if this was some wizard's castle and not a counseling center in a neighborhood shopping mall.

"So if you don't want to involve the police and you don't want to leave him, why *did* you come here?"

"I need some time away from him."

"In a shelter?"

"Yes."

"That's not going to stop it from happening again."

"If I'm away long enough, it might."

"How long is *long enough*?"

"A week . . . maybe two."

Valma shook her head in disbelief. "And he's going to miss you so much, realize how much he needs you, that he'll never lay a hand on you again?"

"Something like that."

"You *really* think that's going to work?"

She said nothing for a long time, then shook her head. "No. I guess not."

"I don't think so either," said Valma.

There was fear in the woman's eyes then as she

most likely realized that she'd just run out of options and would have to return home to a man who would only be enraged by her pitiful attempt at escape.

"But I do think you need some time away from your husband. To heal, if nothing else."

The woman's face immediately brightened with hope.

"You can stay in the shelter for a week . . . *if* you attend daily sessions with a counselor, and join the afternoon support group."

She eagerly nodded in agreement.

"In the meantime I'll pay a visit to your man and set him straight on a few things."

"Be careful," the woman said, her voice edged with concern. "He's got a short fuse. He might not appreciate a stranger in the house, talking about . . ."

"Girl, he doesn't have a choice, and believe me, between me and him, he's the one you should be worrying about."

The house was well-maintained. A smooth lawn of Kentucky bluegrass rolled neatly around edged flower beds and shrubs that were trimmed with all the precision of a bonsai gardener.

No sign of trouble here.

At least not on the outside.

Valma knocked on the door, then waited.

She was about to knock again when the door suddenly opened and a large, good-looking blond-haired man stood there in the doorway with a glass of wine in his hand. "Can I help you?"

She could feel his eyes on her body as they moved down from her thick mane of hair, lingered a moment on her breasts, then continued down to her legs and feet. "I'm here about your wife, Doreen."

"Then she's all right," he exclaimed, with a relief

that almost seemed genuine. "She ran off a couple of nights ago and I've been beside myself ever since."

"Been out looking for her, then, have you?"

He eyed her suspiciously a moment, then said, "You a cop?"

"No, I'm not."

He started closing the door on her, but she put her foot down to block it, then pushed it back open with a strong right arm.

"But I could bring them with me when I come back."

His hand was still putting tension on the door, not trying to close it anymore, but not letting it open up either. He was looking at her now as if sizing her up, trying to gauge her mettle.

He could look all he wanted, but he'd never have a clue.

"I suggest you let me in so we can talk," she said.

"Why should I?"

"Because if you don't, I'll cause you a whole lot of trouble." She stated the words simply, without threat or any hint of anger, as if it were merely a fact.

He took a moment to think about it, then let the door swing open.

She stepped inside.

"So if you're not a cop, what are you?" He finished off his wine in a gulp and put the empty glass down on a table near the door.

"I'm a sort of social worker-slash-marriage counselor."

"Which one are you?" He led her into the living room, which was just as well kept as the outside of the house. Seeing how perfectly maintained the house was, Valma imagined this man had his wife on a pretty short leash. She feared him, and spent her life trying to please him, but never succeeded.

"Some claim I'm more slash than social worker," she said, reflexively smiling to show him her teeth. "Let's just say I help women who need it."

"So that's why you're here, to help Doreen?"

"No." Valma shook her head. "I'm here to set you straight."

"Is that right?"

Valma nodded. "That's right."

"And how are you going to do that?"

"Talk first. If that doesn't get through your thick skull, then something stronger."

"You think you're pretty tough, don't you?"

"You have no idea."

He sat down on the couch and motioned for her to sit in the armchair across from him. After drawing in a deep breath he said, "All right, start talking."

"Doreen came to me for help," she began. "And that's when your troubles began. See, she doesn't want the police involved and, in a way, that makes my job a lot easier. From this point on, I'll be taking a personal interest in Doreen's life, which means if you beat on her again, I'll know about it."

He laughed under his breath.

She leaned forward in her chair, resting her elbows on her knees and cutting the distance between them by half. "For every beating you give her, I'm going to give you one ten times as bad. That means for every scratch, every bruise, every mark on her body . . . every broken bone, you'll have ten of your own to look forward to." She could feel the hairs beginning to rise up along her back, the muscles beginning to ripple under her skin. "And if you happen to kill her one night when you lose control, I'll make sure that you live a long, long time in pain and agony so intense, so relentless, you'll be sorry you didn't take your own life instead of hers."

There was still a look of brash confidence on his face, but she could smell the fear rising up within him.

"I think it's time that you leave," he said.

"Not yet," she said. "I don't think my message has been received."

"Oh, I got it all right." He rose up off the couch and came around to where she sat. "You're just another one of those bleeding hearts who don't have enough going on in their own lives, so you have to worry about everyone around you."

"You haven't heard a word I've said, have you?"

"I've heard plenty." He was leaning over her now, doing his best to intimidate her. "You know, I don't remember inviting you into my house. But I do recall you threatening me, and pushing your way inside. Now, if I decided my home was being invaded, that would give me the right to defend my property, wouldn't it?"

"Meaning?"

"Meaning, there wouldn't be a court in the land that would convict me if I did you some real harm."

"Like what you did to Doreen?"

He looked at her a moment, then said, "Get out!"

"Not until you understand that I will hurt you if you ever lay another finger on that woman."

"I said, get out!" He reached for her then, his hands grabbing for her arm so he could lift her out of the seat and guide her to the door.

But he never laid a finger on her.

She caught his left thumb with her right hand and bent it backward.

"Hey!" was all he said.

Valma could feel the rage surging inside her. She couldn't let it overtake her or she'd have to hide out until dark and run home through the woods. Then she'd have to send someone for the car and even more people's lives would be inconvenienced by this slug. So she kept her anger in check, letting just a hint of it bubble to the surface.

Enough to give him a really good scare.

And send a warning.

Her fangs sharpened inside a slightly lengthened snout. Thick black hair bristled out of the skin of her right arm. The flesh began to ripple and twitch as the muscles beneath doubled their mass. The arm grew in size, at first stretching, then tearing apart the delicate white fabric of her blouse sleeve. Her fingers, still wrapped around his thumb, became gnarled and hairy, and her fingernails grew and darkened into long black talons.

She pulled on his thumb, drawing him close to her. "Maybe now you'll take me seriously."

"Look, I know I got a temper, but sometimes she just . . . she sets me off."

"You're trying to tell me it's her fault . . ." She bent his thumb backward.

"Ow, hey!"

"That she has it coming to her . . ."

"No, ow."

"I don't want to see her hurt again."

"Okay, all right. I won't lay a finger on her. I promise, I swear."

There was a look of fear on his face now. Real terror. At last she was getting through to him. "That's right," she said, bending his thumb back even farther. "Because if you do, I'll make sure you won't have the fingers to ever do it again." She gave his thumb a hard twist and could feel the tendons and ligaments, snapping and tearing, and finally letting go from the rest of the hand.

"Ahh!" His body was stiff from the pain and his mouth was open in a scream.

She let go of his hand and saw his thumb hanging limply and at an awkward angle, as if it was hanging on by the skin alone.

"Doreen will be coming home in a few days. I suggest you make her welcome."

He was cradling his ruined thumb in his hands, but managed a weak nod in acknowledgment of what she'd said.

"And don't trouble yourself. I can let myself out," she said, heading for the front door.

Hopefully, it was still early enough to avoid catching any of the neighbors coming home from work. After all, even though they lived next door to a wife-beating monster, the sight of a partially transmuted werewolf getting into her car and driving away was just the kind of thing that might arouse their suspicions.

Doreen went home after a week in the shelter, her outer bruises healed over, but the inner ones still quite tender. Before seeing her off, Valma suggested one last time that she not return to her husband, but she obviously wasn't listening. They probably missed each other now, so when they got back together, he'd be kind and loving toward her. And then there was the sexual element—neither of them had had any for a week so they'd be especially good to each other, at least for a little while.

But the days turned into a week, and the weeks turned into a month, and it wasn't until July that Doreen dropped by to say hello. Valma thought there would be some bad news, but Doreen was cheerful and laughing, and her skin was tanned and unblemished.

"How have you been?" Valma asked.

"Terrific, everything's been great," answered Doreen. "It's like we've been on a second honeymoon all this time. He calls me 'dear' and 'honey' now . . . Can you believe it?"

"So he hasn't beaten you?"

Doreen looked as if it was the first time anyone had ever asked her such a question. "No, not at all. When I came back to him, he seemed like a whole new person. You know, he broke his thumb at work the day after I left him, and that seemed to have made him a gentler human being. I've had to do a lot of things for him, but he really seems to appreciate them more now, appreciate *me* more . . . if you know what I mean."

"Oh, I know what you mean," said Valma, unconvinced. "It sounds really great."

"It is. I feel like I'm married to a totally changed man."

Valma nodded, knowing the woman was locked into a cycle of abuse that she'd never escape until she did something different with her life, maybe even something drastic. What she was saying now sounded too good to be true and it probably was. The more Doreen went on and on about how great her husband was treating her, the more likely it was that she was hiding something. And even if things were going smoothly between them, all it meant was that there was a seething cauldron of violence and anger simmering somewhere below the surface, just waiting to explode.

"So your husband's thumb is better now?"

"Oh, much better."

"And when does the cast come off?"

"Day after tomorrow. We're going to celebrate with a nice dinner out, and some wine . . . maybe even champagne."

"Wonderful!" said Valma. She hoped things would

be all right, but she didn't have much hope that they would. If the day after tomorrow was Thursday, there was a good chance Doreen would be paying her another visit on Friday morning.

She hoped not.

For his sake.

He looked at his thumb a long time. It wouldn't completely straighten out any more and every time he tried to bend it, a sharp stab of pain shot up his arm past the elbow. The wine was helping to ease a lot of the pain, but there was still a dull ache where the thumb had been reconnected to his hand that refused to go away.

Over the last six weeks he'd been trying to figure out how he'd really broken his thumb, but without much luck. He remembered a woman coming to visit him, who talked to him about Doreen, but after that everything got sort of weird.

He'd gotten into it with the woman, telling her to mind her own business, but she didn't back down. Instead she pushed back, threatening to hurt him if he laid another hand on Doreen.

Imagine that . . . Some bitch trying to tell me what I can and cannot do to my wife.

My wife!

But that wasn't the worst of it.

After she gave him a lecture, she got all weird on him. The first thing he remembered were her eyes turning yellow with two black horizontal slits cut down the middle, almost like a dog's eyes. Then her face started changing, getting longer as if she were growing a snout or something, again like a dog.

He'd tried to move her then. She was sitting in a chair and he tried to pick her up so he could drag her ass to the front door and throw her out of the house, but she'd grabbed his hand before he could touch her and his thumb was suddenly being bent backward at a real unnatural angle.

It hurt like hell, but the thing that really freaked him out was the way her hand and arm were *changing* while she was holding onto him. There was hair all over her arm, and it started getting bigger, as if her arm—just her arm—was turning into something like a man's arm. No, bigger than just a man's arm, since it tore apart her sleeve. It was a huge arm, rippling with muscles like a bodybuilder would have, but the whole arm was covered in thick dark fur.

And this bitch's big, hairy arm wouldn't let go of his thumb, even when he asked her nicely. Even when he heard his bones and shit breaking, she kept bending the thumb back, twisting it like she wanted to tear it away from his hand.

Just the thought of it brought the pain back fresh in his mind. His thumb began to throb. He finished off his glass of wine, and poured himself another.

What the hell could it have been, coming into my house looking like a woman, and then half-turning into some kind of monster just to break my fucking thumb?

If he had to give the thing a name, he'd call it a *werewolf*, even though he knew that was crazy.

That was impossible.

There are no such things as werewolves.

But that's what had fucking happened.

And it was all Doreen's fault.

If she hadn't run away after the last time, letting other people know their business—their *private* business—then none of this shit would have happened. He'd be getting laid tonight and there would be no images of mutating wolf-women breaking off his thumb rattling around in his head and giving him a bad case of limp dick.

He took another hit of wine and looked down between his legs. He'd be lucky to get it up at all tonight, thanks to her.

She could have just left it alone, let me say sorry, and make things up to her like usual. Then we could have been happy again. But no, she had to go running for help, had to make it another bitch's business to know what goes on inside our house.

She had no right to do that.

No fucking right at all.

The bitch!

"Are you coming up here, hon?" Doreen called from the bedroom upstairs. "I'm waiting for you."

He didn't answer.

He went to pour himself another glass of wine, but decided to drink it straight from the bottle instead.

"Hon? Are you there?"

The bitch was making his life miserable, and now he had a no-good gimpy thumb, too . . . thanks to her.

Footsteps on the stairs.

Doreen was on her way down.

Come and get it, baby.

"What's the matter?" she said. "Is everything all right?"

She was wearing a black teddy, a sheer black robe, and bedroom slippers with three-inch heels.

"I'm ready for you, hon," she said, smiling.

Good, 'cause you're gonna get it, bitch.

He got up from the dining room table.

"Why are you holding the bottle like that?"

He didn't answer.

At least not with words.

*   *   *

The call came at two AM Saturday morning.

It was Doreen and she didn't sound good.

"I'm sorry to call you this late," she said. "But the center's help line said I could call this number in an emergency, and I . . ." Her voice broke down, and she began sobbing.

"What happened?" asked Valma.

"I don't know," she cried. "We were going to make love, then . . . then he hit me with a wine bottle. Over and over again . . ."

"All right, never mind that now," said Valma. "Where are you?"

She told her.

"Can you get a cab?"

"I don't have any money with me."

"Don't worry. I'll pay for it when you get here." She gave her the address.

An hour later Doreen was sitting in a chair in the middle of Valma's living room, a reading lamp shining light onto Doreen's head.

Valma was picking granules of glass out of Doreen's skin.

"I want to press charges," Doreen said.

"No," Valma answered. "It's too late for that now."

"Then I won't go back to him. I'll stay with friends out of state, and get a divorce."

"No."

"What?"

"You're going back to him."

"When?"

"In a couple of days." Valma pulled a sliver of glass from Doreen's scalp and patted down the tiny wound with an alcohol swab. "When you're ready."

Doreen cringed slightly at the touch of the swab. "Ready? No, I don't want to go back. It'll only happen again, I know that now."

"No, it won't happen again. In fact I'll guarantee he'll never raise his hand to you again."

"But how?"

Valma stopped working on Doreen's head and pulled up a chair so they were sitting face-to-face.

Doreen waited in silence for an answer.

Valma took a deep breath, let out a sigh, then began. "I wasn't always a social worker."

"Were you a cop, or something?"

"No, I was . . . still am, a lycanthrope."

"A what?"

"A lycanthrope. It just means that I can change my form. You're probably more familiar with the term *werewolf.*"

"I've heard of those."

"Well, that's what I am, what I was, before I came to the city. You see, I used to live in the forests up north, with my pack. We lived on wild animals, mostly, but when they became scarce, we fed on sheep and pigs and livestock, anything we needed to survive."

Valma paused to make sure Doreen was still with her, understanding. The woman's gaze was unwavering.

"One night the farmer caught us killing his ram and he shot at the pack with his gun. We ran, ran like mad dogs in every direction, just to get away. Well, I ran out onto the highway and was hit by a bus. My pack, my family, left me there at the side of the road to die. I managed to crawl into the woods, but I collapsed not far from the road. In the morning the farmer's wife was out for a walk and found me. I was in my human form, well most of my body was anyway, and I thought the farmer's wife would kill me, seeing and knowing what I was. But she didn't kill me. She took me in and helped me.

"The farmer was a bad man, and he beat his wife whenever the mood struck him. The mood struck him a lot, but she never complained about him once, and she never let on that he'd hurt her. That was her strength. The farmer thought he was tough, but she was tougher, stronger. Despite the regular beatings, she nursed me back to health, probably just to have something to keep her mind off her own misery. When I was recovered, and told her I had no way to repay her kindness, she said I could repay her by paying forward and coming to the aid of those who needed my help."

Doreen smiled at the words.

"And so I left her, but not before meeting the farmer in his field one night and tearing the heart out of his chest and feeding it to his pigs."

"Is that what you're going to do to my husband?"

"No. I've got something better in mind."

The smile was still on Doreen's face. "Tell me."

"How would you like to have him live in fear *of you*?"

"That would be a switch."

"I can make it happen for you."

"Please."

"It'll hurt you, more than you've ever experienced in your life, but when it's over, no one will ever be able to lay a hand on you again . . . and live."

Doreen looked at her for a long time through red, puffy eyes. "Are you going to make me like you? A ly . . . lycan-thrope."

"Yes."

"I'd like that."

She returned home a week after she'd left. It was

just after seven and starting to get dark outside. Inside the house, she could smell the heavy scent of fast food hanging on the air.

"Hello," she said. "I'm home."

"It's about time you came back," he said. There was a glass of wine in his hand. It was obvious it wasn't his first of the evening, but it might just be his last.

"I've been good, thanks," she said, mocking him. "How have you been, hon?"

"I see you learned to be mouthy while you were gone."

"Oh, I learned a lot more than that."

"That right?"

"Oh, yeah."

She could see the anger rising in him. His teeth were clenched, his lips parted slightly and trembling, his forehead thickly veined and creased with frustration.

He was drunk, as usual, and he was looking for a fight.

That was fine with her. She could feel her hair bristling down the length of her back, and her fingers growing longer and sharper and more powerful.

He might be looking for a fight.

But she was looking for one, too.

THE DEAD

IN the movie *Dawn of the Dead*, many of the recently
deceased are found milling around a shopping mall
prompting one of the now in the minority living people to comment that "they must have been drawn
here because it was important to them during their
lives."

So much for comments on modern civilization.

What lives on after we have died is obviously subject to debate, but it is reassuring to think that such
concepts as duty, honor, love, and respect might actually continue well beyond the grave.

Whether it is the continuation of the fulfillment of
an obligation, the restitution of an obligation unmet,
or perhaps even just the realization of the necessity
for personal virtue, mere death need not be the ultimate barrier.

BROTHERS IN THE FLESH

by Fiona Patton

Fiona Patton was born in Calgary, Alberta, in 1962 and grew up in the United States. In 1975 she returned to Canada, and after several jobs which had nothing to do with each other, including carnival ride operator and electrician, moved to seventy-five acres of scrubland in rural Ontario with her partner, four cats of various sizes, and one tiny little dog. Her first book, *The Stone Prince*, was published by DAW Books in 1997. This was followed by *The Painter Knight* in 1998 and *The Granite Shield* in 1999, also by DAW. Her fourth book, *The Golden Sword*, was published in 2001. She is working on *The Silver Lake*, the first of a new series.

THE frost-covered roofs of Cerchicava sparkled in the dawn light, giving a deceptively warm glow to the city. The unusually cold winter had cleared the streets of a virulent outbreak of plague but, trading one form of death for another, hundreds of the city's poor had fallen victim to exposure. In a stone hut on the grounds of the Shrine de San Vincenzo, the two men huddled by the fire were grateful for its warmth but knew this would be the last time they would ever benefit from it.

The old man was dying.

The young man would be leaving as soon as he did.

Both were resigned to the inevitable.

Father Bachio Rucella had been a priest at San Vincenzo's for over sixty years, tending the crippled and diseased who came to the shrine for healing. Coll had been under his care for eighteen months, suffering from a terrible, magical wound taken the night Cerchicava's Duc, Giovani de Marco, had embarked on his personal war against the city's necromantic trade. In the pay of the city's premier Death Mage, Coll had betrayed his master to save the life of the Duc's son, Lorenzo, and in doing so had garnered a pardon for himself, but Coll was a "corpse-cutter," one who preyed on the recently dead, "collecting" their flesh for use by the city's necromancers. Involvement in the Death Trade was the most heinous crime possible in Cerchicava and its mages, cutters, markers, even its servants, were damned. No one at San Vincenzo's would even approach him for fear of their own souls except Father Bachio. The old man had brought Coll here, as far from the shrine as possible, fed him, prayed over him, tended the wound in his abdomen which had almost immediately become infected, and kept him alive. Now, with his own strength failing, he'd let Coll stay to see to his few remaining needs in these, his final days.

He began to cough. Coll wiped the blood-flecked spittle from his mouth, listening to the congested rattle in his chest. The old man's lips and fingertips were brushed with blue, his pallid skin stretched over his skull like fine parchment. Coll had seen enough death in his short life to know that it would be soon. He'd told the silent acolyte who'd brought their weekly supplies yesterday, but no one from the shrine had come to tend him, or even to sit by his bedside. They would come after he was dead and

Coll was gone, so he'd attended the priest's Death Watch alone, listening to his faltering breathing all through the long, cold night. Now, as the dawn sun trickled in through the cracks in the shutters, the old man opened his eyes, took one final breath, and without a word, he died.

Coll stared down at him, his dark eyes dull with fatigue. Father Bachio had been a good and pious churchman. He would lie in the mausoleum behind San Vincenzo's, his body wrapped in powerful interment spells to protect it from the Trade, his few possessions given to the poor. The priests would sing a Mass for him every day for a week to ensure his salvation and then he would be forgotten by everyone except the heretic whose life he'd saved.

Coll rose stiffly. He had no illusions about his chances outside the pale of Brother Bachio's protection. Half the Trade would sell him to the Death Mages for a fraction of the price they'd set on his head, the other half would deliver him up to the Holy Scourge—the Church's Militant Order of fanatical priestly knights—in a heartbeat to save their own lives. He had no money, no family, and the Duc only remembered his patronage when he needed him to identify the Trade's working, or dredge up another person to betray.

Opening the shutters, he took a deep breath of the cold, morning air. It was a poor time to be traveling, but if he could make it to Pisario or Riamo, he might be able to begin his life again. There was nothing left in Cerchicava for him but death. He glanced down at the priest. That was all there ever had been. Reaching for a burlap sack, he began to pack up their remaining food.

A few moments later he was interrupted by a sharp knock at the door. Looking up, he was surprised to see a man dressed in a city guardsman's uniform enter instead of the expected acolyte. His face twisted in the usual grimace of disdain, the man barely glanced at the form in the bed, just jerked his head at Coll.

"You're wanted by the Bergo District Watch Captain."

Coll tied a length of rope about the bag before straightening.

"Why?"

The man's eyes narrowed. "Because he sent for you." His hand dropped to the pommel of his sword. "Please, heretic," he said evenly, "resist."

The Bergo Housing District was one of the poorest sections of Cerchicava, its Watch traditionally commanded by drunkards or incompetents. Captain Salvador Caggese was one of the former, although not one of the latter. He came straight to the point.

"The Watch found a corpse outside an alehouse on Via del Badia this morning. It's been identified as Francesco Sarto. Did you know him?"

Coll shrugged. "I knew of him. He owned a warehouse and a couple of tenement houses."

"Was he involved in the Trade?"

"There were rumors that he might be a contact, but there are always rumors about everyone."

"Did he have any powerful enemies?"

"I don't know. Why?"

"He had his belly torn open and his entrails . . . disturbed."

Coll's eyes widened. "Disturbed?"

"Flung about."

"Was anything taken?"

"Nothing. Even the destitute are afraid of the Death Mages and their work."

"I mean, was anything *collected*."

The captain scowled. "That's for you to tell us. The body's at St. Benedito's. Corporal Loperi here will get you in. But work quickly, Sarto's wife wants him interred in the family crypt today, and she won't be too happy if she discovers you've been at her husband's corpse."

Coll regarded him evenly. "If what you think's happened, her priest will have more to cleanse than my touch. Besides, I could care less about Francesco Sarto. Why should I help his wife save money on a purification?"

"It has nothing to do with his wife," the captain snapped. "If the Trade's operating in Bergo, I want it shut down, and you're going to help me, either from outside a cell or inside. Is that a good enough reason for you?"

They locked eyes. After a moment, the ex-cutter shrugged.

"I'll need some money."

The captain's lip drew up in a sneer. "Charging for redemption now, are we?"

"I have to live like everyone else. If I'm to serve the Watch, then the Watch can pay me."

The captain's eyes narrowed, then he shrugged. "Fair enough. The average informant receives ten denari a head. How does that sound?"

"It'll do."

Although the largest place of worship in Bergo, St. Benedito's still wore the musty air of poverty like a shroud. Most parishioners in the housing district couldn't afford to pay even a five percent tithe never mind the fifteen demanded by the Church, and those who could were not predisposed to support a hierarchy whose superiors hunted them down like animals. Its priests supplemented their meager income by renting out their choir to Bergo as a morgue. Corporal Loperi took Coll in the back way, waiting by the door as the ex-cutter approached the body.

Francesco Sarto lay on a stone table in the center of the room. Someone, probably a priest, had draped a canvas sheet over him, but even that tough fabric was soaked through with blood. Coll peeled it back gently, laying it to one side before turning his attention to the body.

The first thing he noticed was the five large bruises around the throat. It looked as if someone had tried to strangle him with one hand. Or possibly held him still while . . . with an involuntary shudder he looked down.

The man's doublet, shirt, even his leather breeches were in tatters, as was the flesh beneath. The intestines were piled on his groin, likely by the Watch for the trip to St. Benedito's, but even they were torn and mangled. If the organs within were in similar shape, it was going to be next to impossible to determine if they'd been defiled. But there was only one way to find out. The scar on his own abdomen aching horribly, Coll plunged his hands into the wound.

An hour later he stood before Captain Caggese again.

"His organs are intact."

"So it wasn't an attack by the Trade, then?"

Although he had half a mind to say no, take his money, and make a run for Pisario, leaving the captain and his—soon to be wiped off—relieved expression, to figure it out for himself, Coll shook his head.

"The Trade's involved, just not in the usual way."

"How do you mean?"

"There's magical residue on the body, but the

wound's too messy. In a straightforward collection an attack like that would damage the item, so it wasn't made by a cutter or any kind of marker working with a cutter. And it wasn't an example killing or a revenge killing either. The first looks like a collection, and in the second . . ." Coll paused.

"What?"

"They wouldn't have wasted the body."

"So what was it, then?"

"A construct killing."

The captain paled. "There've been no reports of a construct stalking Bergo or any other district in the city for over twenty years."

"All the same."

"No, you're wrong. If this wasn't a . . . collection, then it was simple murder. Probably by a drunk or a rampsman."

"Drunks and rampsmen don't use their hands to tear a man's flesh apart. The wound wasn't made by any kind of knife or sword blade. There was no slicing, only tearing, and only a construct has that kind of strength."

The captain pulled a bottle from below his desk and took a deep swallow without bothering to use a glass.

"Who's left in Cerchicava powerful enough to make a construct?" he asked bluntly.

Coll was just as blunt in his reply.

"No one."

The next morning he was awakened by a heavy banging on the door of the dockside shed his ten denari had found him. When he cautiously unbarred the door, he saw Corporal Loperi standing on the pier, his face white.

"There's been another killing."

*   *   *

This time the body was of a youth maybe fourteen or fifteen years old. He was lying where he'd been found, wedged behind a stack of empty wine barrels on Via Talano, two streets down from where Francesco Sarto had been murdered. What was left of his clothes were threadbare, hardly protection against the cold, never mind such an attacker. Even covered in clotted blood, the ruins of his stomach and abdomen could be seen. Coll glanced up at the corporal.

"Who was he?"

"No one knows."

"Well, one thing's for certain . . ." He pried a fine stiletto from the boy's fingers. "He was a cutter."

"So there's still a Death Mage operating in the city," Captain Caggese said woodenly.

"Likely more than one." Coll raised his hands as the other man turned an angry glare in his direction. "You haven't even crippled the Trade in Cerchicava; everyone knows that, even the Duc himself. And for all you know, this creature was made in Pisario, or Rocasta, maybe even in Calegro."

"So why is it here killing people in Bergo?"

"I don't know."

The captain threw a leather purse at him. "Find out."

"How am I supposed to do that?"

"I don't care, just do it. Find out what it is, why it's here, and how to kill it."

"That's not possible. I couldn't even get near anyone in the Trade without ending up just like it."

"So track it down yourself."

"And end up in an alley with my guts spilled out on the ground? You might as well kill me right now."

The captain exploded from his chair. Before Coll

could react, the larger man had him by the front of his jacket. "I'll do just that if you don't obey me," he snarled, spraying alcohol-soaked spittle across Coll's face. "And don't even think about running. I know every gate guard in Cerchicava." The fabric tore under his hand, and with a curse, he flung Coll toward the door. "Find out how to kill this abomination or the Holy Scourge will have a new tenant in its dungeons within the week, ducal pardon or no ducal pardon."

Coll caught himself on the doorjamb and straightened, glaring back at the captain with a cold expression. They stared at each other for a long moment, then the captain slumped. Dropping back into his chair, he picked up the bottle again.

"Look, we need you," he said in a mollifying tone. "You're the only one with any kind of knowledge about this creature. Do it and I'll make sure you get set up, money, a place to stay, whatever you need, all right? Just do it."

"Just do it."

"Just do what?"

Midnight found Coll huddled against a wall on Via del Badia. The purse Captain Cagesse had thrown at him had been enough to buy him a new jacket and a decent meal, but the cold still seeped in through his clothing, making him shiver.

"We need you."

"You need to dry out."

He peered out at the empty street. The news of the killings had swept through Bergo like a fire, and everyone who could was hunkered down behind locked doors and barred windows. He should be doing the same. This was an invitation to suicide.

Something moved across the street. He tensed,

then realized it was just a piece of cloth jammed under a packing crate. He relaxed a little, leaning against the wall so he could watch the street.

For the hundredth time, he wondered why he was still in Cerchicava. Gate guards or no gate guards, Coll knew a dozen ways out of the city, and a dozen more places within its walls where he could hide until the captain had forgotten all about him.

He shook his head. And what then? he asked himself caustically. At least this way he was employed, such as it was.

"I'll make sure you get set up, money, a place to stay, whatever you need."

"Right. If you even remember you said it in the morning."

He turned back to the alley and came face-to-face with another man.

For an instant he saw yellow teeth and a pale, bloodless mouth twisted into a grimace of rage and madness, then he was picked up and flung against the opposite wall. Before he could fall, the figure had him by the throat. Its fingers were icy cold.

He kicked out, and it was like hitting stone. The figure's fingers closed on his windpipe and, even though he knew it would do no good, he scrabbled for the stiletto he'd taken from the dead youth that morning.

The figure raised him up with one hand as it began to tear at his jacket with the other. Its hand found flesh, touched the barely healed wound on Coll's abdomen, and froze.

With pain radiating up his side and black spots dancing before his eyes, Coll dragged at the fingers about his throat, managing to take one shuddering breath before they closed again.

The figure ignored his struggles, pressing its icy fingertips along the outlines of the scar. Then the fingers around Coll's throat eased. Its own throat worked, its mouth opened, and a blast of air burst from between its lips. Coll almost fainted from the smell of it.

"Kill . . . me."

"Wha . . ."

"Kill . . . me . . ."

Its hand caught up Coll's, pressing the stiletto against its chest. The blade went in without resistance through cloth and flesh with a dry, crackling sound, then came out clean. The construct plunged it in again, then again, faster and faster, until Coll's hand began to cramp from the motion. Finally, it stopped. Just able to suck in enough breath to keep from blacking out, Coll stared at it in horror, his skin crawling from its touch.

In life, it had been a young man, around Coll's own age, nineteen or twenty years old. Unlike many such creatures, it had no magical markings on its hands and face, but Coll could feel the heat from the binding spells radiating out from under its clothes. And its eyes, rather than milky white or yellow, were brown with a terrified self-awareness housed inside.

The two stared at each other for one frozen instant, then the construct's face suffused with rage once again.

"Help me!"

It slammed Coll against the wall, over and over, until he heard the crack of ribs under its grasping hand. Coll sagged. The construct raised its fist.

"Ciro."

It paused.

"Ciro. He's not one of them."

Blearily, Coll looked up to see a girl, wrapped in a faded shawl, standing in the street. The creature turned.

"Is . . . Can smell it, can smell *him*."

"No." She came forward to place her hand on its arm. "You can smell his magic on him. He's been touched, but he's not one of *them*."

"He knows. Make him tell me. Make him help me."

"We will, but not here. Bring him with us. Mona will make him tell us."

The creature squeezed his fingers, the desperation in his all too living eyes the last thing Coll saw for a long time.

"Drop him there."

The impact of his body hitting the ground jerked Coll back into consciousness. Resisting the urge to snap into a fetal position, he took a quick inventory. His throat burned like it was on fire, his side where the construct had broken his ribs throbbed in time with the aching in his abdomen, but he wasn't dead and he wasn't bound, not yet. He opened his eyes. His surroundings spun about in a sickening spiral for a moment, then steadied.

He was lying in some kind of windowless room, an oil lamp on each wall illuminating a small circle of plastered stone. He saw the outlines of a door, a few trunks, and a long, high table.

His throat went dry.

A figure moved into his line of sight.

"You still alive, boy?"

He looked up to see an old women with long gray hair and a leather apron over a tattered robe peering down at him. He could see the red glow in her eyes and the discoloration and fine scars on her hands that told of years of necromantic spell-craft. Fear causing his chest to tighten, he nodded mutely.

"Well, that's good. I'd hate to think that Ciro went to all the trouble of dragging a dead body down here. "Sit him up."

Icy hands reached for him. He cringed away from them, but they caught him by the front of the jacket and hauled him to a sitting position against the wall. Coll's knees came up instinctively to protect the wound and his arms went around his ribs. His dark eyes wide and shocky, he stared up at the women.

"What do you want with me?" he rasped.

"Me? I don't want anything with you. It's Ciro who wants to tear the life from your body and Maria who wants to ask you a few questions. The answers might save your life." She cocked her head to one side. "Then again, they might not. Ciro hates the Trade and anyone involved in it." She twirled the stiletto between two fingers, watching it sparkle in the lamplight. "Don't you, Ciro?"

The construct loomed over him. Coll shrank against the wall.

"You did that?" he whispered.

She gave a bark of what might have been laughter. "Old Mona? No. I found him like that, stumbling about in the ruins of Montifero de Sepori's estate. He thinks I might be able to free him. Any ideas?"

Coll blinked. "He's a construct. Can't you just break the binding spells?"

"Normal ones, maybe, but Ciro's a very special construct." She leaned forward. "You see, he never actually died."

Coll went white.

* * *

"My scholars have discovered a new spell-craft with four times the offensive power of the old. It requires the flesh of the living."

Lord Sepori's words to him nearly two years ago echoed in his mind so loudly he thought for a moment that they'd been spoken aloud. He shuddered.

"He was made using necromantic workings," Mona continued, "but he was alive when it was done, and the binding spells make no sense to me. I can't even identify what item was used to work the initial entrapment."

"It requires the flesh of the living."

"The flesh of the living," Coll whispered.

"What?"

He swallowed. "It requires the flesh of the living."

Her eyes widened. "That's not possible."

"It is. He did it. His people found a way."

The girl now stepped forward. "What people?"

"His scholars."

"Who are they? Are they still alive?"

"I don't know."

"Ciro!"

The construct reached for him.

"I don't know! I never met Sepori before the night he died!"

Mona gestured, and the tingling of a coercion spell started up his body. Teeth clenched, he felt it twist inside his throat, but when he opened his mouth, the same words came out.

"I don't know."

The construct stepped back.

"But you do know of them, of *him*," the girl insisted. "You carry the same smell of his workings on your body as Ciro does." Her eyes narrowed. "Who are you? What's your name?"

The coercion spell forced the words from his lips. "Coll."

"Coll what?"

"Just Coll."

"What kind of name is that?"

"A foundling name."

The girl nodded. "What home?"

"Svedali Innocenti."

"Never heard of it."

The words came easier with his cooperation. "It was in Vericcio District. It burned it down when I was six."

"And you went to the streets?"

He nodded.

"Thief or whore?"

His eyes narrowed. "Corpse-cutter."

Mona began to chuckle. Both Coll and Maria turned to glare at her and she smiled back at them, her red eyes gleaming.

"Corpse-cutter indeed," she cackled. "But not any corpse-cutter, oh no, but *the* corpse-cutter, the one who betrayed *him*, Lord Montifero de Sepori, isn't that right, boy?"

He nodded.

"And yet you carry no spell to bind you to him. Why? Do you know?"

He shook his head.

"I'll tell you why. It's because he got sloppy. He got complacent. He thought his power made him invulnerable, his reputation made him untouchable. That no one would ever dare betray him. And he was probably planning to kill you right after the delivery anyway," she added almost as an afterthought. "Still, his loss is my gain."

She drew a knife. Coll shrank back and she gave him a toothy grin.

"Oh don't worry, boy, I'm not going to kill you, or even hurt you all that much. Maria and Ciro need you to help them find those scholars of Sepori's. If they're still alive, that is," she sniffed. "We have a deal, these two and I. I find the way to free Ciro, and they protect me and serve me after their own fashion for their own reasons as you will, but you'll need stronger incentives, won't you, or I'll find the Guard or worse at my door just as Sepori did, eh?

"Maria girl, fetch me that urn?"

Coll scrambled to his feet, his left arm still wrapped about his side. "No."

She raised one eyebrow.

"No. You're not working any necromantic binding spell on me. I'm out. I got out."

"Once in, never out except feet first. Your very first master should have taught you that."

Maria handed her the urn.

"You're as damned as I," she continued as she drew the cork and spilled a small square of flesh into her palm. "As damned as poor Ciro surely is."

"I don't care. That life's behind me. I won't go back."

"How nice that you have the choice."

Ciro reached down and raised Coll up with one hand. He brought his face very close.

"Help . . . me."

"Ciro was a guardsman," Mona continued as she set the urn onto the table. "And a good one, too, from what Maria tells me. They were raised in the

Gervasio Foundling home here in Bergo. Ciro was apprenticed to the Guard and was building a life for them both. He was a young man, a pious man. Sepori stole all that away and turned him into an abomination, a creature who knows only death and hate and damnation; a necromancer's slave preying on the innocent. He never had a choice.

"But you did." She caught Coll in her crimson stare. "How many people have you killed in your, what, nineteen, twenty years? Skulking in some filthy alleyway; your marker with his jack and you with your thin little knives? How many? Do you even know?"

Coll shook his head mutely.

"And afterward, when you washed your hands clean of necromancy with the blood of the Trade? How many have died on your word since that night? How many names given to the Duc and his Guard, how many given to the Holy Scourge?"

Coll met her eyes. "Dozens."

"Dozens. How much of your own blood do you think you'd have to shed to cleanse that from your soul?"

He looked away.

"I don't know."

"How much do you suppose Ciro'd have to shed to cleanse his?" She held up the square of flesh. "Problem is, Ciro hasn't any left, so he'll have to use yours.

"Now you will help us, boy, willingly or unwillingly, but willingly you might finally do something that counts toward redemption someday." She raised the knife. "Hold out your hand."

The great bell atop the San Dante Cathedral had just tolled three as Maria, Coll, and Ciro fetched up beside the blackened gates of Lord Sepori's La Palazzo de Sulla. They stood frozen for an instant. Then, first the construct and then the other two slipped inside, making their way swiftly along the overgrown entrance mall.

It was dark and absolutely silent as if even the birds didn't dare to nest in such a place. Coll shivered in his thin jacket, remembering the blue-and-crimson glow of mage fire battling the orange conflagration that had eventually destroyed the palazzo and Cerchicava's most dangerous necromancer. He'd thought it was all behind him then. He should have known better.

As if triggered by his thoughts, Mona's binding spell tingled over his skin, making the skin crawl beneath the bandaging about his ribs. Gritting his teeth, he forced down the sense of despair. His entire life had been spent surviving in the wake of the powerful: guards, mages, nobles. He'd made his choice each time, to do what he had to do to survive. This time would be no different. He would live; that was all that mattered.

They reached the ruins of the palazzo and Maria turned, her breath puffing out in the cold air.

"Where are we?" she whispered.

Glass crunched beneath his feet. "I think this might have been the rose house."

"The what?"

"The rose house. He had a room made of glass full of roses. He liked roses."

Shaking her head, Maria climbed over what was left of a wall. The others followed silently. They shuffled about in the wreckage while Coll tried to get his bearings.

"I think his study was here, which means the lab stairs must be over there somewhere."

Ciro began to clear away the rubble. After an hour

he managed to uncover the ruins of a wooden door and, with one heave, got it open and flung it aside. He moved forward immediately, but Maria caught his arm before his foot could touch the first step. She turned to Coll.

"Won't there be warding spells?"

"Not anymore."

"Then wait." Holding up a piece of charred wood, she spoke a word, her eyes flashed red, and it began to glow.

"Now."

The glow increased as they descended into the darkened lab. The last time Coll had seen it, Lord Sepori had been standing by his dissecting table holding an urn with a piece of Coll's own flesh inside. His abdomen began to burn and, by the time they reached the stairs, he was almost bent over double. Maria held up the light.

"Search quickly. Look for anything that might have been touched by one of these scholars, or anything that Mona might need."

Ciro pulled out a sack.

They headed back just before dawn. No one on the street paid them any mind, but just the same, they slipped quickly into the abandoned warehouse on Via del Masaccio where Mona made her home and took the cellars stairs at a run, Ciro keeping Coll on his feet with one hand. The mage's wards glowed red as they passed and Coll actually felt a relieved sense of security as they reset behind them but, by the time they entered Mona's lab, he'd reached the end of his strength. Mona pointed him toward a cot, then she and the others turned their attention to the contents of Ciro's sack.

*   *   *

He awoke hours later. Mona was still bent over the pile, but Ciro and Maria had gone. As he stood up groggily, the Death Mage pointed at the door.

"There's a piss pot down the hall, food past that. Eat, then come back."

He scratched at his chin. "Do you have a razor, or a knife, even?"

"No. Here." She handed him the stiletto.

He found the pot, found the food, managed not to slice his own throat, then returned to peer more carefully about the gloomy lab. Many things—the urns—vials, and various knives—were familiar to him, but the several books lying open on the trunk were filled with exotic and colorful drawings of limbs and organs. He squinted down at them.

Mona glanced over. "Maps of the body," she said in answer to his questing gaze. "You can handle them. They won't bite you."

He brought one closer to the lamp.

"Look familiar?" she asked.

"Some."

"That's the abdominal cavity there, intestines, liver, and the like."

"Were they . . . Sepori's?"

"Mine. I drew them. Wrote the text as well. I was apprenticed to a physician who turned out to be a Death Mage. He wanted the entire inner body mapped out. He just about managed it until he was taken. That would be . . . oh, twenty-odd years ago now. This was a dangerous trade even before you came along, boy." She caught him in a penetrating stare. "Can you read?"

"Some."

"Then read me this list. It *was* Sepori's."

* * *

An hour later Maria and Ciro returned, a body now inside Ciro's sack. It hit the ground with a thud. Mona glanced over curiously. "The scholar?"

Ciro nodded.

"Hm. You'd have thought he'd be bigger."

Roberto Ricasoli was an older man, with thinning gray hair and a scraggly beard. Ciro hauled him out of the sack in his nightshirt, and he fell down in a dead faint when he saw Mona in her leather apron. It took two doses of smelling salts and a stiff glass of gin before he stopped babbling in terror. Coll could sympathize. When they finally convinced him that they weren't going to kill him and that they might even pay for his services, he pulled himself together and accepted the spare robe Maria fetched for him. After Mona explained their needs, he approached Ciro with an expression akin to worship.

"I never thought it could be done, he whispered. "Not on this scale. It's magnificent."

Maria caught Ciro's arm before he took the scholar's head off.

"*It* is my brother," she snarled.

Cowering back, the scholar nodded appeasingly. "Brother, yes, of course. My apologies, please."

"Just get on with it."

"I will. I'll . . . need his clothes removed. Um . . . can your other, um, can he get it, I mean him! Him! Get him onto the table?"

Ciro moved forward.

"I . . ." he said, peeling his lips back from his teeth. "Can do it . . . myself."

Ciro's skin was a ghastly white, the binding spells tattooed across his chest, arms, and legs standing out like bright red burns. Maria, her own features pale, held his hand tightly while Ricasoli fussed about, writing down the symbolic components of each spell on a piece of parchment. Mona didn't bother to tell him what the parchment was made of. It would only have distracted him. Finally, he straightened.

"Well, I'm fairly certain I can break the bindings now that Sepori is dead, but um . . . you do know that he . . ." He met Ciro's eyes for the first time. "That *you* won't survive it?"

Ciro nodded. "Just . . . end it."

"Well, I can do that, but I'll need some things from my lab . . ." He made for the door, and this time it was Coll who stepped in front of him.

Mona chuckled. "You don't actually think we'd let you roam about on your own right now, do you?"

"But my things, my books. I can't operate without my books." He drew himself up. "I can't help you without my books."

"Write down what you need. Coll will fetch them for you. Won't you, Coll?"

She didn't press on the binding spell and, with a slight frown, he nodded.

It was strange to be out in daylight. He felt as if he'd been underground for weeks. A light snow had fallen in the night and the early dawn streets were slippery as he made his way to the middle class Lambruschini District where Ricasoli kept rooms. After assuring his hysterical housekeeper that the scholar would be home soon, he convinced her to show him into the man's study and, bent under the weight of half a dozen books, headed back, trying to look nondescript.

With the books spread out around the lab, Mona and Ricasoli managed to identify the spells that had to be eliminated to set Ciro free. Pointing to a particularly complex symbol on his abdomen, the scholar turned.

"This is the cornerstone of the spell's binding power," he explained. "It's the one which constrains the spirit and fills it with rage at the sight of the unfettered. No doubt it's the reason he, er you, feel compelled to . . ." He mimed tearing at the stomach. "You wish to rip it from your own flesh and cannot. It must be removed last and, like the others, it must be burned away, and you will feel it. The more symbols we remove the closer you'll come to what you once were, and the closer you'll come to death. And, once begun, it must be completed. Are you sure this is what you want?"

Ciro nodded at once, Maria more slowly.

Mona cocked her head to one side.

"Can you bear it, girl?"

Her eyes pinched, she nodded. "If Ciro can bear it, I can bear it."

"Do you want a moment alone?"

The two siblings met each other's eyes, then Maria shook her head. "No, do it now. Bring him some peace." She bent and kissed him on the brow, then took his hand. "Just do it."

"Just do it."

Three hours later Coll stood, looking down at the dead guardsman, his face drawn. He'd tried to be as useful as possible. He'd fetched Mona's knives and the herbs and unguents she'd required, kept the fire burning, and sponged away the bits of burned flesh as fast as he was able. Ciro had been in a great deal of pain at the end, but now he had a look of peace that Coll had rarely seen on the faces of the dead. Maria'd held his hand throughout and now she sat slumped beside him, her eyes blank and staring.

"He was so proud when they accepted him into the Guard," she said, after a time. "He was saving up to buy me an apprenticeship at Santa Carma Hospital so we could stay close." She swallowed hard. "He was a good brother. He deserved better than this."

"Father Andre'll perform his purification," Mona answered. "He'll know true peace after that."

A faint cough behind them caused them to turn equally dark expressions toward the scholar.

"What?" Mona growled.

"Um, I know this is perhaps a bad time, but did you want me to do the other one?"

"What other one?"

He pointed at Coll. "Your other construct."

Coll went white. He opened his mouth, but no sound emerged. The room began to spin.

"He carries the same magic within him," Ricasoli continued. He glanced around in confusion. "You knew that, didn't you? I can . . . how do you say . . . um . . ."

"Smell it?"

"More see it, or rather sense it."

Coll found his voice. "No. I'm no . . . construct."

The scholar glanced hesitantly at Mona.

She nodded. "We'll use the cot."

His eyes tightly closed, Coll suffered the scholar to examine him, gritting his teeth as he poked and prodded at his abdomen.

"And you say you removed the, er, item yourself?"

Coll nodded stiffly.

"Astonishing."

"Sepori needed flesh. He thought it was from the Duc's son."

"And that's how you were able to defeat him?"

"No. I just weakened him. When the spell went wrong, the Duc's people defeated him."

"That's not how I heard it told, but never mind. You're lucky to be alive."

"I know."

Ricasoli straightened. "Well, you're not a construct in the traditional sense of the word; your heart still beats, the blood still moves in your veins. And, as you can see, there are no binding spells or symbols on your flesh. However, there have been some dramatic magical changes deep within the organs—concentrated in the liver, of course—which seems to be spreading."

"Will it kill him?" Mona asked.

"I have no idea. This was an accident, or rather an unanticipated occurrence. The spell-craft itself was experimental. I wouldn't know how to combat it, or even if it needs to be. We'll just have to wait and see what it does to him. It may fade, it may spread until, like Ciro, he . . . well you understand. I'd like to examine him again in a few months if I might. Now, about my fee?"

When Ricasoli'd gone, carrying Mona's binding spell and fifty soldi for his services, Coll dressed and came over to help Maria sew Ciro's shroud.

"What will you do now?" he asked her.

She shrugged wearily. "Stay here probably. Serve Mona and learn from her. The more I know about the Trade, the better I can fight it. Ciro would have wanted that." She looked over. "What about you?"

"I don't know."

"You should stay here."

"Why?"

"You don't know what the magic will do to you. Mona could help."

"Why would she?"

"She helped me and Ciro. You need her as much as we did."

"And what would I do? I don't want to serve a Death Mage, not even Mona. I can't go back to that life."

"Who's asking you to?" Mona interjected. "Do as Maria's doing. Learn and fight. I'll teach you how."

"Why would you do that?"

"I'm an old woman," she answered. "Old and tired. I need more than one child to help me keep the wicked world at bay. Besides, I suppose I have as much blood on my hands as you do. Maybe we can cleanse them together."

"But what if I become like Ciro, a construct who only cares about killing?"

"My brother never *cared* about killing!" Maria rounded on him. "He cared about life, he cared about me. Sepori might have defiled his body, but he never touched his soul. That only happens if you let it happen."

"That's not what the priests say."

"The priests have never had to make our choices," Mona answered.

Coll took a deep breath. "All right. You teach me what I need to know to fight the Trade, and I'll serve you . . . for as long as I'm capable."

"Agreed. But first we have to bury Ciro," She rose with a groan. "Where do you want him, girl?"

Maria raised her head. "He was a Guardsman. He deserves to be buried at the Piero Devanza Necropolis."

"The Bergo Watch Captain owes me a favor," Coll offered. "I'll make sure he sees to it. What do you want on his plaque?"

"Ciro Gervasio—he was proud of our past—Guardsman: Bergo District Watch, Cerchicava. Brother to Maria Gervasio."

"Son to Mona Masaccio," the Death Mage added. She looked pointedly at Coll.

"Brother to Coll . . . Svedali."

"Killed in the line of duty," Mona finished. "Now, go and fetch Father Andre, and you to your Watch Captain, boy. Tell him we want Ciro interred by tomorrow noon."

Coll nodded. Together, he and Maria made for the stairs, the warding spells barely whispering across their bodies.

They split up on Via Talano. The city sparkled in the bright dawn sun and far to the south Coll could just make out the boats on the Ardechi River. He shook his head. Three days ago he'd been planning on taking one of those as far away from Cerchicava as he could get, but three days ago he had nothing except his life. Now he had security, purpose, a chance for redemption . . . family.

Breathing the first prayer he'd ever spoken for Ciro Gervasio and Father Bachio Rucella, he made his way along the street to the Bergo Watch House remembering Maria's words:

"He never touched his soul. That only happens if you let it happen."

He wasn't going to let it happen again.

HEAT

by Jean Rabe

When she's not typing away at her out-of-date computer, Jean Rabe watches the goldfish swimming happily in her backyard pond, tugs fiercely on old socks with her two dogs, listens to classical music and noisy cows, and thinks up things to write about. She is the author of ten fantasy novels, including her first hardcover: *Downfall, the Dhamon Saga* Volume 1, and more than a dozen fantasy and science fiction short stories. She lives in rural Wisconsin across from a dairy farm.

THE beads of sweat were thick on Street's face, running into his eyes and down his neck and forming—he was certain—a veritable river that coursed along his spine and spread out at the waistband of his favorite jeans. It didn't help that he was wearing mostly black, a well-lined leather jacket he'd lifted from The Alley on Clark last week, and under that a black T-shirt, long-sleeved. On his feet were leather Reeboks, also taken from The Alley, though these from a visit two months or so back—he'd had plenty of time to break them in. A snug cap, grabbed from a store in the HIP, kept his hair from hanging loose, but it was wool and at the moment only contributed to his discomfort. He felt thoroughly sodden in the clothes, his chest tight from the dry air and the painful cocooning warmth, his nerves on edge. It hurt to breathe.

He glanced down, seeing in the gray half-light spilling in through the cracks in the vent that even the backs of his hands were slick with sweat. *Should've waited till the summer. Damn fool thing to do this now. Summer would've been the time.*

In the summer the air conditioning would be on, rather than the furnace—which on this late December evening was steadily spewing a stream of hot air through the aluminum duct that Street and his friend had carefully and oh-so-quietly wedged themselves into.

You'd think they would've turned down the heat when everybody left and they locked up—which was an hour ago by Street's reckoning. But the furnace was still making the occasional and almost melodic popping sounds that drifted his way.

He blinked the sweat clear from his eyes, stared at his watch, and pushed the stem—it was one of those cheap Timexes he wouldn't have normally lowered himself to pinch. But he'd taken this one because the face glowed green so you could see what time it was if you were in a dark movie theater. *Or,* he thought, *in a frigging hot air duct in the men's bathroom of the Field Museum.*

Aloud, Street whispered: "We'll wait another couple of minutes, Manni. Just to be on the safe side."

"Safe? We ain't safe. We gonna die in here, Street," came a gravelly voice from just behind him.

Street kicked at Manni's face to shut him up, the tip of his shoe instead hitting the duct wall and making a loud "thrum."

"Shit."

"Street . . ."

"Another couple of minutes, I said." Or maybe more now because of the noise he'd just made. "Another couple of minutes, Manni. Keep your mouth shut, forgodssake."

It was actually closer to half an hour before Street popped the vent cover off and eased himself to the floor below, taking in great gulps of the cooler air as he helped Manni and his pillowcases out. Then he replaced the cover without making a sound and held his finger to his lips to keep Manni quiet. Manni retaliated with a different finger gesture, then was quick to use the facilities.

"Manni. Hurry up."

"Hurry? You kept us in the damn vent for hours," Manni shot back. "You can gimme a minute. Ain't never stuck with you in a vent for that long, Street. Ain't never gonna do it again."

Street shook his head and looked out the narrow window. It was snowing outside—hard—and the flakes hitting the glass melted, sliding snakelike down and picking up the lights of passing cars and looking neon against the backdrop darkness. He pressed his face to the glass, which helped to cool him a little. Then he almost reluctantly turned away and caught a glimpse of himself in a long mirror. The overhead light sputtered and tinted everything a dingy yellow. He squared his shoulders and grabbed for a paper towel, dabbing at the sweat on his face.

Street considered himself a handsome man, his smooth skin the color of the Irish Cream coffee he favored at the Starbucks across from his apartment. His six-foot frame was lean and straight, slightly muscular from working out, and with broad shoulders that gave his shadow the appearance of a dagger stuck into the bathroom's tiled floor.

Manni Rizzo was another matter. At least a head
shorter than Street, he was winter-pale, with a shock
of chestnut-colored hair that was perpetually uneven
and that never lay right. He looked unhealthily thin,
save for an odd little paunch of a belly that was
usually accentuated because of the tight-fitting shirts
he insisted on wearing.

"Ready, Manni?" Street glided toward the door
and listened. No clicking of night watchmen's heels.
Nothing. "C'mon. And stay quiet."

Manni grumbled and grabbed for the paper towels,
wiping at the sweat, then discarding them and
quickly following Street out into the first floor of the
museum proper.

To Street's right, he could see the hazy amber glow
from the muted counter lights in the McDonald's. It
didn't seem right, there being a McDonald's in the
Field Museum. Street figured a modern fast-food restaurant had no call to be in a place filled with an-
tiques and long-dead things. Should be some old
sidewalk cafe you might find in nineteenth-century
Germany or France, or better yet, a replica of Chicago's first hotdog stand serving up something smothered in sauerkraut and onions, something of historical
significance to the city. *No place for a friggin' Big Mac
and fries*, he thought. He could faintly smell the
grease from the place.

"Hey, Street." Manni edged by him, tapped his
toe, and looked skittishly around. "Street . . ."

Street ignored him, turning away from the McDonald's and craning his neck around a pole. He was
listening intently, making sure they were alone and
getting his bearings in a museum made ghostly by
the dimmed lighting. *At least they were conserving on
electricity*, he thought. *But it could be pitch-black in here
for all I care. I could still find my way*. Indeed, Street

knew his way around the place well, having visited it every other day for the past three weeks, staying for hours, scoping out everything. Before that, he hadn't set foot in the place since he was a kid dragged here by his mother—who insisted history was good for him.

He knew where the security cameras were, not positioned nearly as well as they could be—and thus giving him and Manni paths they could take without risk of showing up on some television monitor. These paths he'd committed to memory, of course. He also knew which stairs to use, and how far up to go, knew where the loading dock exits were, and the back door in particular that he planned to leave by. Cut across a stretch of parking lot, across a field and to his car parked a few blocks away. He knew that a window in a far lecture hall on the ground floor had loose panes and would provide a secondary way out if something prevented him from getting to the loading dock.

He'd thoroughly cased the place, more diligently than any store he and Manni had robbed in the past several years. Only difference was this wasn't a store. It was the frigging Field Museum, a veritable Chicago landmark. And they weren't after money or Rolexes or electronics, CDs or Nikes or designer clothes this time. This was the Big Time.

Street knew precisely what he wanted. It was two floors up and all the way to the back, in the Special Exhibits Gallery. It was only going to be here another few weeks, which is why he and Manni had to do this now. In the summer there might be another special exhibit worth a second visit—provided this one went without a hitch. It would be a cooler trip. But it wouldn't be any easier than it was tonight. Street suspected that right now there would be fewer guards on duty than usual—two days before New Year's there had to be extra guys on vacation. Only a skeleton crew to contend with.

" 'M still hot," Manni whispered. He pulled his collar away from his neck and fanned his hand in front of his face. "Ain't doin' no more ducts with you in the winter, Street. Should just bust in a back door."

Street didn't reply. But he unzipped his jacket and gained some more relief from the heat for himself. He touched the T-shirt beneath to discover it was as wet as if he'd just washed it in the sink. Sticky. When he put it on late this afternoon and slipped out of the apartment, Leena asked where he was going "dressed so dark and all."

"Me and Manni got some business, Lee," was all he told her. "Be back before midnight."

Good thing he'd glanced through *The Reader* Leena'd brought home last month. Good thing he saw the notice about the museum exhibit. Good thing she made some sort of snide comment about why didn't he rip off something valuable like this rather than the crap he'd been bringing home and fencing. *Should've been Big Time ten years ago.*

"Hey, Street." Tap, tap, tap.

Street roused himself from his musings and motioned for his friend to follow, gliding down one wide corridor, sticking to the south wall, taking a jog and squeezing past Bushman, the huge stuffed gorilla which in life had been on exhibit at the Lincoln Park Zoo.

"Street."

He slipped past a room marked the Sea Mammals Black Box Theater and then cut by the Kid's Field Trip Store.

"Street," Manni repeated a little louder. Tap, tap, tap with his foot. "Ebeneezer."

Street stopped, whirled, and glared. He hated being called by his given name—Ebeneezer. Ebeneezer St. Peter, as in Saint Peter, a moniker that had been passed down by his father and grandfather. He didn't like it. Instead he accepted the nicknames he'd picked up from Leena and friends and enemies, and the aliases he'd created, among them: Christmas, The Christmas Man, 'Neeze, 'Neezer, Scrooge, The Saint of Rush Street, Saint E, E-Pete, E. Z. Street, and his favorite, just Street.

"Manni, keep it quiet, I said," Street hissed. "Quiet and stay behind me."

"I'm thirsty, Street. Can't cool off. Got so hot in that duct, I . . ." Manni gestured past the Field Trip Store and to an arched doorway. The light from a pair of vending machines reflected off the polished floor. Manni swallowed and stared, a deer caught in headlights, Street likened him to.

Street tugged on his friend's arm and pointed to the stairwell at the back. They took the steps two at a time, quiet in their sweat-slippery shoes. Street imagined he heard the squish-squish of his socks against the insoles and felt blisters being born. On the next level he pressed his ear to the door. "Gotta take a different stairway now," he whispered to Manni, nodding with his head to show a surveillance camera up on the wall a few feet that would pick them up if they climbed this one to the next level.

Manni nodded and followed Street out into a main exhibit hall, hugging a pillar to stay out of sight of another slowly-swiveling camera. There was an eerie stillness to this hall that chased a shiver down Street's back. It was the intenseness of the quiet, perhaps, that had finally settled in and decided to bother him. He'd noticed the quiet on the first floor, too, but his ire over the McDonald's, coupled with his nerves at stepping up to the Big Time, had kept him occupied, kept the quiet from niggling at his craw. *Like a tomb*, he thought. Quiet like the mausoleum where his grandfather's ashes were kept. Quiet like the stores they'd robbed after hours. But this quiet was more serious, and inside the thick walls of the museum, they didn't hear the traffic that must be zooming by outside. The other places they'd robbed were up against sidewalks, and the noise of hookers and their marks, sometimes of bums and gang members, intruded—and there was always the sound of the traffic. But not here. Nothing intruded except the sound of their own breathing. *Like a tomb. Best finish this job and get out of here—out to the cold air and the city noise.*

"Geeze, Street. Take a look at that!" Manni broke the uneasy quiet, forgetting himself and practically shouting.

Street elbowed him in the side and instantly regretted taking his friend on this job. Small Time was probably better suited to Manni Rizzo. Radio Shacks didn't pose the threat getting caught in this place did. Street had no intention of doing time in Stateville because of Manni's big mouth.

"Look at that, Street." The words a faint whisper now.

"It's Sue."

Manni cocked his head and strained to hear Street's soft voice.

"Sue. The T-Rex skeleton. It was in the paper. Don't you read? They called it Sue after some farmer's wife." Street had seen the colossal thing every other day for the past three weeks. The towering monstrosity gazed down at them through empty sockets, the silence wrapped tightly around the thing and stretching out to Street. The shadow it cast in the dim light wavered.

Another shiver, then Street thrust his nervousness aside. *Just bones. Not even bones, actually. No big deal.* He thought he should have been impressed by Sue. But it was just a collection of fossils, he told himself, just dead matter. It wasn't even the dinosaur's real head that was poised above them. It was a plaster replica. The real thing was on the next floor up, along with a printed explanation that it was too heavy to set on the skeleton.

Manni was watching the surveillance camera, then without warning skidded out after it swung to the left, darted onto the display and knelt at Sue's foot.

"Manni!" a whispered shout from Street. "What the hell are you doing? We ain't here to mess with the dinosaur."

"A souvenir," Manni shot back. "I'm gonna give this to my old man. Late Christmas present. Pappa Rizzo'll love this."

"Forgodssake, Manni."

"Just a foot bone's all," came the muted reply. "Ain't no one in the museum gonna miss it." Then he was back at Street's side, clinging to the pillar and holding up his prize.

"What if that thing had tipped over?"

Manni shrugged and put the fossil in his pocket. "Thing wasn't gonna tip over, Street. Really had to work at it to get it, though. All wired up. Had to cut it and . . ."

Street glared at him.

"We should get goin', Street, I think I hear somethin'. Maybe a guard."

Street tugged Manni through the North American Birds exhibit, then turned and cut down through the

World of Animals display. Out of the corner of his eye, he saw a night watchman, uniform pressed, ID clipped to his pocket, flashlight held out and beam bouncing ahead of him, soles clicking rhythmically against the floor.

Must've heard Manni's "Look at that!" "Shit," Street hissed.

The watchman angled the light through the bird exhibit, and he paused, as if he was debating whether to go down the aisle for a look-see. He trained the light on the floor, and Street sucked in his breath. The beam didn't quite reach to where they were. *Had the watchman indeed heard Manni? Or had they dropped something along the way? A pillowcase? No. Manni had both of them tucked under his belt. Maybe the sweat. All that sweat, maybe some had run off, leaving a trail on the tile.*

But after a moment the watchman retreated, heels clicking away, light bobbing and then disappearing. Street and Manni let out a collective deep breath, and Manni looked innocently away to avoid his friend's icy stare.

Then Street was heading south, past a display of stuffed lions, one standing and the other lying on a rock. The Lions of Tsavo, they were called, subject of a movie Street remembered seeing quite a few years back—*The Ghost and the Darkness* with Michael Douglas. Male lions, it didn't seem right to Street that they didn't have their manes on. *A McDonald's and male lions that looked like female ones,* Street mused. *And a dinosaur with a plaster head rather than the real one. Museum's got some problems. Well, it's gonna have another one 'fore the night's out—it's gonna be minus some real expensive stuff.*

Street gestured with his head and Manni kept up with him, passing the Africa exhibit and the African

Resource Center, then cutting through the Ancient
Egypt Display.

"Street!" Manni whispered. "Look at this!"

Hadn't the man ever been to a museum before? Street
groaned as Manni skidded past him. *Now this place
really did look like a tomb*—more so now with the
dimmed lighting then when Street had been through
it during the day. The quiet was thick here, too, the
soft slapping of Manni's tennis shoes echoing eerily.
Street let out a deep sigh, this sound, too, unnerving.

"Hate the quiet and the heat," Street whispered.

The heat was oppressive in this exhibit—and dry,
a condition he'd noted here during the day, probably
to preserve everything or to make the patrons feel
like they were in an Egyptian desert. *I'll give you
one minute, Manni,* he thought. *One minute, then we're
upstairs. And no more Big Time jobs for you, Manni
Rizzo. Better enjoy tonight.*

Manni was struggling to take it all in—the images
of bronze and stone, a funerary boat that Street knew
from a previous visit belonged to Senwosret III.
There were two chapel rooms from the tombs of
Unis-ankh and Netcher-user, and fortunately Manni
wasn't interested in these. He was heading straight
to a sarcophagus, making oohing and ahhing sounds
as he made a move to touch the thing inside. Street
shot forward, his hand grabbing Manni's just in time.

"Motion sensor," Street said.

Manni shook his head. "Already looked. There
isn't a motion sensor on anything in here."

"You're an idiot, Manni. You wanna see the mummies? You come back during regular hours. Take a
tour or something. Understand? Stare at Sue and the
Bushman and anything else you want to. I ain't
gonna do no time 'cause you're making like a school-
boy." Street shook his head for emphasis and paced

in front of a catlike statue, the ears of which were badly chipped. It was said to be one of the finest Egyptian representations of a cat ever found, a scarab set on its forehead, a sacred eye appearing on its chest. Street thought it was ugly. "You gotta be taking this serious, Manni."

Manni nodded and ground the ball of his foot against the tile floor. " 'M sorry, Street. Let's go get the jewels and get out of here." Behind Street's back, he dug his penknife into the cat statue's head, retrieved the scarab and thrust it into his pocket. "Merry Christmas, Pappa Rizzo," Manni whispered.

They cut across Stanley Field Hall and slipped into the display on Ancient North America and Mesoamerica. Street lost Manni for a moment—he'd jimmied the door on the Field Museum Store, rushed in, and retrieved a denim "Eye of Horus" baseball cap, a Sue keychain, and a pen with a rubber lizard on the top.

"Dammit, Manni."

Manni grinned sheepishly and plowed ahead, through the Yates Exhibition Center and . . . paused when he heard music. "Street . . ." he whispered.

"I hear it."

"Boz Skaggs. 'Lido Shuffle.' "

Street pressed his friend up against a wall and stepped past, craning his neck around a corner and seeing a small room where a lightbulb hung down over a small wooden table. There was a radio, a deck of cards, and two guards drinking Dr. Pepper and chatting.

"*Trib* says Jordan's thinking about coming back," the one with his back to the doorway said.

The other shook his head, his policeman-like hat almost falling off. "Speculation. Just something to sell papers. Jordan ain't coming back. And the Bulls ain't never going to be great again. Your deal, Mick."

Street recognized the one named Mick when the fellow turned to grab the deck. He'd been the one with the flashlight, the one that had almost caught them by the North American Birds.

Mick called one-eyed jacks wild and took a pull on the soda. "Be good, though, it would, if Jordan did come back."

Street stared at the men, certain they couldn't see him from his shadowy vantage point. A moment more, then he backtracked, Manni on his heels, until they were at the Museum Store again.

"Now what?" Manni said. "The stairs are past that room, you said. And to get to the jewels we gotta . . ."

"Take a different way," Street cut in. On his previous trips to the museum the door had been closed to that little room, and Street hadn't realized guards would be there now—or that they'd have left the door open. Shouldn't they be patrolling? Shouldn't they be protecting the museum from folks like him and Manni? *Well, mark up another thing to complain to the alderman about—lax museum guards. Probably getting twelve bucks an hour to play poker and listen to the Boz. If he ran the museum, things would be different.*

"There's more stairs back here, Manni. C'mon."

Manni adjusted the brim on his new hat and gestured for Street to lead the way. Through the Eskimos and Northwest Coast Indians section they went, pausing at a temporary exhibit—Kachinas: Gifts from the Spirit Messengers. Arrayed in glass cases were colorful carved wooden figurines. Kachinas, Street had learned when he read the signs last week. They were supposed to symbolize spirit messengers and act as intermediaries between the Hopi Indians and the supernatural realm. Thought to provide rain and improve crops in a harsh desert land, the dolls were often given to children and women to strengthen their religious beliefs. On the spur of the moment, Street decided these had to be valuable.

"This case, Manni. Don't see any motion sensors."

Manni concurred, thoroughly examining the case and the floor around it before pulling out his penknife and wires and going to work. A few heartbeats later a dozen of the figures were inside one of the pillowcases. "Papa Rizzo'll . . ."

"Go to our fence if he wants one of these, Manni. The damn dinosaur bone's enough."

"Street . . ."

Street gave his friend a baleful look.

"It ain't about gettin' presents for my dad."

Street turned away, but Manni tapped on his shoulder. "Street . . ."

A raised eyebrow, still the glare.

"Street, I think I heard something. One o' them watchmen. Listen."

Street did, picking through the still-unnerving silence and detecting a repeated "shush." He slipped back down the corridor to the guard room. Mick and his friend were just finishing a hand. Street listened again. The "shush" was slightly louder, closer. He turned and practically ran back to Manni.

"It's another guard. I knew they'd have more than two," Street said, his voice so soft Manni couldn't catch all the words. "A smart guard. No leather heels. Don't think he has a flashlight either. I didn't see him. But I'm sure he didn't see me either."

Manni snatched up another doll, and looked to Street for advice. Into the pillowcase with it, then the last two from the shelf joined it. "You want we should find a place to hide?"

Street drew his lips into a thin line and pointed to the far corner, where a faint light glowed from behind a glass panel on a metal door. "Service stairs," he mouthed. "Move."

Manni did, trying to be quiet, but the dolls softly clacked together in the pillowcase. Then more noise intruded on the otherwise silent museum, the creak of the doorknob being turned by Manni's sweaty fingers, the metal groan the door made when Manni tugged it open.

"Quiet!" Street hushed, knowing Manni couldn't do anything about the dolls or the door, and wondering why had they stopped for the damned Hopi trinkets to begin with. It hadn't been in Street's original plan. "Move. Up the stairs." He heard a "shush" before he fell in behind Manni and closed the door behind him. His fingers fumbled for a moment, trying to find a lock. There wasn't one. So Street pressed his ear to the door, feeling the cool metal against his face. He didn't hear anything beyond it.

A glance through the window panel. Nothing. No movement. No flashlight beam. There was only the dim light in this stairwell, the only sound the soft clacking the dolls made as Manni hurried up the steps.

The dolls. They weren't part of the plan, Street cursed. Maybe there was a motion sensor after all. Maybe there was some silent alarm that was triggered when they busted into the case. Maybe the dolls were so valuable that something had been rigged to them to alert a guard.

He took the stairs three at a time, wondering if they should leave at this moment, be content with the Hopi spirit dolls. But there was Leena to consider, and the jewels upstairs. This was the Big Time, Street knew. And if he was going to be Big Time from here on out, he better follow through with the job.

Upstairs, Manni was waiting for him. He took off the ball cap and jacket, stuffing both in the pillow-case. "To keep the dolls quiet," he mouthed.

Street's expression didn't soften, and Manni looked nervously at him. The the pair was moving away from the door, through the Life Over Time section and past the McDonald's Fossil Preparation Lab. Sue's head came into focus to their right, the dimmed lighting playing over the massive skull. *Nothing should be that big*, Street mused.

The quiet had returned in force, at the same time relaxing Street and setting him to sweating again. Manni was moving ahead of him now, past a kiosk that said something about Tibet, past the Art Lacquer of Japan, around the corner and through a Maori Meeting House, which seemed unreal in the darkness and the quiet.

The quiet broken by the softly groaning metal of the opening stairwell door.

"Street . . ."

Waggling fingers encouraged his friend to move faster.

They were into the Marae Gallery now, the Pacific Spirits section to their right.

"Shush" Street heard. "Shush, shush, shush, shush." Regular, coming from somewhere behind him. Manni heard it, too, and he almost dropped the pillowcase with the Hopi dolls.

"A guard's coming. Street . . ."

Street circled round and entered the Tibet gallery, Manni so close behind him he imagined he could feel the shorter man's breath on his back.

"Shush, shush, shush, shush."

"What the hell is that?" Street whispered, not intending to speak the words aloud. Regular, like footsteps, but different. He'd decided the "shushing" pace seemed too slow for a guard, and there was no flashlight. He pushed Manni up against a corner, his dagger-eyes telling his friend to stay put.

Then he was edging out into the main gallery, looking, listening, seeing a shadow pass by the Art Lacquer of Japan store. Too short for a guard—unless the dimness distorted the figure. An odd thought crossed Street's mind. Another thief? Someone who'd gotten the idea to break into the museum this night, too? Anger grabbed him, and he headed toward where he last saw the figure. Street spun around the corner, intending to confront his competition. Feet flying across the tile, sweat dripping from his face, he closed the distance.

Shush, shush, shush. The figure stopped and turned, stepped away from a partition perhaps so it could better see in the dim light. Or perhaps so it could better be seen.

Street swallowed hard and felt his heart hammer in his chest. A dozen things assailed him, all terrifying. The silence of the place settled in again, more profound than ever before. And the heat assaulted him. It was the heat he'd noticed in the Egyptian display, the dry heat he thought would either preserve the antiquities kept there or make the patrons think they were in the desert. The heat emanated from the creature.

Manni, Street tried to say. But nothing came out. The heat of the desert had settled in his throat, and he couldn't work up enough saliva for even one word.

Shush, shush, shush. The creature came closer. It was a mummy, not so physically impressive as the ones on the movie screen, but more terrifying because it was real. No more than five feet tall, and slight, the thing shambled forward, just as Street managed to find the will to take a few steps back.

With it came the heat, and an odor of chemicals and age and death and things Street couldn't put a name to. The shushing sound came from its bandaged feet moving across the tiled floor. The creature seemed unable to pick its feet up, but shuffled along on straight legs, straight arms held out to its sides. Perhaps it couldn't bend them because the wrappings were so tight, Street thought. Or perhaps its limbs had been locked in place by whatever ancient man embalmed it.

After a moment more, Street tried to tell himself the thing was not to be feared. It was slow, small, and without a weapon. Its face was bandaged and so it couldn't really see. Maybe it followed Street by smell, like some bloodhound. Maybe it was the mummy Manni had tried to touch, and had inadvertently disturbed.

"S–s–sorry," Street managed when he worked up some spit. "Didn't mean to disturb you." He backed away as the mummy shushed forward. Then he took in a great gulp of air and spun on the balls of his feet, finding the courage—or more likely propelled by the fear—to get back to Manni's side.

Shush, shush, shush, came the soft sound from behind him.

Damn dead thing's slow, Street realized by the time he'd found Manni, who had edged away from the corner despite Street's instructions. *Can't keep up with us. Gotta get out of here. Can't catch us, so slow.*

"Street?"

"It's not a guard," Street said, the words coming hard, as his throat was still desert dry.

"What . . ."

"You don't want to know, and I haven't the time to tell you. Gotta get out of here, Manni." He wasn't whispering any more, wasn't worried about someone hearing him.

"The jewels."

"Forget the jewels. We got the dolls and . . ."

Manni vehemently shook his head and brushed by Street, heading to the back of the hall where the Special Exhibit Gallery stretched. Even in the muted light, Manni could see the sign: Kremlin Gold—One Thousand Years of Russian Gems and Jewels. "If there ain't no guard, I ain't leavin'. Look at this!"

On display were thousand-year-old icons excavated on the Kremlin grounds. Behind glass cases were diamond- and sapphire-bejeweled crowns of the tsars. Manni pointed toward a separate case, one clearly attached to motion sensors. Inside were a pair of Imperial Fabergé eggs.

"This is what we came for, Street. This was your idea." Manni knelt by the egg case, tugging free his knife and wires, setting to work on the motion detectors. "I'm gonna show one o' these to Papa Rizzo 'fore we hock 'em."

Shush, shush, shush.

Over the pounding of his heart and his labored breathing, over Manni's incessant prattle, Street heard the damn shushing. *No wonder the guards were playing cards,* he thought. *Why'd they need to patrol this place when they had a mummy to do it for them? And why did he go through the Egyptian exhibit?* He could've taken Manni another way, though longer. Had he wanted to impress Manni by taking him past the various exhibits?

And how could a mummy be walking around in the museum? He knew better than to tell himself it was a security man dressed up. The heat that pulsed from the thing, that he was feeling now, the scent that came with it, the way it moved. It was real. *Why was it after them?*

Shush, shush, shush.

"Manni!"

"Got past the sensor. Got the case open," Manni reported. He reached inside and carefully retrieved an egg.

"Manni, did you take anything from the Egyptian display?"

He retrieved the second egg. "And if I did? If I did I ain't splittin' it with you. We'll split the jewels and the dolls. I just picked up a little souvenir for Papa Rizzo."

Street felt his stomach rise up into his chest. "You took something."

He didn't see Manni nod and shrug, didn't see him move to another case and set to work on that motion sensor. But he heard the shush, shush, shush, felt the heat becoming more intense, saw the mummy come from around the corner.

No eyes? It had eyes, Street discovered. A hellish green glow came from behind the bandages on its face.

All of your organs are removed, Street mentally told it. He'd read all about embalming on one of his numerous trips to the museum. *They're sitting in some jar somewhere. You can't move without organs. You can't move 'cause you're dead. Dead, dead, dead.*

Shush, shush, shush.

"Manni! Forgodssake, Manni!"

His friend turned, sapphire crown in hand. "Gotta be quiet, Street. Gotta be . . ." The crown slipped from his fingers, striking the tile. The bag with the eggs followed. And then the bag with the Hopi dolls. Manni's fingers trembled and grabbed at the air.

"What'd you take?" Street was practically shouting. "What'd you take from downstairs?" He tried to say more, but his throat was desert-dry, his tongue swollen and filling his mouth. Sweat poured down his forehead and into his eyes.

Manni's fingers fumbled in his pockets, eyes wide and locked onto the hellish green ones of the mummy. "That's real, ain't it, Street? That's . . ." Then Manni's words were gone, too, swallowed up by the heat that pulsated from the nearing mummy. His fingers touched the scarab, the one he'd pried from the cat statue. He pulled it out and held it as the mummy passed by Street, bringing the unbearable heat with it.

Here, Manni tried to say, thrusting the scarab at the creature, which clumsily held out a bandaged hand. *Take it.*

The creature did, but continued on, forcing Manni back against a display case that held a ruby-encrusted necklace. It pressed its chest against Manni's and the heat became an overwhelming force, wrapping around Manni tighter than the bandages that were around the creature.

Manni gasped, his legs buckling. He couldn't fall, the mummy held him in place, the green eyes boring into his. *Street*, he tried to say. *Street*!

Street was there, having found the will to move his feet. He grabbed at the mummy's shoulder, intending to pull it away from his friend. But he quickly withdrew his fingers. Scalding hot, the surface of the mummy was. His fingertips were blistered.

"Manni . . . omigod, Manni."

Street stared as blisters formed on Manni's face, the kind you'd get from being too long under a desert sun. Manni's too-pale skin was bright red and peeling, his lips were deeply cracked, his eyes fixed on the mummy.

"Manni . . ."

The mummy stepped back, and Manni fell to the floor. He was still alive, Street could tell, his chest rising and falling and his fingers twitching. But he wouldn't be able to go anywhere soon.

The green glow of eyes caught Street.

"No." Street whirled, feet flying over the tiled floor, as he dashed toward the service stairwell. There were cameras, and he raced by them, not caring if his image was picked up. Hoping his image would indeed be picked up. "No, no, no."

Shush, shush, shush, he heard coming from behind him—and from in front of him.

Another one? Street's mind cried in disbelief. There, at the stairwell doorway, was another mummy. This one slightly taller than the other, and not so well preserved. It was missing its left hand and the bandages were dark at its abdomen, as if something had gone awry in the embalming stage. It generated the same heat, which came at Street like a fist.

He gasped as the force of the heat struck him from the front, crumpled when the heat came at him from behind, completely cocooning him. For only an instant the coolness of the tile floor registered against his back, then the heat overwhelmed him.

"Suffocating . . ." he gasped before his words were taken again. The mummies looked down at him, green eyes glowing through the gauze. Shush, shush, shush. They stepped back.

Street heard a clicking now, rhythmic and getting louder. Someone was coming up the stairs. A flicker of light bouncing through the window and against the ceiling signaled the approach of a night watchman. It was the one called Mick.

The watchman didn't give the mummies a second glance, seeming far more interested in Street.

"Thought someone was prowling around," Mick said, staring down at Street and shaking his head. Mick made a tsk-tsking noise.

Street tried to say something, but his tongue filled his mouth and wouldn't cooperate.

"We'll get you an ambulance," Mick said. "After I get these fellows back to the Egyptian exhibit."

Street managed to raise an eyebrow, the gesture painful on his sunburned face.

"From the Fifth Dynasty," Mick explained. There was some amount of pride in the night watchman's voice. "Don't know their names. But they were Unas' guards. Don't have anything of Unas' on display downstairs. See . . . the guards were lax in life, let some thieves slip in and steal all of the pharaoh's riches. So they're making up for it all in death, their repentance so to speak. Their way of trying to pave themselves a path to the afterlife." The guard slapped the taller mummy on the back. "They guard the museum's treasures right well. And we don't have to worry about them killing anyone. See, I think they want to keep thieves alive to give 'em a chance to repent, too."

Mick voiced a clipped laugh and the mummies' eyes seemed to glow a little brighter.

Street closed his eyes and surrendered himself to the heat.

SHE DWELLETH IN THE COLD OF THE MOON

by James Lowder

James Lowder is the author of a half-dozen novels, including *Prince of Lies* and *The Ring of Winter*. His short fiction has appeared in various anthologies and magazines, sometimes alongside his reviews and essays. As an editor he's helmed such diverse anthologies as *The Doom of Camelot*, *Realms of Valor*, and *The Book of All Flesh*. He also serves as executive editor for Green Knight Publishing's book line.

MI Tzu-hsia's patrols had a horrible precision to them. Four times a day, at exactly the same hour, she set out from one corner of her two-mile stretch of beach and marched in ever-tightening spirals until she reached the large shale slab that marked the exact center of her demesne. Then she walked the pattern's reverse with the same coldly measured tread. As she shuffled along, she scanned the ground for signs of life—dragon gull eggs, smoke crabs, tide beetles, even sprouts of dune grass. When she found any living thing, she smothered it between her rotting palms or ground it beneath her oozing, gray-fleshed heel.

Mi Tzu-hsia had declared war on the living for the

same reason she never tired of her ceaseless patrols. She was dead, and had been for three years.

Her only occupation was marching a spiral of destruction upon the black sand beach. That was enough to fill her time. Each night the sea deposited seedpods and crawling things that threatened to take up residence above the tidal wash. The sunrise brought creeping vines and swift-footed lizards from the jungle to challenge her carefully maintained border. Mi Tzu-hsia rebuffed all such incursions with efficiency. Even the other living dead exiled to the Isle of Fei knew better than to trespass on her beach.

So it was a noteworthy event when Mi Tzu-hsia heard voices late one night. They echoed from a desolate cove beyond her domain's northernmost fringe. At first she dismissed the sound as the distant roar of dragon gulls. The birds could be quite expressive, particularly when voicing a claim to a whale corpse or seal carcass freshly discarded by the waves. But then the murmurs became shouts, followed by a clatter of metal on stone.

Though she was loath to do so, Mi Tzu-hsia broke from her pattern. She padded steadily across the black sands until she came to a boulder at the cove's edge. From that vantage, neither hiding nor drawing attention to herself, she silently spied a quintet of men crowded around a ship's boat.

Their lanterns were hooded and the moon shone only faintly, but night was as day to Mi Tzu-hsia's dead eyes. She saw from the gilt piping on their robes that three of the men were guards from the emperor's court in Yitu. One huddled nervously within the boat, oars at the ready. The second soldier was obviously in command. His imperious manner would have revealed his station, even had his silk vest not hung heavy with medals and badges of rank.

The remaining guard—a short fellow with a porcine face and bloated gut—struggled with an armload of twisted metal rods, splintered poles, and tattered canvas flags. He heaped them in an untidy pile next to the remaining men, a pair of unfortunates in prison rags.

"Please, superior sir," one of the prisoners moaned. "At least leave my medicines. If you do not, you change the emperor's sentence against my master from exile to death."

He gestured to his fellow convict, who knelt by his side in stoic silence. Dirty, bloodstained bandages covered this other man's hands and masked his eyes. The rest of his many wounds were unbound. Bruises had turned the yellow skin of his face to an ugly purple-black. Weeping lash marks crisscrossed his back. Burn blisters welled on his calves.

For his selfless plea, the first prisoner received a kick to the ribs. "How I implement the emperor's sentence is my decision," the commander said. "Do not waste your breath in pleading."

"Better you save that breath to power your screams. You will be doing plenty of that once the walking corpses find you." The pig-faced soldier snorted a laugh and dumped a very large copper bowl onto the pile of junk. The resulting clatter made even Mi Tzu-hsia start a little. "If you work fast enough," the pig-man added, "perhaps you can fashion your scrying cauldron into armor."

"We will need such armor ourselves if we dawdle any longer," the oarsman hissed. "Were any of the dead men sleeping, that racket has surely roused them."

"Such creatures do not sleep," the commander noted with casual authority. "But we will go. The time has arrived for these frauds to meet the minions of Leng Tu." The name was bitter in the man's mouth, and he spat it as if it were wine gone to vinegar.

Mi Tzu-hsia narrowed her unblinking eyes at the mention of Leng Tu, God of Destruction. Had she been alive, her devotion to the Warlord of the Ebon Moon would have incited her to choke the life from anyone who uttered his name with disdain. Such passion no longer fired her heart. In death, a stolid logic of self-interest had taken possession of her.

The emperor's men carried fighting hatchets—blessed silver, more likely than not. Mi Tzu-hsia knew that such weapons would snap her bones and splatter her poisonous flesh. In three years of unlife, her body had decayed in places to something only slightly more firm than jade paste. Even now her fingers left greasy smudges where they rested upon the boulder at her side.

Had the soldiers trespassed upon the section of beach Mi Tzu-hsia claimed in the name of Leng Tu, violated that sanctuary from life, she would have attacked them without hesitation. To assault them now would be pointless. The Ebon Warlord would revenge himself upon the commander for his insult, or allow Mi Tzu-hsia to do so once he formally accepted her into his Host. But that honor would never be hers if she squandered her gift of unlife and allowed her limbs to be shattered in a meaningless scuffle. Leng Tu's black heart held no place for fools, just as his undead army held no place for broken wretches.

So Mi Tzu-hsia catalogued the disrespectful soldier as someone to be given singular, horrible attention when Leng Tu finally brought the living world to grief, and then set about to wait with the patience known only to the dead. The soldiers would depart soon enough, leaving the doomed men behind. As an offering to the Ebon Warlord, the prisoners would surely gain the dark god's full attention. The extermination of two mortal men would sing her praises in music more to Leng Tu's liking than the feeble notes she had wrung from birds' throats and lizards' spines. The song might even be discordant enough to secure her place in the Host of the Damned.

At last the ship's boat slipped away from the beach and glided toward the lantern lights that marked the presence of a war junk off in the darkness. The receding slap of the oars and the waves' constant susurrus couldn't mask the sobbing of one of the prisoners. "As barren as the face of the moon," he wailed, clutching a handful of black sand.

"An apt enough analogy, friend Bo," replied the man with the bandaged eyes. He pushed himself up on trembling arms. "For we know this place, like the moon above, holds nothing we need fear."

"But, Master Yuen, I have met sailors who claim to have seen the dead walk here," Bo said as he helped the older man to his feet. "They seemed level-headed sorts, not drunkards or dolts or fools prone to wild tales."

Fearfully, the servant gazed into the night. Had the moon been a bit brighter, Bo's vision less blurred by tears, he might have recognized the proof of those sailors' stories moving silently toward him through the jumble of tide-worn boulders to his left. Yet Mi Tzu-hsia, enfolded as she was in the night's gloom, escaped the unfortunate man's sight. To the dead woman, there could be no more absolute proof that Leng Tu smiled upon her mission of slaughter.

"Men see what their passions allow them to see," Master Yuen said, his voice taking on a singsong quality it always seemed to possess when he was imparting a lesson to Bo. "This is true even of the emperor. Did we not show him with our scrying cauldron that the Host of the Damned does not exist, that no warring armies of Darkness and Light tread upon the moon? Yet he refused to see the truth we laid so clearly before him."

These words had remarkably different effects upon the two who heard them. The inflexible denial of the Host's existence paralyzed Mi Tzu-hsia, and the calm certainty with which that denial was delivered stopped her in her tracks like some giant hand. She hesitated, poised on the verge of striking, at the very edge of the tumbled boulders.

The lesson's familiar, pedantic tone banished Bo's sorrow, just as his master had intended. A slight annoyance displaced that despair, an exasperation born of the younger man's belief that he was simply too dim to understand all that seemed so obvious to Master Yuen. Bo expressed that irritation by half-heartedly kicking the large copper bowl the soldiers had left with them. "The ability to spy upon the moon does us precious little good now," he said. "Once we find the makings of shelter, we might use the scrying cauldron for cooking, I suppose."

"We will worry about food tomorrow. Tonight," Master Yuen noted wearily, "we should find someplace to hide. Someplace where we won't be so exposed to the night." He gingerly touched his bandaged eyes with his equally wrapped and ravaged hands. "I am afraid you will need to lead me, friend Bo."

The servant retrieved one of the sturdier bamboo poles, handed it to his master, and directed him toward the jungle. Mi Tzu-hsia watched them disappear into the green, her mind awhirl with the terrible notion that the Host of the Damned was a myth. It could not be so.

With halting steps Mi Tzu-hsia marched from the shadows and away from the boulders. Her sudden movement startled a smoke crab come to investigate the seeming bounty of carrion. She crushed the tiny creature on reflex alone and continued on, never realizing she'd left her work half-done. Its shell steaming and soot smudged from its internal fires, the crippled creature clung to life long after Mi Tzu-hsia disappeared into the life-choked jungle that dominated so much of the Isle of Fei.

The sun hung directly overhead, searing the jungle canopy and turning the air below furnace hot. Mi Tzu-hsia could feel a heat rising within her, too.

It had started as a dull resentment of the mass of green surrounding her. She tried to ignore it, but after only a few steps into the jungle, three years' habit took hold. An urge to destroy overwhelmed thoughts of her human prey, and Mi Tzu-hsia set about exterminating everything in her path. As the night retreated and the dawn claimed the horizon, though, she found herself barely advanced a dozen yards. True, a swath of withered plants and the carcasses of a few sluggardly animals marked her wake. Yet her work had left the merest of scars on the jungle's verdant face, one that would be healed before a month had passed.

From the white *mujin* flowers that bloomed just beyond the dead woman's reach to the monkeys and moths that darted too swiftly for her death-slowed reflexes, the jungle taunted Mi Tzu-hsia. Every sturdy tree fanned her resentment. Every call of unseen bird or beast threatened to blow those smoldering ashes into anger, rage even. As quickly as she recognized that emotional heat for what it was, she tried to quench it.

The dead—those worthy to join the Host of the Damned—knew such feelings to be the trappings of life, and thus traps to their kind. Leng Tu's promise of destruction was not voiced in anger, was not a threat or a curse. It was a cold statement of fact: Death, not life, controlled the world's fate. And the Ebon Warlord's army would visit that doom upon the living.

The Host of the Damned drilled ceaselessly upon the moon's barren surface. The passing of the army blighted that bright orb for part of every month, driving the divine forces of Huaxushi before its dark advance. From a single faultless soldier on the first day of Creation, the Host had grown to cover half the moon. With each passing year, the ranks swelled, and the mortal world trembled at their shadow. Emperor and pauper alike prayed nightly that Leng Tu's search for new soldiers go unrewarded, that this not be the hour in which the Host's weight cracked the Pillars of Heaven and brought the moon crashing down upon them.

Mi Tzu-hsia's prayers ran contrary to those of the living. It was her goal to be that final new recruit, for her weight to shatter the heavens and spill the undead army upon the world like so much cleansing rain. Now, encircled by such infuriating, unconquerable life, the dead woman envisioned the jungle in the aftermath of that storm. The certainty that all would be ruined in time allowed her to go on without killing everything in her way. That, Mi Tzu-hsia decided, was not her role here. No, she would seek the exiles out, prove to the elder that Leng Tu's minions did indeed rule the moon, and then send the Ebon Warlord their dying screams.

Yet it was not a sound of agony that helped her locate Bo and Master Yuen late that same afternoon.

It was one of joy—or rather, one that was intended to bespeak joy.

"She came once more to me, to me,
Within that sacred wood.
My heart again did beat, did beat,
As she and I there stood."

The song was a familiar one, a simple story of love lost and love regained that was heard as frequently in Yitu's royal court as in her countryside. The singer had reached the final verse, in which the errant lovers reunited, and was doing his best to fill the twilight with its message of hope. His sepulchral voice, though, lent the song an unintended air of the macabre. The hopeful words rang false from his desiccated lips. His black, leathery tongue transformed the lovers' chaste passion into something quite obscene.

Mi Tzu-hsia lurked in the shadows and watched as the thing brought the song to a wheezing close. He had been dead far longer than she had, and his body was little more than a skeleton armored in a desert-dry drumhead of skin. Yet he acted as if he were still one of the living. Like some contented rustic he shuffled across the clearing to a rough hewn and rickety table. There, he set about preparing the evening meal for himself and the two guests he had lashed to nearby poles.

"I cannot express how much joy this gives me," the dead man said as he slipped on a pair of thick gloves. Humming, he entered a small fenced-in garden and picked some vegetables, which he then divided between three platters. He was careful to keep the food clear of his poisonous flesh. "A feast, and friends to share it with."

From the way Master Yuen slouched against his

bonds, he appeared to be unconscious—whether from exhaustion or his wounds, Mi Tzi-hsia could not tell. His servant, Bo, was not so fortunate. The younger man stared with eyes that had clearly witnessed too much. He whimpered and groaned in turns. When his captor approached with a plate, Bo snapped his teeth like an angry hound.

The dead man maintained his façade of perfect host. He flashed what was supposed to be a charming smile and took a bite from an overripe cucumber. The gesture was meant to prove the meal's palatability. Bo missed any such reassuring notion; he could not take his eyes off the bulge of food as it worked its way down the dead man's throat, eventually disappearing behind his ribs. Somewhere in his fear-splintered mind, the servant imagined chunks of his own flesh making the same journey, and began to giggle madly.

"Oh, dear," said the dead man. "And I was so hoping—"

The shattering of his skull prevented him from completing that sentiment. Before the body hit the ground, the deadfall branch came down again, snapping spine and stick-thin arm alike. The broken pieces continued to move, attempted to pull themselves into some semblance of order, even as Mi Tzi-hsia methodically splintered the larger bones. The club could not destroy the living dead thing—only blessed silver could loose a soul from an animate corpse—but it could render him harmless.

One eye glared up from a fractured, jawless face at Mi Tzu-hsia as she stepped over the ruined corpse and approached the now-silent Bo. The servant did not cry out, did not seem to recognize the threat posed by the oozing hand reaching for his throat. Mi Tzu-hsia could see that the servant's mind had fled.

Even if he did know something about his master's ability to spy upon the moon's surface, he would be no help to her now.

Bo's final sound in life was one of relief, not pain, though Mi Tzu-hsia tried not to let that fact disappoint her. She turned her attention to Master Yuen, who seemed to be fighting up toward consciousness from some great depth. A sharp prod with the branch elicited only a grunt. A second rap under the chin made him snap his head back, loosening the bandages around his eyes. Finally Mi Tzu-hsia broke the vines binding him to the pole. The fall to the ground seemed to drag him the rest of the way up to awareness.

"Have you changed your mind, then?" Yuen managed at last. "If you free us, my servant can tend to your wounds. They cannot be as fatal as he described. Even lepers may be treated now with some success." He struggled to stand, to force his body to fill the role of teacher his voice had already reclaimed. "The Arts will fully banish even that curse one day."

Mi Tzu-hsia tried to speak: *The moon . . .* But her long-unused voice would not form the words. They stuck in her throat like barbed things.

Stumbling forward, Master Yuen reached out to steady himself. Mi Tzu-hsia stepped aside, ready to let him fall, but the man caught his balance. "Friend Bo," he called out. "I need you."

Again Mi Tzu-hsia struggled to form the question. Again she failed.

"Come, come, Bo," Yuen continued. "No need to sulk. I knew the fellow could not be the monster you described, that he would let us go." He reached up to straighten the remaining bandages on his face and only succeeded in unraveling them further. No eyes looked out upon the world, only burned and empty sockets. "Admit you were wrong," he continued, a merry chiding in his voice. "There is no shame in that . . ."

The man's cheerful tone, despite his situation and the tortures he had obviously endured, and her own inability to speak finally goaded Mi Tzu-hsia into a frenzy. She clamped one rotting hand over Yuen's mouth. The living flesh sizzled at her touch, the sound drowning out the man's startled yelp.

The temptation to kill him filled Mi Tzu-hsia, but she drove it away. To murder him now would be to allow her passions to rule her. It would mean leaving the question he had planted in her thoughts unanswered. She owed it to herself, to Leng Tu, to disprove the man's lies. The Ebon Warlord would understand why the man's death, like the destruction of the world itself, would have to wait, if only for a little while longer.

Her course decided, Mi Tzu-hsia set about tending Master Yuen with the same stolid determination she applied to denying life a place in her demesne. With the large shale slab as a foundation, a lean-to soon rose up on the beach to protect the invalid from sun and storm. The wood for the structure came from the dead man's camp in the jungle, as did a supply of food and fresh water, and the gloves with which Mi Tzu-hsia could handle them without further poisoning her prisoner. The large copper cauldron and the rest of the materials the soldiers had left behind rested in a heap by the sick man's pallet.

Master Yuen lay unconscious for more than two days. Mi Tzu-hsia used that time to resume her patrols and drive away the few living things that had taken advantage of her brief absence. Whenever she came near the lean-to, she found Yuen ranting and fever-racked. She did nothing to lessen his suffering beyond that which would keep him alive long enough to reveal the scrying cauldron's secret. By the dawning of the third day, it was clear that he was indeed strong enough to fight off the poison, despite the grievous wounds inflicted by the emperor's men.

Mi Tzu-hsia forced Yuen to eat and drink, and cleaned his wounds as best she could. From the dead servant's clothes, she made bandages to once more cover the gaping pits where Yuen's eyes had been. He was delirious, so no words were yet necessary, but Mi Tzu-hsia practiced the few she would need when he finally regained his senses.

That preparation was soon put to the test. On a night when the light of Huaxushi shone as only the thinnest of slivers on the moon, a night very much like the one on which Mi Tzu-hsia had died, Master Yuen finally broke free of the sickness.

"Friend Bo?" he called weakly. This in itself was not unusual—he had summoned his servant many times in his delirium—so Mi Tzu-hsia continued her rounds. Yet she came quickly to Yuen's side a moment later, when he added, "I hear the hiss of the surf. Why have we come back to the beach?"

At the sound of her approach, little more than a soft shuffle of sand beneath her feet and a guttural rumble of words being formed in a throat still unused to the task, Master Yuen held out a hand. "I am glad you are still with me."

"No," rasped Mi Tzu-hsia. "Servant . . . dead."

Master Yuen stifled a cry of pain at the news. "For the best," he said, though even Mi Tzu-hsia could tell he did not seem to believe it. "So I have you to thank for my rescue," he added after a time. "I am Master Yuen of the—"

"No," Mi Tzu-hsia interrupted, before Yuen could begin the long process of polite introduction. "Show . . . me . . . moon." At the man's puzzled look, she clanged the copper bowl. "Show . . . Host."

Slowly Master Yuen sank back onto his pallet. "Did the emperor send you?" he asked, then laughed at his own question. "No, he is surely done with me. You must have been watching when his men abandoned us here."

Mi Tzu-hsia fought back the urge to strike him. Instead she rapped the bowl again. "Show."

"The apparatus is damaged," Yuen replied. "At best I could merely give you a glimpse—"

"Yes . . . glimpse."

Following Master Yuen's directions, delivered even now with his usual singsong intonation, Mi Tzu-hsia filled the copper cauldron with clean water. Carefully she positioned the bowl in the black sand so that the water captured the moon's reflection. She stared at the darkness in that reflection, at the sickle of light clinging to the moon's edge, and listened to Yuen speak a simple incantation. Then the reflection was gone. In its place appeared a cold, blasted landscape, a place of dust and craters and nothing else, no minions of Huaxushi, no Host of the Damned.

"No . . . dead," she said as the vision of the moonscape disappeared. "No . . . Host."

Yuen's scarred lips twisted into a smirk of satisfaction. "Correct. The moon is nothing more than a lifeless ball of rock, lit by the reflected light of the sun." He shook his head sadly. "If the emperor had believed his eyes as readily as you do yours, I would not be here now. And he had hours in which to study the moon, days."

The words cut through the fog of confusion clouding Mi Tzu-hsia's thoughts. "Days," she said. "Show . . . days."

"Not unless you can repair the full apparatus," Master Yuen said. He closed his eyes, accepting the gentle tug of sleep, then added, "Assuming the soldiers left us all the parts."

Long after Master Yuen had drifted off, Mi Tzu-hsia crouched next to the lean-to and struggled with the vision the scrying cauldron had presented. The Host had to exist. That alone would explain her awful rebirth, would give meaning to the past three years of unlife. Yet the cold logic of the dead demanded she accept what she had seen. The truth had been offered to her. She should accept it and move on.

At dawn, a dragon gull landed at the corner of Mi Tzu-hsia's demesne. The rainbow-scaled bird watched the dead woman cautiously, pausing now and then to scratch at the clean black sand, so perfect for nesting. Within a week, it had claimed that patch of beach for its own, just like half a dozen of its kind did in other places nearby. And with them, after a time, came the decapedes that preyed upon unattended gull eggs, and the other small creatures of the island.

Mi Tzu-hsia's patrols were over. Work on the scrying apparatus now consumed her hours, along with tending Master Yuen himself. From time to time, as she fetched food from the dead man's garden in the jungle, or vines and bamboo for use in repairs, she would chase away a lizard or spoil a nest. Mi Tzu-hsia told herself that she would withhold judgment until Yuen gave her more than a glimpse of the moon, but she had surrendered her belief in the Host.

She had fallen into her new role as caregiver with little thought, surprised only at the ease with which she accessed the storehouse of her experiences as a living woman. She had been mother to six children, wife to a minor bureaucrat. Even in the imperial city, where they had been fortunate enough to live, disease and disaster were commonplace. Ministering to the sick was simply a fact of life. Mi Tzu-hsia had tended to family and friends in their dying hours, just as her friends had cared for her in her final days, after the miscarriage of her seventh child brought on hemorrhaging from which she did not recover.

Her work on the scrying apparatus resurrected many of those memories, and seemed to promise the rediscovery of a feeling she had long ago given up for lost: joy. The emotion itself was still beyond her reach, still hazy and half-felt, but Yuen's optimism and self-assurance reminded her of its potential presence in everything. Even though his wounds had begun to fester, he remained defiant in his happiness.

"There is nothing in death for me to fear, Lady Mi," he said one evening, as Mi Tzu-hsia worked quietly on the apparatus. "No, the gods have left our fate in our own hands. Like magic, we may do with it what we will."

"Yet still there is much suffering in the world," Mi Tzu-hsia sighed, her voice ragged still, but stronger from practice. "It cannot all be self-inflicted."

"True. Fools inflict more pain on others than themselves. Take us, for instance, and our plight." Though blind, he turned his head as if taking in the moonlit beach around them. Like many of his mannerisms, this dramatic pause had been made habit by long years of teaching. "We are both brought to this sorry place by superstition."

Mi Tzu-hsia merely grunted her assent. She had yet to find a way to tell Yuen of her true nature. Because she had died in blood on a moonless night, a sign that she might be one of Leng Tu's chosen, superstition demanded her body be ferried across the Wushan Straits and left untouched on the Isle of Fei. She had, as the old stories predicted, risen up as one of the walking dead. Yet Yuen believed her to be a leper driven from the mainland, not at all the monster she surely had been.

Perhaps his belief had more power than she would have credited not so long ago. Mi Tzu-hsia had lately felt the stirring of her long-slumbering humanity. Should she be able to finish these last few adjustments tonight, she might just feel that joy Yuen seemed capable of inspiring in her.

"After I attach the last of the flags and catch the moon's reflection in the water, is there anything left to do?"

When Yuen did not answer promptly, Mi Tzu-hsia was not alarmed. A sickness beyond the dead woman's feeble ability to heal had dug its claws into his chest and legs. He faded now and then; it would not be long before he was dead.

Mi Tzu-hsia wondered idly if he might come back as she had. She looked up at the full moon, brilliant and golden against a cloth of star-dotted sable. *No,* she thought, *to return one must die on the last night of the old moon, when Leng Tu's army is at its strongest.*

She chided herself for the superstitious thought, though not even Master Yuen had been able to fully explain why sometimes the dead did arise. Magic turned upon the unfortunate souls by evil men, he had suggested, or a powerful guilt over some wrong done in life that prevented the dead from resting. Yet Mi Tzu-hsia could think of no great wrong she had ever perpetrated, nor anyone who might hate her enough to deny her soul rest.

"One more task," muttered Master Yuen, breaking his companion from her reverie. "Yes, one more task after you tie off the flags and position the cauldron."

He sat up, jaw clenched with the effort. Mi Tzu-hsia was at his side instantly. "You must rest," she said kindly. "Conserve your strength."

"I've nothing left to save it for," he replied. "It is time to go, I think. Which brings us to your final chore." He opened his arms. "An embrace, my friend."

"My sickness—"

"Can hurt me no longer," Yuen interrupted. "I can scarcely feel the aches I have already cultivated." He opened his arms wider. "Come, Lady Mi, I grow weak."

Cautiously Mi Tzu-hsia moved into the blind man's embrace, held him tight as he spoke the simple incantation to activate the scrying device. She thought she could feel the magic of those words, or perhaps it was just the power of a living thing held close. They remained huddled together for a time, two fragile creatures supporting one another. At last Master Yuen turned and kissed her gently upon the cheek. "Even the dead can find redemption," he whispered through poison-tainted lips, and then was gone.

When Mi Tzu-hsia finally lowered Yuen's corpse to the ground and moved to the copper cauldron, nestled nearby in its complicated web of poles and ropes and flags, she saw what she had expected to see: an image of a desolate plain. A sudden sorrow overwhelmed her, grief for the loss of her friend and for all the pointless destruction she had wrought in the three years before his arrival.

The image in the scrying cauldron did not change until the rising sun made it fade. With the dying of the day, it returned, just as it did every night. For days and weeks, Mi Tzu-hsia stood in silent contemplation of its stark, seemingly undeniable truth. At last, though, something began to encroach upon the bright vista. "The shadow of the world," Yuen had called the moon's darkness, nothing more. Yet as that darkness crept across the barren ground reflected in the water, Mi Tzu-hsia saw something else: the vanguard of a vast army, nightmare creatures marching in horrible formation, keeping the moon as bleak and lifeless as her beach had once been.

The Host of the Damned.

The minions of Leng Tu were not warring against the Army of Huaxushi, but Time itself, biding the hours until they fell upon the world. Yuen had looked only into the light, and like those he despised, had seen only what he had wanted to see.

Mi Tzu-hsia overturned the scrying cauldron, frightening a rat that had come to feast on Yuen's unattended corpse. With one of the splintered poles, she attempted to spear the scavenger, but it scampered behind the lean-to and escaped. The dead woman stopped and looked around at her demesne. Gull nests were heaped everywhere. Creeping vines ate away at the border with the jungle. She was surrounded by life.

The scream that welled up from deep within her, that rang out in the darkness clutching the world, was very much the cry of a living thing.

Mi Tzu-hsia knew the truth of this, felt it in her rotting bones. Even as she staggered across the black sands, away from her failed kingdom of death, she sent up a mad, fearful whisper to Heaven—a prayer that this night not see the end of the Ebon Warlord's quest for recruits, that tonight the Pillars of Heaven once more hold his terrible army at bay.

THE UNDEAD

THE noble vampire has become a rather common-place character in the current canon of fantastic literature. Sometimes he casts himself as detective, like P.N. Elrod's P.I. Jack Fleming or Joss Wedon's Angel, while other times he just retakes his place in normal society like Tanya Huff's author Henry Fitzroy or Chelsea Quinn Yarbro's Count Saint-Germain.

True, certain precautions must be taken, strict dietary requirements and a bit of behavioral modification to avoid bad habits that might feel instinctual, but when it comes right down to it, society would appear to welcome more whole-heartedly the modern vampire rather than the habitual smoker or the bottom-feeding journalist.

Needless to say this is a far cry in terms of social acceptance from the days of Stoker's dank and musky tomb-bound Dracula.

SCELERATUS

by Tanya Huff

Tanya Huff lives and writes in rural Ontario with her partner, six cats, and a chihuahua who refuses to acknowledge her existence. Her latest book, out for DAW in May of 2003, was the third in the Keeper Chronicles called *Long Hot Summoning* and she's currently working on the first of three books spinning the character Tony off from her Blood series (DAW spring 2004). In her spare time she gardens and complains about the weather.

"MAN, this whole church thing just freaks me right out." Tony came out of the shadows where the streetlights stopped short of Holy Rosary Cathedral and fell into step beside the short, blond man who'd just come out of the building. "I mean, you're a member of the bloodsucking undead for Christ's sa . . . Ow!" He rubbed the back of his head. "What was that for?"

"I just came from Confession. I'm in a mood."

"It's going to pass, right?" In the time it took him to maneuver around three elderly Chinese women, his companion had made it almost all the way to the parking lot and he had to run to catch up. "You know, we've been together what, almost two years, and you haven't been in church since last year around this time and . . ."

"Exactly this time."

"Okay. Is it like an anniversary or something?"

"Exactly like an anniversary." Henry Fitzroy, once Duke of Richmond and Somerset, bastard son of Henry VIII, fished out the keys to his BMW and unlocked the door.

Tony studied Henry's face as he got into his own seat, as he buckled his seat belt, as Henry pulled out onto Richards Street. "You want to tell me about it?" he asked at last.

They'd turned onto Smithe Street before Henry answered. . . .

Even after three weeks of torment, her body burned and broken, she was still beautiful to him. He cut the rope and caught her as she dropped, allowing her weight to take him to his knees. Holding her against his heart, rocking back and forth in a sticky pool, he waited for grief.

She had been dead only a few hours when he'd found her, following a blood scent so thick it left a trail even a mortal could have used. Her wrists had been tightly bound behind her back, a coarse rope threaded through the lashing and used to hoist her into the air. Heavy iron weights hung from burned ankles. The Inquisitors had begun with flogging and added more painful persuasions over time. Time had killed her; pain layered on pain until finally life had fled.

They'd had a year together, a year of nights since he'd followed her home from the Square of San Marco. He'd waited until the servants were asleep and then slipped unseen and unheard into her father's house, into her room. Her heartbeat had drawn him to the bed, and he'd gently pulled the covers back. Her name was Ginevra Treschi. Almost thirty, and three years a widow, she wasn't beautiful but she was so alive—even asleep—that he'd found himself staring. Only to find a few moments later that she was staring back at him.

"I don't want to hurry your decision," she'd said dryly, "but I'm getting chilled and I'd like to know if I should scream."

He'd intended to feed and then convince her that he was a dream but he found he couldn't.

For the first time in a hundred years, for the first time since he had willingly pressed his mouth to the bleeding wound in his immortal lover's breast, Henry Fitzroy, allowed someone to see him as he was.

All he was.

Vampire. Prince. Man.

Allowed love.

Ginevra Treschi had brought light back into a life spent hiding from the sun.

Only one gray eye remained beneath a puckered lid and the Inquisitors had burned off what remained of the dark hair—the ebony curls first shorn in the convent that had been no protection from the Hounds of God. In Venice, in the year of our Lord 1637, the Hounds hunted as they pleased among the powerless. First, it had been the Jews, and then the Moors, and then those suspected of Protestantism until finally the Inquisition, backed by the gold flowing into Spain from the New World, began to cast its net where it chose. Ginevra had been an intelligent woman who dared to think for herself. In this time, that was enough.

Dead flesh compacted under his hands as his grip tightened. He wanted to rage and weep and mourn his loss, but he felt nothing. Her light, her love, had been extinguished and darkness had filled its place.

His heart as cold as hers, Henry kissed her forehead and laid the body gently down. When he stood, his hands were covered in her blood.

There would be blood enough to wash it away.

He found the priests in a small study, sitting at ease in a pair of cushioned chairs on either side of a marble hearth, slippered feet stretched out toward the fire, gold rings glittering on pale fingers. Cleaned and fed, they still stank of her death.

". . . confessed to having relations with the devil, was forgiven, and gave her soul up to God. Very satisfactory all around. Shall we return the body to the Sisters or to her family?"

The older Dominican shrugged. "I cannot see that it makes any difference, she . . . Who are you?"

Henry lifted his lip off his teeth in a parody of a smile. "I am vengeance," he said, closing and bolting the heavy oak door behind him. When he turned, he saw that the younger priest, secure in the power he wielded, blinded by that security, had moved toward him.

Their eyes met. The priest, who had stood calmly by while countless *heretics* found their way to redemption on paths of pain, visibly paled.

Henry stopped pretending to smile. "And I am the devil Ginevra Treschi had relations with."

He released the Hunger her blood had called.

They died begging for their lives as Ginevra had died.

It wasn't enough.

The Grand Inquisitor had sent five other Dominicans to serve on his Tribunal in Venice. Three died at prayer. One died in bed. One died as he dictated a letter to a novice who would remember nothing but darkness and blood.

* * *

The Doge, needing Spain's political and monetary support to retain power, had given the Inquisitors a wing of his palace. Had given them the room where the stone walls were damp and thick and the screams of the those the Hounds brought down would not disturb his slumber.

Had killed Ginevra as surely as if he'd used the irons.

With a soft cry, Gracia la Valla sat bolt upright in the Doge's ornate bed clutching the covers in both hands. The canopy was open and a spill of moonlight patterned the room in shadows.

She heard a sound beside her and, thinking she'd woken her lover, murmured, as she reached out for him, "Such a dark dream I had."

Her screams brought the household guard.

He killed the Inquisition's holy torturer quickly, like the animal he was, and left him lying beside the filthy pallet that was his bed.

It still wasn't enough.

In the hour before dawn, Henry carried the body of Ginevra Treschi to the chapel of the Benedictine Sisters who had tried to shelter her. He had washed her in the canal, wrapped her in linen, and laid her in front of their altar, her hands closed around the rosary she'd given him the night they'd parted.

Her lips when he kissed them were cold.

But so were his.

Although he had all but bathed in the blood of her murderers, it was her blood still staining his hands.

He met none of the sisters and, as much as he could feel anything, he was glad of it. Her miraculous return to the cloister would grant her burial in their consecrated ground—but not if death returned with her.

Henry woke the next night in one of the vaults under San Marco, the smell of her blood all around him. It would take still more blood to wash it away. For all their combined power of church and state, the Inquisition did not gather their victims randomly. Someone had borne witness against her.

Giuseppe Lemmo.

Marriage to him had been the alternative to the convent.

He had a large head, and a powdered gray wig, and no time for denial. After Henry had drunk his fill, head and wig and the body they were more or less attached to slid silently into the canal.

As Lemmo sank beneath the filthy water, the sound of two men approaching drove Henry into the shadows. His clothing stank of new death and old, but it was unlikely anyone could smell it over the stink of the city.

"No, no, I say the Dominicans died at the hand of the Devil rising from hell to protect one of His own."

Henry fell silently into step behind the pair of merchants, the Hunger barely leashed.

"And I say," the second merchant snorted, "that the Holy Fathers called it on themselves. They spend so much time worrying about the Devil in others, well, there's no smoke without fire. They enjoyed their work too much for my taste and you'll notice, if you look close, that most of their *heretics* had a hefty purse split between the Order and the Doge after their deaths."

"And more talk like that will give them *your* purse to split, you fool."

Actually, it had saved them both, but they would never know it.

"Give who my purse? The Hounds of God in Venice have gone to their just reward." He turned his head and spat into the dark waters of the canal. "And I wish Old Nick the joy of them."

His companion hurriedly crossed himself. "Do you think they're the only dogs in the kennel? The Dominicans are powerful, their tribunals stretch all the way back to Spain and up into the northlands. They won't let this go unanswered. I think you will find before very long that Venice will be overrun by the Hounds of God."

"You think? Fool, the One Hundred will be too busy fighting over a new Doge to tell His Holiness that some of his dogs have been put down."

Before they could draw near the lights and crowds around the Grand Canal, Henry slipped into the deeper darkness between two buildings. The Dominican's Tribunals stretched all the way back to Spain. He looked down at Ginevra's blood on his hands.

"Drink, signore?"

Without looking at either the bottle or the man who offered it, Henry shook his head and continued staring out over the moonlit water toward the lights of Sicily. Before him, although he could not tell which lights they were, were the buildings of the Inquisition's largest tribunal outside of Spain. They had their own courthouse, their own prison, their own chapel, their own apartments where half of every *heretic's* possessions ended up.

It was entirely possible they knew he was coming or that *something* was coming. Rumor could travel by day and night while he could move only in darkness.

Behind him stretched a long line of the dead. He

had killed both Dominicans and the secular authorities who sat with them on the tribunals. He had killed the lawyers hired by the Inquisition. He had killed those who denounced their neighbors to the Inquisition and those who lent the Inquisition their support. He had killed those who thought to kill him.

He had never killed so often or been so strong. He could stand on a hill overlooking a village and know how many lives were scattered beneath him. He could stand in shadow outside a shuttered building and count the number of hearts beating within. He could stare into the eyes of the doomed and be almost deafened by the song of blood running through their veins. It was becoming hard to tell where he ended and the Hunger began.

The terrified whispers that followed him named him demon so, when he fed, he hid the marks that would have shown what he truly was. There were too many who believed the old tales and he was far too vulnerable in the day.

"Too good to drink with me, signore?" Stinking of wine, he staggered along the rail until the motion of the waves threw him into Henry's side. Stumbling back, he raised the jug belligerently. "Too good to . . ."

Henry caught the man's gaze with his and held it. Held it through the realization, held it through the terror, held it as the heart began to race with panic, held it as bowels voided. When he finally released it, he caught the jug that dropped from nerveless fingers and watched the man crawl whimpering away, his mind already refusing to admit what he had seen.

It had been easy to find a ship willing to cross the narrow strait at night. Henry had merely attached himself to a party of students negotiating their return to the university after spending the day in the brothels of Reggio and the exotic arms of mainland whores. Although the sky was clear, the moon full, and the winds from the northwest, the captain of the schooner had accepted their combined coin so quickly he'd probably been looking for an excuse to make the trip. No doubt, his hold held some of the steady stream of goods from France, Genoa, and Florence that moved illegally down the western coast to the Spanish-controlled kingdom of Naples and then to Sicily.

The smugglers would use the students as Henry intended, as a diversion over their arrival in Messina.

They passed the outer arm of the sickle-shaped harbor, close enough that the night no longer hid the individual buildings crouched on the skirts of Mount Etna. He could see the spire of the cathedral, the Abbey of Santa Maria della Valle, the monastery of San Giorgio, but nothing that told him where the Dominicans murdered in the name of God.

No matter.

It would be easy enough to find what he was looking for.

They could lock themselves away, but Henry would find them. They could beg or plead or pray, but they would die. And they would keep dying until enough blood had poured over his hands to wash the stain of Ginevra's blood away.

Messina was a port city and had been in continuous use since before the days of the Roman Empire. Beneath its piers and warehouses, beneath broad avenues and narrow streets, beneath the lemon trees and the olive groves, were the ruins of an earlier city. Beneath its necropolis were Roman catacombs.

As the students followed their hired torchbearer from the docks to the university, Henry followed the scent of death through the streets until he came at last to the end of the Via Annunziata to the heavy iron gates that closed off the Piazza del Dominico from the rest of the city. The pair of stakes rising out of the low stone dais in the center of the square had been used within the last three or four days. The stink of burning flesh almost overwhelmed the stink of fear.

Almost.

"Hey! You! What are you doing?"

The guard's sudden roar out of the shadows was intended to intimidate.

"Why the gates?" Henry asked without turning. The Hounds preferred an audience when they burned away heresy.

"You a stranger?"

"I am vengeance," Henry said quietly, touching the iron and rubbing the residue of greasy smoke between two fingers. As the guard reached for him, he turned and closed his hand about the burly wrist, tightening his grip until bones cracked and the man fell to his knees. "Why the gates?" he repeated.

"Friends. Oh, God, please . . ." It wasn't the pain that made him beg but the darkness in the stranger's eyes. "Some of the heretics got friends!"

"Good." He had fed in Reggio, so he snapped the guard's neck and let the body fall back into the shadows. Without the guard, the gates were no barrier.

"You said he was ready to confess." Habit held up out of the filth, the Dominican stared disapprovingly at the body on the rack. "He is unconscious!"

The thin man in the leather apron shrugged. "Wasn't when I sent for you."

"Get him off that thing and back into the cell with the others." Sandals sticking to the floor, he stepped

back beside the second monk and shook his head.
"I am exhausted and his attorney has gone home.
Let God's work take a break until morning, for
pity's . . ."

The irons had not been in the fire, but they did
what they'd been made to do. Even as the Hunger
rose to answer the blood now turning the robe to
black and white and red, Henry appreciated the
irony of the monk's last word. A man who knew no
pity had died with pity on his tongue. The second
monk screamed and choked on a crimson flood as
curved knives, taken from the table beside the rack,
hooked in under his arms and met at his breastbone.

Henry killed the jailer as he'd killed the guard.
Only those who gave the orders paid in blood.

Behind doors of solid oak, one large cell held half a
dozen prisoners and two of the smaller cells held one
prisoner each. Removing the bars, Henry opened the
doors and stepped back out of sight. He had learned
early that prisoners would rather remain to face the
Inquisition than walk by him, but he always watched
them leave, some small foolish part of his heart hoping
he'd see Ginevra among them, free and alive.

The prisoner from one of the small cells surged
out as the door was opened. Crouched low and ready
for a fight, he squinted in the torchlight searching for
an enemy. When he saw the bodies, he straightened
and his generous mouth curved up into a smile. Hair
as red-gold as Henry's had begun to gray, but in
spite of approaching middle-age, his body was trim
and well built. He was well-dressed and clearly used
to being obeyed.

On his order, four men and two women shuffled
out of the large cell, hands raised to block the light,
bits of straw clinging to hair and clothing. On his
order, they led the way out of the prison.

He was using them to see if the way was clear, Henry realized. Clever. Ginevra had been clever, too.

Murmured Latin drew his attention back to the bodies of the Dominicans. Kneeling between them, a hand on each brow, the elderly Franciscan who'd emerged from the other cell performed the Last Rites. "In nomine Patris, et Filii, et Spiritus Sancti. Amen." One hand gripping the edge of the rack, he pulled himself painfully to his feet. "You can come out now. I know what you are."

"You have no idea, monk."

"You think not?" The old man shrugged and bent to release the ratchet that held the body on the rack taut. "You are the death that haunts the Inquisition. You began in Venice, you finally found your way to us here in Messina."

"If I am death, you should fear me."

"I haven't feared death for some time." He turned and swept the shadows with a rheumy gaze. "Are you afraid to face *me*, then?"

Lips drawn back off his teeth, Henry moved into the light.

The Franciscan frowned. "Come closer."

Snarling, Henry stepped over one of the bodies, the blood scent wrapping around him. Prisoner of the Inquisition or not, the monk would learn fear. He caught the Franciscan's gaze with his but, to his astonishment, couldn't hold it. When he tried to look away, he could not.

After a long moment, the old monk sighed, and released him. "Not evil, although you have done evil. Not anger, nor joy in slaughter. I never knew your kind could feel such pain."

He staggered back, clutching for the Hunger as it fled. "I feel nothing!"

"So you keep telling yourself. What happened in

Venice, vampire? Who did the Inquisition kill that you try to wash away the blood with theirs?"

Over the roaring in his head, Henry heard himself say, "Ginevra Treschi."

"You loved her."

It wasn't a question. He answered it anyway. "Yes."

"You should kill me, you know. I have seen you. I know what you are. I know what is myth . . ." He touched two fingers to the wooden cross hanging against his chest. ". . . and I know how to destroy you. When you are helpless in the day, I could drag your body into sunlight; I could hammer a stake through your heart. For your own safety, you should kill me."

He was right.

What was one more death? Henry's fingers, sticky with blood already shed, closed around the old man's skinny neck. He would kill him quickly and return to the work he had come here to do. There were many, many more Dominicans in Messina.

The Franciscan's pulse beat slow and steady.

It beat Henry's hand back to his side. "No. I do not kill the innocent."

"I will not argue original sin with you, vampire, but you're wrong. Parigi Carradori, the man from the cell next to mine, seeks power from the Lord of Hell by sacrificing children in dark rites."

Henry's lip curled. "Neither do I listen to the Inquisition's lies."

"No lie; Carradori admits it freely without persuasion. The demons hold full possession of his mind, and you have sent him out to slaughter the closest thing to innocence in the city."

"That is none of my concern."

"If that is true, then you really should kill me."

"Do not push me, old man!" He reached for the Hunger but for the first time since Ginevra's death it was slow to answer.

"By God's Grace, you are being given a chance to save yourself. To find, if you will, redemption. You may, of course, choose to give yourself fully to the darkness you have had wrapped about you for so many months, allowing it, finally, into your heart. Or you may choose to begin making amends."

"Amends?" He stepped back slowly so it wouldn't look so much like a retreat and spat into the drying blood pooled out from the Dominicans' bodies. "You want me to feel sorrow for the deaths of these men?"

"Not yet. To feel sorrow, you must first feel. Begin by stopping Carradori. We will see what the Lord has in mind for you after that." He patted the air between them, an absentminded benediction, then turned and began to free the man on the rack, working the leather straps out of creases in the swollen arms.

Henry watched him for a moment, then turned on one heel and strode out of the room.

He was not going after Carradori. His business was with the Inquisition, with those who had slowly murdered his Ginevra, not with a man who may or may not be dealing with the Dark One.

" . . . *you have sent him out to slaughter the closest thing to innocence in the city.*"

He was not responsible for what Carradori chose to do with his freedom. Stepping out into the square, he listened to the sound of Dominican hearts beating all around him. Enough blood to finally *be* enough.

" . . . *seeks power from the Lord of Hell by sacrificing children in dark rites.*"

Children died. Some years, more children died than lived. He could not save them all even were he willing to try.

"You may choose to give yourself fully to the darkness. Or you may choose to begin making amends."

"Shut up, old man!"

Torch held high, head cocked to better peer beyond its circle of light, a young monk stepped out of one of the other buildings. "Who is there? Is that you Brother Pe . . .?" He felt more than saw a shadow slip past him. When he moved the torch forward, he saw only the entrance to the prison. A bloody handprint glistened on the pale stone.

The prisoners had left the gate open. Most of them had taken the path of least resistance and stumbled down the Via Annunziata, but one had turned left, gone along the wall heading up toward the mountain.

Carradori.

Out away from the stink of terror that filled the prison, Henry could smell the taint of the Dark One in his blood.

The old man hadn't lied about that, at least.

Behind him, a sudden cacophony of male voices suggested his visit had been discovered. It would be dangerous to deal further with the Inquisition tonight. He turned left.

He should have caught up to Carradori in minutes, but he didn't and he found himself standing outside a row of tenements pressed up against the outer wall of the necropolis with no idea of where the man had gone. Lip drawn up off his teeth, he snarled softly and a scrawny dog, thrown out of sleep by the sound, began to howl. In a heartbeat, a dozen more were protesting the appearance of a new predator on their territory.

The noise the monks had made was nothing in comparison.

As voices rained curses down from a dozen windows, Henry ran for the quiet of the necropolis.

The City of the Dead had tenements of its own; the dead had been stacked in this ground since the Greeks controlled the strait. Before Venice, before Ginevra, Henry had spent very little time with the dead—his own grave had not exactly been a restful place. Of late, however, he had grown to appreciate the silence. No heartbeats, no bloodsong, nothing to call the Hunger, to remind him of vengeance not yet complete.

But not tonight.

Tonight he could hear two hearts and feel a life poised on the edge of eternity.

The houses of the dead often became temples for the dark arts.

Warding glyphs had been painted in blood on the outside of the mausoleum. Henry sneered and passed them by. Blood held a specific power over him, as specific as the power he held over it. The dark arts were a part of neither.

The black candles, one at either end of the skinny child laid out on the tomb, shed so little light Henry entered without fear of detection. To his surprise, Carradori looked directly at him with wild eyes.

"And so the agent of my Dark Lord comes to take his place by my side." Stripped to the waist, he had cut more glyphs into his own flesh, new wounds over old scars.

"I am no one's agent," Henry spat, stepping forward.

"You set me free, vampire. You slaughtered those who had imprisoned me."

"You may choose to give yourself fully to the darkness."

"That had nothing to do with you."

Holding a long straight blade over the child, Carradori laughed. "Then why are you here?"

"Or you may choose to begin making amends."

"I was curious."

"Then let me satisfy your curiosity."

He lifted the knife and the language he spoke was neither Latin nor Greek, for Henry's father had seen that he was fluent in both. It had hard consonants that tore at the ears of the listener as much as at the throat of the speaker. The Hunger, pushed back by the Franciscan, rose in answer.

This would be one way to get enough blood.

Then the child turned her head.

Gray eyes stared at Henry past a fall of ebony curls. One small, dirty hand stretched out toward him.

But the knife was already on its way down.

He caught the point on the back of his arm, felt it cut through him toward the child as his fist drove the bones of Carradori's face back into his brain. He was dead before he hit the floor.

The point of the blade had touched the skin over the child's heart but the only blood in the tomb was Henry's.

He dragged the knife free and threw it aside, catching the little girl up in his arms and sliding to his knees. The new wound in his arm was nothing to the old wound in his heart. It felt as though a glass case had been shattered and now the shards were slicing their way out. Rocking back and forth, he buried his face in the child's dark curls and sobbed over and over, "I'm sorry, I'm sorry, I'm sorry."

" . . . *confessed to having relations with the devil, was forgiven, and gave her soul up to God.*"

"And I am the devil Ginevra Treschi had relations with."

Loving him had killed her.

When he woke the next evening, the old Franciscan was sitting against the wall, the shielded lantern at his feet making him a gray shadow in the darkness.

"I thought you'd bring a mob with stakes and torches."

"Not much of a hiding place, if that's what you thought."

Sitting up, Henry glanced around the alcove and shrugged. He had left the girl at the tenements, one grimy hand buried in the ruff of the scrawny dog he'd wakened and then, with dawn close on his heels, he'd gone into the first layer of catacombs and given himself to the day.

"Why didn't you?"

" 'Vengeance is mine,' sayeth the Lord. And besides . . ." Clutching the lantern, he heaved himself to his feet. ". . . I hate to lose a chance to redeem a soul."

"You know what I am. I have no soul."

"You said you loved this Ginevra Treschi. Love does not exist without a soul."

"My love killed her."

"Perhaps." Setting the lantern on the tomb, he took Henry's left hand in his and turned his palm to the light. The wound began to bleed sluggishly again, the blood running down the pale skin of Henry's forearm to pool in his palm. "Did she choose to love you in return?"

His voice less than a whisper. "Yes."

"Then don't take that choice away from her. She

has lost enough else. You have blood on your hands, vampire. But not hers."

He stared at the crimson stains. "Not hers."

"No. And you can see whose blood is needed to wash away the rest." He gently closed Henry's fingers.

"Mine . . ."

The smack on the back of the head took him by surprise. He hadn't even seen the old monk move.

"The Blood of the Lamb, vampire. Your death will not bring my brother Dominicans back to life, but your life will be long enough to atone."

"You are a very strange monk."

"I wasn't always a monk. I knew one of your kind in my youth and perhaps by redeeming you, I redeem myself for the mob and the stakes I brought to him."

Henry could see his own sorrow mirrored in the Franciscan's eyes. He knew better than to attempt to look beyond it.

"Why were you a prisoner of the Inquisition?"

"I'm a Franciscan. The Dominicans don't appreciate our holding of the moral high ground."

"The moral high ground . . ."

"Christ was poor. We are poor. *They* are not. Which does not mean, however, that they need to die."

"I didn't . . ."

"I know." He laid a warm palm against Henry's hair. "How long has it been since your last confession . . . ?"

"The Tribunal's buildings were destroyed in an earthquake in 1783. They were never rebuilt. When I went back to Messina in the 1860s, even I couldn't find the place they'd been."

Tony stared out into the parking garage. They'd been home for half an hour, just sitting in the car while Henry talked. "Did you really kill all those people?"

"Yes."

"But some of them were bad people, abusing their power and . . . that's not the point, is it?"

"No. They died because I felt guilty about what happened to Ginevra, not because the world would have been a better place without them in it, not because I had to kill to survive." His lips pulled back off his teeth. "I have good reasons when I kill people now."

"Speaking as people," Tony said softly, "I'm glad to hear that."

His tone drew Henry's gaze around. "You're not afraid?"

"Because you vamped out three hundred and fifty years ago?" He twisted in the seat and met Henry's eyes. "No. I know you *now*." When Henry looked away, he reached out and laid a hand on his arm. "Hey, I got a past, too. Not like yours, but you can't live without having done things you need to make up for. Things you're sorry you did."

"Is being sorry enough?"

"I haven't been to Mass since I was a kid, but isn't it supposed to be? I mean, if you're *really* sorry? So what kind of penance did he give you?" Tony asked a few moments later when it became obvious Henry wasn't going to elaborate on how sorry he was.

"Today?"

"No, three hundred and fifty years ago. I mean, three Hail Marys aren't gonna cut it after, well . . ."

"He made me promise to remember."

"That's all?" When it became clear Henry wasn't going to answer that either, he slid out of the car and leaned back in the open door. "Come on, TSN's got Australian rugger on tonight. You know you love it."

"You go. I'll be up in a few minutes."

"You okay?"

"Fine."

"I could . . ."

"Tony."

"Okay. I could go upstairs." He straightened, closed the car door, and headed across the parking garage to the elevator. When he reached it, he hit the call button and waited without turning. He didn't need to turn. He knew what he'd see.

Henry.

Still sitting in the car.

Staring at his hands.

SLAUGHTER

by P.N. Elrod

P.N. Elrod has written over sixteen novels, edited two anthologies, and contributed to several others in the science fiction and fantasy genres. She is best known for her vampire/detective series, *The Vampire Files*, featuring undead detective Jack Fleming. She has cowritten three novels with actor/director/writer Nigel Bennett who played LaCroix in the TV vampire cop series *Forever Knight*. When she has the time, she may be found lurking at various sci-fi cons all over the country scarfing chocolate and talking non-stop about writing.

"HE calls himself Slaughter. None of the guys knows his real name."

The self-named Slaughter was at a booth a few yards from where Gordy and I were seated in the dimly-lit nightclub. More than half in shadows, Slaughter had his back to a wall, but in Chicago that was just healthy habit for certain guys. He'd popped up out of nowhere, and had apparently, without any fuss, taken over the running of one of the lesser businesses that were under Gordy's protective eye. Well, it had something to do with protection. I rarely asked Gordy for details about his work. If he wanted me to know something, he'd say.

"So what's the story?" I asked, pretending to sip

at a coffee. It was only coffee, too; Prohibition being a not-so fond memory meant you could order the best from Brazil without getting something else in the cup. Coffee and booze were the same for me: undrinkable. Thrift and principle dictated I not waste money or booze.

Gordy was slow to reply, being a careful man with his words, never using many and often given to understatement. He frowned slightly over his drink, which was also free of alcohol. When on a business call he never had so much as a short beer. "Sent some boys here last night to collect the club's usual cut. They came back empty. None of 'em's talking much, and what they don't say makes me think he's like you."

Another vampire? He'd caught my full attention. I looked more carefully at Slaughter, trying to see any sign of kinship. That would be impossible unless I got close enough to discern the absence of a heartbeat or unless he happened to walk in front of a mirror.

"Can't tell anything from here," I said, anticipating the question.

"Time for a word. I'll lead, you watch him." Gordy wore caution like a suit, which was why he'd lasted so long in the mob, and tonight I was his insurance. If Slaughter was like me, no ordinary bodyguard would be enough.

We left our table; Gordy's broad back blocked my view of a sizable portion of the club for a few moments. He was taller than me and a lot wider, all of it muscle; people stared and some whispered recognition. Not many bothered to notice me, which was how I preferred it.

Slaughter watched our approach. He was young, reasonably handsome, on the good side of his twenties, all dark eyes, tight mouth, and pale skin, but lots of guys in the mob were like that. His suit was sharp, expensive, and looked like it was wearing him. I tried to pick up his heartbeat, but too much general noise prevented anything so subtle.

"Slaughter. You know who I am," said Gordy from his height. It was not a question. "We need to talk."

Slaughter gave a half-smile to show he was amused, not intimidated. Wise men were respectful to Gordy; the rest tended to disappear without a trace. "Do we?"

"Yeah. Find a quiet place."

More smile. Slaughter's gaze flicked at me. He'd see a tall, lean man in a flashy double-breasted suit and silk shirt, Fedora hat pulled low, probably the gang boss' pilot fish, errand runner, bodyguard, or all three. No one important. When he focused back on Gordy, I could tell I'd conned another one. "Okay, come to the back."

We threaded past the tables, drawing a share of attention away from the dance music and the couples drifting around the floor by the band. The ripples faded along with the noise as Slaughter preceded us into the manager's office.

Gordy paused at the door. "Where's Herm?"

Until last week Herm Foster had been running things here.

"He left," Slaughter answered with a straight face. "Greener pastures."

We went in. It had all the usual office stuff, plus a long couch. A large-busted blonde girl was sprawled on it, fast asleep, her arm thrown across her eyes to shut out the light. She wore a dark red evening dress, cut low, and it looked like she'd been wearing it for at least three days. Slaughter went over and tapped the back of his hand against her hip. She woke slow and looked pitifully hung over.

"Out," he ordered. "Go clean up. Come back tomorrow."

She blinked, her eyes smudged and disoriented. It took her a moment to find her feet and then she tottered like a drunk. I could smell no booze on her, though. Ghost-pale, her heart was racing too fast, trying to pump blood that she didn't have. I put an arm out to steady her. Slaughter didn't bother.

"You go home and stay there," I murmured when she looked at me. I focused hard, but the effort was unnecessary; she was still more than half under Slaughter's influence and shifted loyalties easily enough. She nodded agreeably, her eyes blank now. I gave her more than enough for cab fare. "I mean it. Go rest up, get yourself well again, and don't come back."

Gordy caught my glance. Yeah, he'd spotted the clumsy bruising and red marks on her throat, too. He had the most poker of poker faces, but I could tell he was pissed. That wasn't even close to how I felt, but I kept my reaction to myself, this was his show for the present.

She nodded some more and left, choosing her steps one at a time like an old woman.

Slaughter had a narrow eye on me during the exchange, but I didn't think I'd tipped my hand. If he took me for a mob mug with a soft spot for females, all the better. He sat behind the desk, seeming to be at ease with himself and what to him should have been dangerous company. Gordy took a chair, and I shut the door so we wouldn't be disturbed. I remained on my feet, still playing bodyguard.

Slaughter spared me another dismissive once-over and beamed a smirk at Gordy. "So you wanna talk? What about?"

"This club is run by Herm. I picked him. Who picked you for his place?"

"I did. It was a sweet setup, so I moved in. Herm decided he should leave. He told me to expect you to notice."

"He was right."

"You got nothing to worry about. I'm running things the same, maybe better. No fights, no problems with the cops. Everything's copacetic."

"Except for the weekly payment."

Slaughter flashed his teeth. They were very white, but otherwise normal appearing, as were mine. "Yeah, I decided I don't need your kind of insurance after all. I'm glad you came by so we could straighten this out."

Gordy studied him a long time. He could take the spine out of most men when he gave them the cold eye, but this guy seemed immune. "You are not being very smart."

"Maybe, but I'm getting rich."

"At my expense. Such matters are not tolerated. If you want to keep the club, you have to pay for the privilege. That's how things work in this town."

In the silence I heard one heart beating, one set of lungs pumping: Gordy's.

Slaughter shrugged. "Those rules don't apply to me."

"To you more than most."

"Uh-uh. What do they call you? Gordy? You're gonna listen to me from now on." Slaughter leaned forward over the desk, fixing Gordy with a good hard stare. He had emotional strength behind it, had worked himself into a little anger, which was dangerous. Though it helped to hammer a point home, too much rage can shatter minds. I should know. Gordy's expression had gone as blank as the girl's.

I stepped in before things went over the edge, slipping a .38 revolver from my coat pocket and putting it between them. "Lay off," I ordered Slaughter, my voice wonderfully calm.

The unwelcome reminder of my presence startled him. He rocked back, eyes blazing. "Hey!"

"Fleming?" began Gordy, puzzled. He made a vague movement toward the gun he packed under his left arm, then stopped.

"It's all right," I said. "He's covered. He was working a persuasion move on you. Might be better if you let me take it from here."

He bit off further questions, trusting my judgment. That's why he'd asked me along. He quit his chair and got out of my way.

Slowly standing to bring us level, Slaughter turned his persuasive stare full on me. "You're gonna to listen to me, punk. You have to listen to me, understand? From now on I'm the only voice you can hear."

I felt a little pressure inside my skull, like the air when there's a weather change. Nothing I couldn't ignore.

"You are gonna listen and do everything I say . . ."

Familiar words. I'd used them myself countless times. It's a great way to get out of speeding tickets.

"You must listen—"

And it doesn't work on me. "The hell I will. Sit down and shut up." I cocked the gun and matched the muzzle level with his left eye. "Don't argue, just do it."

That thoroughly broke his concentration, and his mouth dropped open with shock. I wondered how experienced he was, if he knew he could survive a bullet. I had, lots of them, but getting shot hurts. Whether he was informed or not, Slaughter retreated, lowering himself into his chair, his hands out slightly in placation. The keystone of all his confidence was quite gone.

An intake of breath from him, a sniff. He was checking me for booze. He knew how that could interfere with hypnosis. What else had he figured out?

"You can't do this," he said, dumbfounded, maybe a little hurt. It's a tough moment, that awful one when you realize you're not all-powerful.

"How old are you?" I asked.

"Huh?"

"Your age. I won't ask again."

"Huh. Twenty-five."

"You got this dumb in just twenty-five years? Amazing."

"Who the hell are you?"

"To you, kid, I am Mr. Fleming."

"You don't call me kid."

"How old do you think I am?"

"Who the hell cares?"

"This dumb and bad manners. What a world."

"You—"

But he didn't get a chance to finish. I vanished first, cocked gun and all. Though invisible to Gordy, Slaughter would be able to see me in this state—as an amorphous gray cloud—so I wasted no time hurtling through the bulk of the desk to get behind him. When I reappeared, I was leaning over his shoulder, my mouth close to his ear and the cold muzzle pressed to his temple hard enough to bruise.

"You be quiet now, new boy," I whispered, trying to be as scary as possible. It didn't take much, I was in the mood and had seen enough movies to know how it was done.

Though he no longer used his lungs regularly, Slaughter caught his breath. "Oh, shit, you're—"

"Yeah, I'm the undead welcome wagon for the Windy City. And you've been putting your foot wrong ever since you crawled out of the woodwork. You're making certain people unhappy." A pause to let it sink in. I straightened enough to check on Gordy. His slab of a face was impassive, but I could tell he was highly amused by my act.

Slaughter tried to twist toward me. "Jeez, I didn't mean anyth—"

"Shuddup, kid. This piece has a hair-trigger and lead hurts just as much as a wooden stake. You can't vanish faster than I can shoot."

He made like a statue. Maybe he didn't know about our relative immunity to bullets.

I eased back, giving him an opening to jump me. He didn't take it. Going around the desk in the normal way, I hitched a hip on the front, keeping the gun well in sight. I eased it off cock, but kept it aimed on him. Used to be I didn't bother carrying, but Chicago is a tough place, even for a vampire, as Slaughter was beginning to find out. I looked him over, the same as he had for me, only I didn't make the mistake of underestimation. He was inexperienced, but every bit as physically dangerous as I when it came to supernatural abilities like strength, speed, and vanishing. What he'd done to the collection boys and the blonde girl indicated he knew how to manipulate minds. I hoped he would listen to sense before he really hurt anyone.

"You made a messy start, Slaughter, nothing that can't be fixed, but only if you decide to play smart. You can begin by apologizing to Gordy. Tell him you're sorry for being such a rude son-of-a-bitch."

Too off-balance to argue, Slaughter made a handsome, word-for-word apology. He probably didn't mean it, but he was obeying orders. Just what I wanted. "That's good. So—how long since you died?"

He glanced walleyed at Gordy.

"He's wise to us," I added. "Answer."

"About a month."

"How'd it happen?"

"I don't wanna say. It was in a fight, that's all."

One's death is always a very personal experience. For me, it was singularly unpleasant and violent, and even after a year I could still get a bad case of lock-jaw when the topic came up. "Okay, never mind. Who made you?"

"Nobody made me, it just happened."

I gave a short laugh. "And the stork delivers babies from under cabbage leaves. Come on and spill, we're all grown-ups here. Who was she?"

"No one."

"Was it a he, then?"

That made him mad. "You son-of-a—" He saw my expression and a twitch of my hand reminded him about the revolver. He thought better about finishing and settled back. "It was a girl."

"Where?"

"Here in town, the south side. Thought she was hooking a drunk. Saw her in an alley, looked like she was kissing him, then she—there was blood on her mouth. It was sick. I was gonna chase her off, but that didn't happen."

"What did?"

"She came after me instead. When she looked at me . . . I wanted her to, so she did. We did. I don't wanna say any more." He'd gone beet red.

"No need. But sometime during this enchanting encounter you exchanged blood, right?"

He nodded.

"And then you got killed sometime after. And then you woke up."

"Yeah. That's how it was. What about you? She do you, too?"

"No. The lady I was with had a greater sense of responsibility. You get a name, where she lives?" If his story was true, I wanted to find this careless girl. Vampires are damned rare, and the few that I knew were levelheaded and conscientious about their second chance at living and especially about bestowing the possibility on others. They didn't just leap out of alleys and attack people for blood, nor casually exchange it. Stupid behavior like that gets you noticed. Even in these days of electricity and scientific skepticism you might run into a would-be Van Helsing who's more than happy to rid the world of a medieval kind of bloodsucker. It had nearly happened to me once.

"I don't know where she is," said Slaughter. "That was months back. I forgot about it until the night I woke up. I guess she made me forget."

"She didn't tell you what to expect, what to do?"

"I figured it out. I remembered what she did and how she did it. It wasn't hard. I read that book about Dracula, but it was fulla crap. I can't turn into a bat."

I snorted. "You can do more than enough as it is. You've been abusing the privilege, taking this place over."

"It beats rolling drunks."

Thus did I get an idea of why Slaughter had been in that particular alley when he met the other vampire.

"Besides, how else am I supposed to make a living? The guys in the bread lines can work days, I can't. I'm flat on my keister the whole time."

"You've got options, but stealing isn't one of them. It annoys people."

"That's what he does." He pointed at Gordy. "Why do I have to be any different?"

"Because I said so. Use your common sense. You get yourself noticed and you get yourself dead. You think we're the only ones watching you?" That, so far as I knew, was a lie, but anything to keep this idiot in line.

"There's others? Like us? Where?"

I just smiled. "They can turn up at the damnedest times—and you won't spot them coming. You didn't know what I was until too late. There's plenty who would have staked you on sight. Just your good luck I'm willing to give you a chance to clean up your act before they come calling."

"Why should they bother? Or you? I'm not hurting you. Who the hell do you think you are to march in my place and tell me how to live? You some kind of king vampire around here?"

"Only when it comes to the dumb ones. Don't be dumb, kid. You've got a lot of great years ahead so long as you wise up fast. Gordy might not mind you running this place, but you have to follow the rules just like everyone else."

"Huh. What can he do to me if I don't?"

"He just waits for the sun to come up—you work out the rest from there."

Gordy played it through with an appropriate cold-faced stare. I knew him to be a good egg when it suited, but he was also a killer. He showed that side now.

Slaughter scowled, but gave a sullen nod. He only half-understood, half-believed. "So just like any other mug, I pay him and he doesn't kill me?"

"That's all there is to it. Beyond that, you live like a normal human being and keep your nose clean."

"How am I supposed to be normal? I'm not!"

"If I can get away with it easy enough, so can you."

"Why should I?"

"Figure it out. Your answer will tell you how long you'll live. Lay off the hypnosis until and unless you really need it to stay alive, the headache ain't worth the trouble. And you stop feeding from women like you've been doing."

"I gotta eat!"

"Then you go to the stockyards like the rest of us."

"What?"

"Plenty of cattle there, or hadn't you figured that out yet? They got blood to spare, and it's less risky. You can have all you want then. You ever use another woman for food, I'll twist your head off. And you know I can do it."

Even if the interview wasn't exactly satisfying to everyone, at its conclusion Slaughter looked like he'd behave himself for a while. He grudgingly provided a general location for the vampire who'd used and made him. Gordy and I left the club, climbed into his big car, and drove to his own place, the Nightcrawler Club.

"Don't trust that weasel," I said.

"Never," he agreed. "I see his kind plenty. He'll go along until he thinks he's wise enough, then watch out. I'll have people keep tabs on him in case he gets cute."

"Or at least until he's broken in on this new life he's got. The change is a hell of a thing for anyone to handle. It still gets to me sometimes."

"No excuse. He's trouble. His type don't learn easy. Maybe never."

"Yeah. But I gotta give him a chance. I see myself in him, and I don't like it. If things had gone different, I might have needed someone like me to knock some sense into my skull."

"You're too easy on Slaughter and too tough on yourself. You were never that dumb."

"I might have been if I'd lived in his shoes. What is he? Some poor schmuck who never had anything and now he can have everything for the asking. He's got the world in his hands, but he doesn't know how heavy it is."

"And you did when it happened to you?"

I shook my head. "It hit me different. I'd known what I was in for, but I made mistakes I'm still wincing over. I want to stop Slaughter before he trips."

"He's already tripped. You're just trying to stop him from landing too hard."

We spent the remains of the evening in Gordy's office while he made phone calls trying to find the mystery lady. Not having a name for her, coupled with a second-hand description made the task fairly hopeless, but Gordy had more eyes in this town than Argus. If he wasn't in the mob, he'd have made a hell of a detective.

"Anything?" I asked after returning from a round at the blackjack tables in the private room downstairs. I was down five bucks, but I'd enjoyed the game. Sooner or later I'd win it back with interest.

He lifted one large hand an inch to indicate frustration. "Bupkis. She could be in a different state by now. Or Slaughter made her up."

"He doesn't strike me as being too imaginative. Maybe he killed her."

"No reason to think that yet."

"No," I said. "No reason at all."

I left in the wee hours, driving to the stockyards. It's

dirty and it stinks, but I don't have to breathe regularly. The blood is plentiful and there for the taking, fresh on the hoof. I fed well, and I fed deep.

When I straightened from my crouch over the flowing vein I'd opened in a cow's leg, I saw Slaughter on the other side of the enclosure fence. I'd not heard him; he must have gone invisible and floated in.

He looked disgusted. "How can you do that?"

"Because it tastes good." I wiped at my mouth with a handkerchief.

"There's better stuff than that for guys like us."

"And we need too much of it too often. You'd kill the girl."

"Then take a little from a lot of girls. They don't have to know."

"That's rape."

He smirked. "Not if you make them want it."

"You're not a real man doing that."

"Don't tell me you've never tried. You ever kill anyone? Don't tell me you haven't."

"I've never killed . . . for blood."

He snorted and spat.

"Slaughter, why do you set yourself up to make people want to punch your nose into the back of your head?"

"A fancy-pants like you wouldn't last a minute with me."

He'd missed the point behind the question. Disappointing, but I'd more than halfway expected that. "Appearances are deceptive."

"Then prove it."

Much as I wanted to turn his smug face inside out, obliging him would do neither of us any good. We were evenly matched; it could go either way. And no matter who won, I'd lose any chance to straighten him out.

"We're not enemies, Slaughter."

"I think we are . . . because of what we are."

"We're a couple of guys standing around in cow shit."

"We're goddamn vampires, you son-of-a-bitch!"

"So?"

"You nuts or something? The things we can do—we can *own* this town! Don't you see that?"

"Yeah. From the first night I woke up, then I decided I didn't want the worry. I got my piece of the world; it's more than enough for anyone, and I keep my nose clean. You should do the same."

"Or Gordy the goon comes after me?"

"You're starting to get it." I vanished from within the cattle pen and reappeared only a pace or so from Slaughter. He was less surprised this time, but still scowled. Maybe he thought I was showing off.

"Gordy has to find me first," he said, as though trying to convince himself. "No one knows where I hide during the day."

I laughed a little. "You sure about that? Your life could depend on it. In fact, it does already. Just give us an excuse."

"Goddamn cow-sucker."

"Don't knock it till you've tried it."

"You can't make me."

"The idea is for you to do it on your own. Wet nurse ain't in my line. You think I couldn't force you? I'm older and stronger than you—" A lie, but believable to anyone who'd read *Dracula*. "—I wouldn't even break a sweat . . . but I'm trying to give you some respect."

A flash from his eyes. Was it suspicion or had I finally touched the right nerve?

"You've been through the wringer and had it tough," I continued. "I'm not talking about your life before your change, but what happened after you woke up dead. You were smart enough to figure things out and survive. That tells me you've got the smarts to get along without abusing others."

"What's it to you?"

"Respect for another bloodsucker. There's not a lot of us walking around. We look out for each other. I'm willing to teach you the rest of the stuff you need to know, but to put it like the high-hatters, I 'don't suffer fools gladly.' You think it over. If you decide you're not a fool, then look me up. I'm usually at the Nightcrawler Club. Just ask for Jack Fleming."

Slaughter made no answer, but he wasn't sneering, so that was some progress.

"I'll see you around," I said. He was between me and the street. If I walked past him, he'd might bump my shoulder or something to provoke a fight.

Entertaining as that might be, it was late and my suit had seen enough wear for one evening. I vanished again and flowed swiftly away, not reappearing until I was clear of the pens and well onto the sidewalk.

He followed me. A gray cloud that only I could see sieved through the fence, bumbled around for a moment, then solidified into his shape. By then, I was in my car and driving off. I didn't bother to wave good-bye.

At exactly sunset I woke as usual, but not in the usual spot at home. There, I had a fairly well-hidden sanctuary in the basement of my partner Escott's house. But because of Slaughter, I'd steered clear of its shelter in favor of an even better hidden bolt-hole in a tobacco shop. It was in an upstairs storage room that backed the office where Escott ran his not-too-busy detective agency. In a long box hidden beneath a lot of other boxes I was safe for the day. The only access was through the shop below or through a concealed panel in the common wall of Escott's back room. Only he and I knew about it.

Leaving the small bag of my home earth behind, I dematerialized and flowed through the wall, going solid again in the tiny rest room. Ingrained caution made me pause and listen before moving another inch. It paid off; someone was in the outer office. He was being quiet, but when I concentrate I can hear a gnat belch.

It wouldn't be Escott; he was out of town running an errand for a client, nor would it be another client. I'd made a point of locking the door before turning in. Next time I'd buy a heavy bolt to beef things up.

Deciding to be wary, I vanished and pushed my way through until I was just behind whoever was there. Serve him right if I gave him a heart attack.

The general grayness of my perception took on form and color as I gradually went solid.

The man turned out to be Gordy. His back was to me, his massive frame seated in one of the fortunately sturdy chairs by Escott's desk. Something must have come up for him to be here waiting for me. Normally, he'd just phone at sunset.

And he'd phone me at home. He didn't know I'd be here. He knew nothing about the box above the shop.

But Slaughter might—if he'd followed me from the yards.

"Gordy?"

No jump of surprise. Gordy turned like a machine, raising his gun to my chest level. His eyes were blank; his whole face was empty of thought. I dove in fast and grabbed his arm. The big .45 boomed twice before I could wrest it away from him, blasting craters in the plaster. He tried to get it back, but I gave him a hefty gut punch to distract him, shouting his name right in his ear.

He didn't quite double over. I had to pop him again, harder. That did the job. His knees hit the floor, but he still made a single-minded reaching motion for the gun. I shouted at him again, this time making eye contact.

"Listen to me, goddammit!"

He halted in mid-motion.

"Wake up, Gordy! Come out of it. You don't hear him anymore."

He blinked and shook his head like a drunk, but awareness finally flooded back. "Jeez, Fleming— what the hell . . . ?"

I sagged. "That goddamn little son-of-a—" The sudden shock of adrenaline that was trying to pound a hole in the top of my skull vented itself in multi-colored phrase for a brief time. When coherency returned, I apologized to Gordy for getting rough.

"No problem," he said, slowly boosting himself into the chair. "But you didn't have to use a sledge-hammer on me. I just wanna know why. How come I'm here?"

"Weasel-boy got to you."

"The hell you say."

"He sent you over to drill me." I held out the gun.

He gingerly took it and sniffed the muzzle. He looked at the holes I'd have to patch up before Escott got back. Evidently no one had heard or bothered to do anything about the noise of their making.

"You know what day it is?" I asked.

"Wednesday."

"Try Thursday night."

"I lost a whole damn day?" He never raised his voice. Any other man would be smashing furniture. "How the hell—"

"Hypnosis. He messed your mind up good. I can find out more, but I'd have to put you under myself."

He thought about it. Taking his time. "You won't make me quack like a duck?"

"I don't do that to friends."

His head wobbled, indication that I'd amused him, and marginally relaxed. "Okay. What do I do?"

"Just sit comfortable . . ."

It didn't take long to jog the whole business from Gordy's memory. Slaughter had turned up at the Nightcrawler not long after our cozy chat over the stockyards fence. He'd located Gordy and put him under, then gave him careful instructions to go to a place called the Escott Agency. There he was to wait and kill me as soon as I showed myself in the evening. Afterward, he was to return to the Nightcrawler like nothing ever happened. Slaughter would be waiting there for him.

I made sure Gordy remembered everything when I woke him up.

"Little son-of-a-bitch," he muttered. It was unanimous now.

"Simple but effective. If you got caught, you'd take the fall, and never know why. Wanna make book that he's going to be all set to give you fresh orders?"

"Nope. But even if I'd shot you, you wouldn't have died. Ain't that right?"

"A metal bullet's ugly, but not enough. Slaughter doesn't know how hard we are to kill."

"Then we show him how it's done."

"He might be watching outside."

"Hell."

It wasn't likely, being so soon after sundown, but

neither of us wanted to risk that Slaughter hadn't found a temporary resting place in some nearby attic or cellar. He'd have gotten up at the same time as I, and had only to find a view of the street to see how things progressed for his mobster puppet.

"Have a gander," I said, nodding at windows.

Gordy peered through the blinds. "Don't see nothing, for what that's worth."

"Not a red cent. We'll have to play this out, just in case."

"Why bother? Come back with me and let's just go after him."

"He's too hard to catch. He finds out we're onto his game, he vanishes—literally—and leaves town to set up someplace else. He'll kill, if he hasn't already. His next target could be you. He might hypnotize you again. He seems to like controlling people."

Eyes grim, Gordy nodded, accepting the possibility. "Can you do anything?"

"I got an idea . . ."

Gordy drove himself back to the Nightcrawler. That he'd left behind his usual chauffeur and strongarm again indicated Slaughter's not-too-subtle influence. I had a more clandestine exit via the tobacco shop, wafting invisibly past the last customers. One of them shivered when I brushed too close and joked that someone must be walking over his grave. I'd never thought that observation to be particularly funny.

I floated outside and streamed down the still-busy street until I found what seemed to be an alley at least a block away and there went solid. I felt a little naked without my hat, but if Slaughter came by the office and noticed it gone from the desk, he might get wise. My missing body could be explained, though. Gordy would feed him a line that I'd vanished upon expiring. Dracula had done so, after all. Never thought I'd be grateful for its inspired misinformation.

Hailing a cab, I got a ride to the Nightcrawler and had the driver drop me in the building's rear alley. I paid him off and vanished, aiming for Gordy's private suite, ghosting up the side of the building to ease through the wall. I don't like how it feels going through bricks and mortar, plaster and lathe, but it beats the brittle resistance of glass.

If Slaughter saw me in this state, the game was up. There was no way I could tell where he might be either. Chances were he'd be waiting in Gordy's office for his return with the news of my death. Gordy was of the opinion that Slaughter would be in the big chair behind the desk all set to take over. I had no reason to disagree. Slaughter must have mistaken my position in the scheme of things, thinking that I was really in charge of this mob. It would never enter his head that I might be hanging around out of friendship. Slaughter would judge me by his limits; he sure as hell wouldn't have any friends: only enemies and people he could control.

Eventually, I thought myself home safe, feeling the general shape of the area around me. Materializing, I puffed relief. It was a large closet and pitch-dark. Without even a faint outside source of light I was as blind as anyone else would be given the circumstance. I struck a match, careful to hold it clear. If I singed any of Gordy's custom-made suits, he would not be happy.

In the five seconds before the match burned down, I found what I wanted: a stubby, sawed-off shotgun high on a back shelf. Gordy assured me it was still properly loaded with some special shells he'd made up. We'd used it once before to deal with a vampire, and the memory was anything but pleasant. My fingers shook as they closed over its chill weight.

Wood can truly damage us or guarantee a kill. You just have to know to use it, whether it's a stake in the heart, a club to the skull, or small beads loaded into a shotgun shell. On a normal human, the latter would probably do less damage than rock salt, but for guys like me and Slaughter, it's a slow ugly death. Press both barrels against the chest and pull the trigger. Messy, but effective.

Maybe I wouldn't be able to do it. I'd killed before, by accident, in cold blood, and in the madness of rage. I wasn't proud of myself, and on those rare, awful days when I was stupid enough to get caught away from my home earth, the dreams ate through my helpless brain like acid. Slaughter was bad news, but was he worth another dent in my already battered conscience? Perhaps all he needed was an almighty scare and some sense beaten into him. That I could do and no problem.

But Gordy would want him dead. In these matters Gordy was usually right.

First get the drop on Slaughter, then decide.

Easier thought of than done.

I eased open the closet door, ears flapping. It was clear, but the next room over was Gordy's palatial office, and there I heard activity, but not conversation. I pressed against the wall. At least three people, two of them breathing. Slaughter, Gordy, and one of the strongarms? That wasn't right. We'd agreed to keep this party exclusive. Slaughter may have added a third guest.

Then one of the breathing persons released a long, delicious moan of gratification. The timbre was female, and I thought I understood what was going on, having enjoyed the pleasure myself, both giving and receiving.

Hugging the shotgun close, I bulled invisibly through the wall. When I went solid, pure shock froze me for an instant.

Slaughter had one of the cigarette girls on the couch, sprawling over her. He'd pawed the top half of her brief costume away, and buried his mouth deeply, greedily in the soft part of her throat. Her face was toward me, glowing, absolutely glowing from the pleasure of dying, lids squeezed shut, her arms wrapped tight around him. She moaned again, turning it into a sigh.

Across the room stood Gordy, hands to his sides like a soldier at silent attention. He should have been oblivious to the scene, but there was a terrible awareness in his expression. He'd been ordered to watch; he'd been ordered to do nothing. He looked at me, hope and fury in his white-rimmed eyes.

I couldn't shoot Slaughter without risking the girl. Had to move fast, he was draining her dry. I had to hold him in place to keep him from vanishing. On Gordy's desk lay a metal letter opener, thin-bladed, fragile, not too sharp, but effective with enough force behind it.

Not bothering to be quiet, I swiftly swapped the shotgun for the letter opener and closed on Slaughter just as he began to rise up to see the source of the noise. Blood was smeared all over his lower face. The whites of his eyes were suffused with blood from his feeding. They flashed scarlet in flat-footed surprise.

I drove in hard with the blade, slamming it into his side.

Shrieking fury and pain, he staggered to his feet, clawing at it. I grabbed his arms above the wrists and tried to twist them behind him. The metal in his body kept him from vanishing, but he was still capable of a hellish fight. We danced around the room, wrecking furniture. I kept him busy, waiting for Gordy to snap out of his spell and grab the gun. I yelled his name over the screaming, hoping that might work. He was still rooted in place the next time I spun around.

Slaughter managed to make a grab for the letter opener, and pulled it partway out. I punched a fist against the side of his skull. Any other man would have dropped, the bones caved in, not this guy. It slowed him, but he didn't stop trying to break free.

I dragged him toward the desk, toward the shotgun.

Roaring, he threw himself in the same direction, trying to get me off balance. I was too used to dealing with ordinary humans, not anyone with strength equal to my own. He tore one arm free and managed a solid, gut-bruising punch that made me grunt, then went for the gun, falling bodily on it.

His other arm wrenched from my grasp. He had the gun. I tried to lock him up in a full-nelson, but he shifted us in a clumsy waltz until he faced Gordy.

"Lay off or I scrag him!" Slaughter snarled, the barrels centered on my friend.

He'd follow through. Gordy's eyes told me as much. I broke off the wrestling hold and slapped both hands around Slaughter's skull. Then I twisted hard and sharp. I'd never done it before, wasn't sure if it would even work on Slaughter.

But I heard and felt the awful wet crack of bone and cartilage. Slaughter made a sick-making gagging noise and abruptly turned into dead weight. I let him fall. He dropped straight down, his only sound now a grunt as the air left his lungs. He lay on his belly, but his head was turned halfway around, his blood-red eyes stared at me.

"Jeez." Gordy, no longer frozen, shook into his normal posture. "Jeez, that bastard . . ."

I slumped relief, but for only an instant, hurriedly pulling the gun from under Slaughter's body.

Gordy came over and glared down. I'd never seen him angry. He always held it in behind a stone face. Not this time. I backed up a few steps, anticipating an explosion. God knows he was entitled. While I checked on the girl, he glared down at Slaughter for what seemed a long moment, then straightened and turned toward me.

"She okay?" His voice was calm as always, but I heard his heart booming, almost filling the room for me.

I pressed a fresh handkerchief against her neck wounds. They were larger than they had to be and still freely seeping. Slaughter had missed tearing fatally wide anything major in his greed, but it was likely more a matter of luck than care. "She needs a doctor to patch her up, but she should be fine."

"I know someone," said Gordy. "This guy. Is he dead? All the way dead?"

No heart or lungs working, no way for me to tell. I'd played possum a few times and gotten away with being taken for a corpse. Slaughter might be doing the same. Or he could be immobile from his injuries, unable to move, and—with the knife in him—unable to vanish and heal. I'd been in that position as well, and its dire helplessness was the worst. All you can do is scream within your mind until insanity brings a kind of ease, until death finally comes. We don't die fast. Maybe it's the price we pay for all the life we get after cheating death the first time.

"I don't know," I said. "There're ways to make sure."

"We make sure."

Gordy saw to a doctor, who wanted to know the cause of the girl's strange injury. Gordy told him a crazed customer got too fresh and bit her, which was close enough to reality. He said the customer had been dealt with and would not be returning. Later, I'd have to have a private talk with the girl and make sure she only remembered what we wanted her to know; for now, Gordy and I had other things to do.

He knew how to dispose of inconvenient bodies. I'd been with him on only one such expedition, taking care of another vampire's corpse. We would do the same again, with me along to make sure there was no sudden revival of the body. About an hour later, after a quiet phone call to arrange a truck and a boat, we were on our way. Slaughter's corpse was to be dumped so far out in the lake that even the fish would have trouble finding him.

Gordy and I rode in the back of the paneled truck, a carpet-wrapped bundle between us. His men would wrap a couple of hundred pounds of chains and weights to it, but only after loading it onto the boat.

Dim light filtered in from the small windows set in the truck doors, not much for Gordy, but plenty for me. He looked a lot calmer now, almost satisfied.

"Just realized something," he said.

"Oh, yeah?"

"You told Slaughter you'd twist his head off if he used another girl for food. I didn't know you meant it."

"Me neither."

"Maybe we should take his head off the rest of the way. Just to be sure."

"Maybe. Wait till you're on the boat. Easier to clean up after."

"Yeah."

"You had this ready," I stated. I still held the shotgun, playing bodyguard. "Wood in the shells, all that."

"Yeah."

"Why?"

"In case you ever got stupid," he said without apology.

"Okay." Well, he was honest. "I don't blame you. Jerks like Slaughter give vampires a bad name."

Gordy's head wobbled. Laughter. Then he sobered. "There's still another one out there. The one who made him, if he was telling the truth."

"Yeah," I said. I puffed air, and stared out the small windows on the doors. No moon. It was dark even for me. "So . . . what're you doing the rest of the night?"

A HOLLYWOOD TRADITION

by Brian M. Thomsen

Brian M. Thomsen has been nominated for a Hugo, has served as a World Fantasy Award judge, and is the author of two novels, *Once Around the Realms* and *The Mage in the Iron Mask*, and more than thirty short stories. His most recent publications as an editor include several anthologies in collaboration with Marty Greenberg for DAW Books, including *The Reel Stuff*, *Mob Magic*, *Oceans of Space*, and *Oceans of Magic*, and as a co-author with Julius Schwartz on his memoirs entitled *Man of Two Worlds—My Life in Science Fiction and Comics*. He lives in Brooklyn with his lovely wife Donna and two talented cats by the names of Sparky and Minx.

THE writer from Milwaukee hated these trips, especially the ones toward the end of a given project where there were still so many loose ends to tie up. The money from the advance as well as an additional early d&a payment were almost already used up, requiring him to adhere to an exceptionally tight travel and research budget that necessitated the use of city buses instead of taxis or car rentals, and roach motels instead of Hiltons and Hyatts. (He often wished that Motel 6 would set up a few outlets inside of the LA city limits, but such was not the case.)

This time the loose ends were a few legal releases

that had to be signed by some of his interviewees before his litigation-wary publisher would allow their revelations to be included in his upcoming star bio (he secretly wished that all of his subjects were dead), and a few necessary neighborhood photos that he had decided to shoot himself and save the expense of permissions (the star was abroad and his palatial Beverly Hills mansion was easily visible from the street).

Airline rates and discount fares necessitated a seven-day stay for the three days of work that had to be done, and with three days left before his return to the frozen north of Wisconsin in January, and the obligations of the almost fully paid-for book already met, the writer turned himself to his next matter at hand, namely figuring out the subject for his next book that could command enough money up front to keep him and his family out of debt for at least the length of time it took to write the first draft.

He had already proposed three subjects to his editor: the French New Wave, the European Exile Community in Hollywood during World War II, and Vancouver: Hollywood's Northernmost Suburb. Each was met with excitement, respect, enthusiasm . . . and a polite "No" after a review by sales and marketing. They wanted something BIG, HOT, and COMMERCIAL. As to subject matter, they had no suggestions but reiterated their faith in his ability to come up with a project worthy of his six-figure advance . . . but until then no Big Idea, no blockbuster . . . no blockbuster, no contract . . . no contract, not a single red cent.

In the past the writer picked his subjects from his own passions, or—in at least one case—by simple dumb luck. His most successful book to date was inspired by a conversation with a soda jerk. That had led to his first major bestseller, and he was quite desperate to repeat it. His future career as a "working writer" probably depended on it.

A "Rooms for Rent Cheap" shingle outside of a mansion located at the junction of two bus lines had caught the writer's eye on his way to a research meeting for which he got stuck with both the check for the drinks-turned-dinner engagement and the embarrassment of an over-the-limit Visa warning with nary a lead to the new work, and, despite the lateness of the hour, he decided to check out the accommodation and expense of the place in hopes of saving a few bucks, and at least killing the hour's lag time between connections.

The mansion was better than he remembered it. Very "Norma Desmond"; creepy yet elegant in a way that captured both the glory of yesteryear and the decay of the passage of time.

With any luck, the writer thought to himself as he rang the bell, *I'll be met at the door by some bald old German who will inform me that the mistress of the house can't be disturbed as she is playing cards with Mr. Fairbanks (Junior not Senior, of course) and Mr. Cooper (Jackie not Gary, for the same reason). I'll be invited in and treated to some dark and devilish revelation from Hollywood's past that will catapult me back onto the bestseller list . . . or maybe it will just be an old Mexican maid who was the former mistress of Selznick, Mayer, or Warner (maybe all three) with tales of romance and naughtiness of the Tinsel Town of yesteryear . . . or maybe it will just be a rooming house ten dollars cheaper than my current digs.*

He heard footsteps approaching down a long hallway as it started to rain behind him.

No matter what, I'll try to stretch this to fifty-five min-

utes, he thought, *or at least till the rain stops. You'd think this neighborhood could afford bus shelters.*

The casting department had either gotten it wrong or perhaps a Von Stroheim type was unavailable. The door was opened by a fellow of slight build in an out-of-style waistcoat that seemed to have been left over from some old Hammer film. Maybe the call had gone out for Peter Cushing types instead.

"Dear me. Oh, dear, it's starting to rain," the fellow dithered. "Come inside. You're probably between buses. You would think with the amount of taxes people pay around here they could afford bus shelters. Step inside, step inside . . . unless, of course, you don't want to. I assume you are here about a room."

"Uh, yes," the writer replied, both amused and relieved at the little man's antics.

"Well, I guess Mister Drake Ladd was right about placing the sign out where it could be seen at the bus junction. Long-term or short-term?"

"Short-term," the writer replied, adding "for now."

"That's what they all say," the fellow dithered. "Everybody comes out to Hollywood for a while and stays a lifetime, some even longer. You sir, and your face is familiar, I would say, are here on business."

"Correct," the writer replied. "I'm a writer, and this is sort of a research trip."

"A writer?" the fellow said, immediately taken aback. "Of books, I hope."

"Well, yes, of course. I'm just finishing one and getting ready to find something new to strike my fancy," the writer said guardedly. "When you said 'of books,' I was just wondering, as opposed to what?"

"Why, a no-good journalist of course," the fellow explained. "You know, one of those confidential tabloid fellows, out to dredge up all sorts of sordid tales, not to say that there aren't plenty of such tales around, some even related to this house."

"Do tell," the writer replied, trying to appear interested without appearing eager.

"Indeed," the strange fellow replied, his hand straightening out a few loose locks from his just-gray and thinning widow's peak that seemed to be losing a war of attrition with his balding pate, then abruptly changed the direction of the conversation. "But where are my manners? Come into the parlor and I will fetch you a cup of tea. There's no one around presently, but I can fill you in on the rates and all, that is, if you are interested in such things."

"Indeed," the writer replied, only afterward hoping that the fellow who he surmised was the butler or caretaker did not notice the touch of mockery in his own response.

"Indeed," the fellow replied, with a reassuring smile, and led the writer into the parlor where he was instructed to take a seat while the tea was fetched.

When the Cushing-esque fellow returned with the freshly brewed tea, the writer slipped into curious tourist mode.

"You mentioned something about sordid tales connected to this house," the writer mentioned, taking a sip of his tea as the fellow took a seat across from him.

"You might say that," he dithered. "I did."

"Why?"

"Well, the original owner was connected to a sort of scandal back in the silent era. He was a casting director who worked with all of the biggies, Mack Sennett, D. W. Griffith, all of the biggies."

"Do tell," the writer urged.

"Well, I guess if you miss your bus, there is always another in an hour."

"Indeed," the writer agreed, "and it is raining and I might like another cup of tea."

"And there are the details of your possible stay . . . but first the story. You see, the master of this humble abode first came to Hollywood at the beginning of the so-called 'Roaring Twenties' having briefly worked in the European film industry under such luminaries as George Melies and F. W. Murnau."

The writer subtly reached into his pocket and turned on a mini tape recorder. The fellow was probably mixing and matching names from the past based on stories his master had told him. Undoubtedly, the old geezer who owned the place, "the master" as this quaint fellow called him, had to be ancient and therefore unlikely to protest the appropriation of his name as a source.

"Perhaps your chair is uncomfortable," the fellow offered, interrupting his tale. "If you don't mind me saying so, you appear to be a bit fidgety."

"No," the writer replied quickly, "please do go on."

"Well, nowadays many don't remember Mack Sennett, but at one time he was the most powerful man in all of Hollywood. He had worked under D. W. Griffith in New York City, back when that was the center of the film industry—well, really there and New Jersey if you counted Thomas Edison and all—and Sennett was really the first major moviemaker to set down stakes in this area. The Keystone Kops,

Charlie Chaplin, Fatty Arbuckle, Harold Lloyd all worked for him. He was the King of Comedy or at least that was how he referred to himself, and as with every king there had to be a queen, and Mack's was Mabel Normand.

"Now, you have to realize that the movie business was still in its infancy and every day brought about new changes and innovations to filmmaking. Even the so-called experts were still making it up as they went along. This month, everybody made ten-minute comedies, next month twenty-minute tragedies, three-hour epics, etc. This week they needed actors who could be anonymous clowns, next week they needed personalities, and so it went.

"Sennett's problem initially was that he was trying to do everything, and as a result he always had his hands full as each day brought along some new problem that had to be solved. One of his biggest problems was his sometimes collaborator/sometimes fiancée Mabel Normand who had set her heart on three different goals: one, to be Mrs. Mack Sennett; two, to be the biggest star in the entire moving pictures industry (that was what they called it in those days); and three, to have the best time possible every day for the rest of her life.

"As the story goes, one day Mr. Sennett was confronted by two major problems that required his immediate attention. His discovery, Charles Chaplin, was threatening to quit unless all creative control of his performances was ceded to him, and Mabel was threatening to walk out on both him and the company unless he could find a way of making her more distinctive on screen.

"Now no one is disputing that Mabel Normand was an attractive woman with a face that was very pleasing to even the most discriminating eye. The problem was the technology at that time never allowed for a flattering enough picture of her. Her features would wash together in the gray/white/black palette of colors of the camera man's work (this was before anyone had even coined the word cinematographer) which did little to satisfy her desire to be a one-of-a-kind.

"The filmmaker was at his wits' end and was about to deal with his problems through self-lubrication with grain alcohol (I don't recall if this was during Prohibition or not, not that that ever mattered in the film industry) when a distinguished European gentlemen by the name of Drake Ladd entered his life."

"Now, you probably have never heard of the name Drake Ladd . . ." the fellow interrupted his story for a moment.

"I'm afraid not," the writer replied, taking a moment to jot down the name on the pocket-sized notepad that he always carried with him. "Does he own this house?"

"Indeed, he does," the fellow said, pausing just a moment with a close-lipped smile finally punctuated by an all-too-appropriate lightning flash and thunderclap that seemed to have come from just outside the window. "And his contribution to the silent film industry was invaluable."

"Ladd offered his services to Sennett as a consultant, having worked with some of Europe's great filmmakers, or so he claimed. Sennett was about to give him the brushoff when an idea came to him. He told Ladd that if he could solve the two problems of the day, namely Mabel's and Chaplin's, he could have his choice of several jobs on the lot. Drake Ladd accepted the challenge.

"Now it is important to note that at the time that Ladd and Sennett made their acquaintance, the day's filming was already over, and the California moon had already made her appearance in the sky. Sennett fully expected to awake the following morning with his problems still intact and, with any luck, no sign of the optimistic Drake Ladd.

"Morning came, and Sennett made a point of arriving at the studio a little later than usual in order to avoid any new altercations with his prima donnas. Both however were waiting for him, both in surprisingly good moods. Apparently the ubiquitous European had paid them both visits the night before to very positive results.

"Chaplin apologized for being unreasonable and agreed to return to work, and did so directly. After the soon-to-be-world-famous 'little tramp' left, Sennett quickly turned his attention to the now quite serene object of both his affections and future profits who, with a soft smile asked if he noticed anything different about her.

"It was then that he realized that her skin seemed whiter than ever, almost corpselike. Initially, he thought that perhaps she had taken to some sort of opiate or other narcotic, and feared that perhaps the European had opted to drug his leading lady.

"Mabel just laughed at the thought, and explained that the charming Mr. Ladd had suggested that the theatrical makeup that was designed to make her 'more of a ravishing beauty,' his words according to her, would be more effective if she paled her complexion naturally to improve its contrast for the film's grey scale, and with a coquettish toss of her head, she, too, returned to work.

"I feel it is necessary to interject here that, given the absence of color film techniques at the time,

Ladd's natural pale complexion method became quite popular among all of the stars, men and women alike. After all, everyone wanted to have features that stood out without two pounds of pancake on their faces.

"Needless to say, Sennett didn't know quite what to make of the work of a mysterious European known as Drake Ladd, but, being a man of his word, he waited in his office for Ladd to show up and claim a place on the payroll.

"Drake didn't show up until the early evening, explaining that business elsewhere and the lateness of the hour in which he retired on the previous evening, having met with both Mr. Chaplin and Miss Normand, had resulted in him oversleeping that morning and playing catch-up for the rest of the day.

"Sennett admitted that the European had indeed risen to the challenge that had been presented to him, and he was now prepared to keep his end of the bargain by offering him a place on the studio payroll as a special consultant and problem solver.

"Sennett was surprised at the ease with which Drake Ladd seemed to deal with the studio's problem stars, and he himself found Ladd very difficult to disagree with, many times embracing positions in arguments that he recalled previously being diametrically opposed to, such as allowing Ladd to set his own hours, have free run of the set, and be paid in cash.

"As Mabel the star became more and more compliant, Mabel the fiancée became more and more distant. Sennett initially didn't really notice. He was much too busy with holding on to the film empire that was just beginning to come apart as new competition began to surround him and eat away at his controls. Ladd seemed to become less available to solve the troublesome problems of the stars, and Sennett suspected that he was perhaps now in the employ of some of the other rising movie moguls that had sunk roots into Tinsel Town. In no time at all talkies were all the rage and Sennett was on his way out of town, a dismal failure."

The writer looked up from his notes for a moment and with a moment's hesitation interrupted the fellow's tale.

"But what was the scandal?" he asked, hoping not to appear to be a scandalmonger or even worse a dreaded journalist.

"Oh, I'm sorry," the host dithered. "I skipped over it. Let me backtrack just a little."

The writer detected a mischievous gleam in the old fellow's eye and pretended not to notice that his host seemed to enjoy playing with him like a playful feline who gently batted around a favorite mouse.

"Sennett, when all else was beginning to fail around him, had once again decided that he really wanted to marry Mabel Normand. The only problem was that she no longer seemed to have any time for him. Her career was also on the skids and rumor had it that she was seeing another man.

"Sennett surprised her in her apartment one night, having spied Ladd entering the premises, but when he got inside, Ladd was nowhere to be found, though he did notice the telltale bruising of a fresh love bite on his on-again, off-again fiancée's neck.

"He decided to hire a private detective to catch the two together, but despite statements and promises to the contrary, all he wound up with was a collection of photos of Mabel apparently alone in her apartment practicing some sort of love scene.

"Sennett confronted Ladd with the allegations and offered to buy him off if he would stop seeing Mabel. He agreed, but at a price, a rather exorbitant one at that."

"How exorbitant?" the writer queried.

"Well let me put it this way, how much do you think this house is worth?"

"Wow!"

"The agreed-upon price left Sennett on the verge of bankruptcy, but at least he still had Mabel. Or so he thought.

"Ladd kept his word, as would any gentleman of European extraction or otherwise, and never saw Mabel again. In reality she was just a convenient dalliance to sate his appetites and a new object of his affections was easily enough found. Unfortunately, such was not the same for Mabel. She showed no interest in returning to Sennett and spent the rest of her days looking for the nirvana that she felt being in the mysterious European's presence. I believe that she eventually died of a drug overdose of some sort.

"Sennett's company went under, and various others who had dealings with Ladd also seemed to come to bad ends. Names like Fatty Arbuckle and William Desmond Taylor to name a few. Ladd's name seemed to mean bad luck and misfortune. Others credited him with leading otherwise sane performers astray. Supposedly Sarah Bernhardt took to sleeping in a coffin after having an affair with him, and some link Bela Lugosi's eccentricities and drug addiction to a stint where the two spent time together during one of the star-studded cavalcade films, *The Big Broadcast*, I believe it was. Among the inner circles of the movers and shakers he began to be looked upon as a jinx, though this never stopped them from occasionally calling upon him to, how shall I say, put the bite on a troublesome star who didn't know his place. This was before the age of super-agencies like CAA, of course.

"Ladd didn't care. He had this house and all of Hollywood at his disposal. For one with tastes such as his, his appetite was easily sated."

The writer looked at his watch and realized that he had just missed another bus, and that the rain was still coming down. He hoped that the master of the house would arrive soon so that he could make some renting arrangements. He was sure the butler had plenty more tales of Hollywood to tell.

"Wow," the writer reiterated, "and Ladd is still around?"

"Indeed," the fellow replied.

"He must be ancient."

"At least," the fellow replied, standing up and drawing closer to the writer as if to retrieve the now empty cup and saucer from his hands.

"How long have you known him?"

"An equally long time," the butler said, a sinister grin evident on his face. "I'm very well-preserved."

The writer laughed. "I suppose you have a full staff of servants to keep this place going."

"Oh, no," the fellow replied, his eyes trained on the writer as if waiting to detect some sort of reaction, "Drake Ladd doesn't believe in domestics. One might say he prefers take-out."

"So you are his secretary?"

"No," the fellow replied. "I am he."

"But you can't be," the momentarily dense writer insisted. "You can't be much more than sixty, and even then . . ."

"I am much more than sixty," he replied, "and even as a vampire, I pride myself on being, how do you say, well preserved."

The writer's jaw dropped as he noticed the tooth-some smile of his host, the widow's peak hairline, and the gentle point of both of his ears, as he realized that his host's dinner hour had probably just arrived, and he was set as the main course.

Drake Ladd laughed as if reading his guest's mind.

"You have nothing to fear," Ladd said. "I won't harm you. Though I have not yet supped, I have no desire to place you on the menu. We'll call it professional courtesy. We are, after all, two of the same, metaphorically speaking, of course."

The writer was torn. He had always been insulted when allusions were made to his work being parasitic . . . then again, what's an insult or two when survival is at stake.

"Please don't take it as an insult," the host reassured, adding, "I was merely stating a fact. I thought I recognized you from a picture on one of your book jackets. We have a lot in common. We are not alone in this regard. After all, Hollywood itself is a vampire."

The writer fingered the chin whiskers that always seemed to grow faster when he was on the road, trying to at least give the impression that he was considering the metaphor at hand.

The host shook his head, obviously aware of the lack of understanding on the part of his guest.

"Come, come," he scolded. "I had taken you for an educated fellow, particularly on matters concerning Tinsel Town." The vampire massaged his brow for a moment, and snapped his fingers when a new illustration of the matter at hand came to him. "Surely you have driven on Mulholland Drive, that lovely stretch of road that starts out by the HOLLYWOOD sign."

"Of course," the writer replied with a bit of uncertainty.

"Well, who was it named after?"

With nary a mental effort, the writer replied, "William Mulholland."

"Who was?"

"A politician?" the writer answered with a hesitation.

"The superintendent of the L.A. Water Department," the host corrected. "He is the one who came up with the plan to provide irrigation for this area by draining off the reserves from the Owens Valley. When it comes to real estate, particularly California real estate, water is the lifeblood of the land, and L.A. sucked Owens Valley dry."

The host took to his feet, and extended a hand of friendship to the writer.

"I'm sure we will get along fine," the vampire replied, "and I'm sure that we will be able to come to terms on a reasonable rent for you."

The writer took the host's hand, which was as cool as cemetery granite, and gave it a firm shake of agreement.

"I believe that you mentioned that you are currently finishing a project, and looking at your options for the next one?"

"Yes," the author replied, his hand still clasping the cool and finely manicured humanlike paw of the bloodsucking predator before him.

The vampire gave a firm yank, drawing the writer closer so that he could now just see the sharp teeth that hid behind his host's cordial smile.

"Good," the vampire said with a predatory hiss. "We have much to discuss. It is about time that I give back something to the community that has kept me so hale and hearty."

"What do you mean?"

"It is time for the true stories of Hollywood to come out. The myths behind the legends, so to speak . . ." The vampire then set his blood-red eyes on the author and added, ". . . and you shall be my collaborator, the means to my message."

The writer found himself incapable of saying anything but "yes."

"Good," the bloodsucker replied. "The split on earnings will be fifty-fifty of course. My share, of course to be donated to charity, giving back to the community as I mentioned."

"Of course," the writer agreed.

"Indeed, others might be willing to contribute too, perhaps in exchange for . . ."

"Confidentiality?"

"Discretion." The vampire chuckled and added, "and there are more than a few folks around the industry that I would love to see you put the bite on, in the manner that you have proven yourself so adept at in the past."

With a final conspiratorial shake, the vampire released his guest's hand.

The writer replied silently with a conspiratorial smile of his own in agreement.

What went around comes around, and all accounts must be eventually settled.

There would always be a predator waiting to feed on the lifeblood that had fed on those that had come before.

Who was he to argue with a Hollywood tradition?

INTERCESSION

by Chelsea Quinn Yarbro

Chelsea Quinn Yarbro is the author of more than sixty books, among which are the Saint-Germain cycle of vampire novels.

TO the very worthy and most faithful Passionist monk, Andres del Cruzado, at the Monasterio de la Nuestra Señora, la Reina del Cielo at Antioquia, Audiencia de Santa Fe, the respectful greetings of Rogerio, manservant to el Conde de San Germanno, currently residing at Portobello, Audiencia de Panama.

The Church detained my master a number of months ago, and I have been subsequently unable to locate him or receive any news of his welfare. Recent inquiries have suggested that you may know where he is, for you have long kept the records of incarceration at your monastery and, in that capacity, have access to many more records of suspected heretics. I am writing to you in the hope that you will tell me where I may find him, and the reason for his detention.

I must here make bold to tell you that el Conde is no heretic, although he is not a communicant of your Catholic faith, for those of his blood come from the

Carpathian Mountains in Hungary, and in such places, the Greek Church is maintaining the mission of Christ against the forces of the sultan and all the Ottoman followers of their false prophet. Those of his heritage have defended that land from the might of Islam and offered havens to those fleeing oppression and slavery. He has done nothing to disgrace your Church, nor to bring any others to act against it; he has upheld the Church wherever it has flourished, and has given to its causes readily and generously; those acts are recorded and known. If you will review the records of Don Ezequias Pannefrio y Modestez, Corregidor, Audiencia de Lima of his time in Cuzco, as well as the Presidencia de Acapulco, for his time in the Audiencia de Mexico, you will see this supported in all his official obligations: he has long maintained cordial and respectful dealings with your Church.

For many months I have tried to find out what became of my employer after he called upon Obispos Trineo y Alfia and Apuesta y Fogon in Portobello in the Audiencia of Panama, shortly before he was scheduled to sail back to Spain. That day was April 16th, in 1649, one day before his ship, *El Testigo da Fe*, was to leave for Cuba and Cadiz, with ports of call in Bilbao and Calais. The ship departed four days later, but my master was not on it, and indeed, no one can tell me where he is since that hour when he called upon the obispos.

Surely, good Frey, you understand why I must find my master. I am obliged to serve him, and I cannot do this if I cannot reach him. I have undertaken to maintain his business ventures in his absence, but I cannot do so without his guidance. For that reason I implore you, tell me what you know, that I may do my duty to him, see that he is not, through some oversight or misplaced zeal, mistreated or held for crimes he did not commit. I know pursuing this matter takes you away from the work you do for the Glory of God, so I am including a payment to your monastery in the sum of twenty-five gold reals, not to pay for your time, which would disgrace your vocation, but to help your Order continue your Christian enterprises in the New World, even as my master himself would do were I missing and he searching for me.

For your assistance on my master's behalf, and with my gratitude for any information you are able to provide me, I am most humbly at your service, and thankful to God for your willingness to hear me,
                              Rogerio, manservant
At Portobello, Audiencia de Panama, the Feast of the Holy Trinity, June 22nd, in the Year of Grace 1652

To the most respected, devoted Passionist monk, Frey Andres del Cruzado, of the Monasterio de Nuestra Señora, la Reina del Cielo at Antioquia in the Audiencia de Santa Fe, the grateful salutation from the manservant of el Conde de San Germanno, Rogerio.

How very gracious of you to answer my letter of the last Feast of the Holy Trinity, and I am thankful for your information, which is most welcome, for it finally tells me that my master is yet alive, and that you, of the Church, know it.

But I fear I must impose on your charity again, and ask you where the Convento dell' Agonia is located. I understand that your Order supervises the convento, and the inmates living there. If I knew the location of the convento, I might be able to arrange something with the prior that would allow some communication with my master regarding his financial dealings, particularly his shipping ventures which are extensive and in need of close supervision. If he cannot give me his orders, then at least he can provide me with the authority to act on his behalf, which, in turn, will enable me to do all that might be done to keep his ships sailing.

Those who are imprisoned may sometimes receive visits from such members of their households as the Church deems appropriate to their welfare, and I would like to put such a petition before you at this time. I do not seek this to subvert the purposes of the Church: I believe it would be useful for me to do all that I can to carry out my master's instructions, not only because his ships carry cargo for Spain, but because he has long given certain preferential attention to goods commanded by the Church, and thus has brought about a mutually rewarding arrangement that I must suppose it is his intention to continue.

Good Passionist, I ask you to advise me. I am prepared to leave Portobello and move to a city more conveniently located to my master, but if this is not the wish of the Church, I will, of course, remain where I am, or take up residence in a place that the Church approves. Yet I do not know what course to take that will bring about the resolution to my perplexity. How am I to present these requests that they may be heard with compassion and an appreciation of mutual benefit? I thank you for any recommendations you may offer in this regard. And I am sending you fifty gold reals for your Order, as a demonstration of my sincerity and thanks for your attention in regard to my request. I am also hoping that this will help to defray any expenses my master may incur while residing at the convento, and ask, that if I have reckoned insufficiently, I may know the appropriate sum in your next letter.

I have sent this letter with the messenger Dalcut de Cartagena, who has long been employed in this capacity and was recommended to me by Frey Pascual of San Tomasso, a member of your Order, and a most worthy cleric in his own right, and who has often employed Dalcut as his personal courier. Dalcut has been paid to carry this to you and to bring your message back with all due haste so that we may exchange letters in a more timely manner. I shall expect your answer within six weeks of your receipt of this, which, you will agree, will be beneficial to both of us.

With my evening prayers of gratitude and my morning prayers of industry, I thank you for your efforts, and I beseech Heaven to reward you for all your kindness to me in helping me to better serve my master, for as the servant of man must model himself on the servants of God, so I am thankful for your excellent example. With devotion and Grace, I may approach your excellence.

Rogerio, manservant

At Portobello, Audiencia de Panama, January 24th, the 1653rd Year of Grace

To the most reverend Frey Cirilo de San Ysidro, Passionist, Prior of the Convento dell' Agonia, Passionist, near Popayan, Audiencia de Quito, the respectful greetings of Rogerio, manservant of el Conde de San Germanno, and upon whose behalf I now address you.

Your name was provided to me by a member of your Order and I have, of my own decision, made up my mind to approach you in the hope that you will be good enough to alleviate the many apprehensions that have come upon me since my master disappeared into the hands of the Church. I have spoken personally to all those religious in Portobello who might be able to advise me, and without exception, they recommended I address you, stating my concerns.

Since the unfortunate incarceration of my noble employer, I have sought to have his charges made clear and his case brought before proper authorities, all to no avail. I have been given many names with the assurance that such persons can and will assist me, but thus far, all have been fruitless, but for the most generous information provided by your good Passionist Brother, Frey Andres del Cruzado of the Monasterio de Nuestra Señora la Reina del Cielo, who has informed me that you, at the Convento dell' Agonia have my master in residence there; since I have been given your name and direction, I have taken the advice I have been given. This letter is the result. I pray that you will be the one to decide to uphold the law of the Viceroyalty and your Order, and address the great wrong that has been done to my master.

To be specific, my employer was detained by Church authorities and imprisoned at Portobello in the Audiencia de Panama on April 16th, 1649, and was covertly carried from there on a day I cannot yet name. He has been held incognito in what I have reason to hope now is your Convento dell' Angonia. If you will confirm this, I may, in my duty to my master, do my utmost to bring about his release and exoneration from all charges made against him. I plead with you to send me an answer quickly by the messenger Dalcut de Cartagena, who carries this to you. He has been most reliable and discreet in these matters, and you will find him spoken of most favorably by all manner of men in your Church. I ask you to entrust all communication to him, and to permit him to travel as soon as you have penned your answer to me. Much time has passed, and although I do not doubt that my master's soul has benefited from your good examples, I fear his businesses have need of him. If he cannot come himself, pray ask him to send authorization to me to continue on his behalf his ongoing work.

I am sending eighty gold reals to you as a donation to your convento, and with the hope that they will mitigate the cost of keeping my master among you; with these reals for his support, he need be no charge on you and at the same time need not live in a style unlike the one to which he has long been accustomed. I pray that if you need more for your work or for the benefit of my master you will inform me so that I may attend to providing the amounts you deem necessary.

In addition to providing funds for his keep, I would ask you to permit me to correspond with my master, so that I can act with the benefit of his experience and knowledge of his wishes in the matters of businesses he had undertaken in many parts of the New World. If correspondence isn't possible, then I ask that you permit me to inform him of what I have done, so that he may be kept abreast of the activities of his ships and shipping businesses. For example, I would like him to know that *La Luna Negra* has put into Maracaibo, Audiencia de Santo Domingo, for repairs, and that *Los Lobos del Yermo* has had to have new masts fitted on her, and now lies in the harbor of Veracruz, Audiencia de Mexico, awaiting orders for her next voyage, as she is no longer on the schedule that she once kept, and *Santa Clara de Assisi* has taken her routes for the time being, and is presently bound for Cadiz, Bilbao, Calais, and Bruges before returning to Havana and Portobello. These, and many other matters, are in need of his attention. If I proceed blindly, I fear I will make decisions counter to those my master would make, and I seek his council, or, barring that, his declaration that I may act on his behalf according to my own thoughts.

For any information you can provide me, I will be most grateful. I may have to travel on my master's behalf, and if that is necessary, the servants of this household will know how to find me, if I must be found. Of course, if my master has need of me, I am prepared to journey to him at any time, and to put myself at his disposal for as long as he has need of me. I pray this will persuade you of my earnest desire to aid my master, who is blameless of all accusations against him. I swear this on the bones of my family and of the saints who guard and protect all who come to them.

> Rogerio de Cadiz, manservant
> to el Conde de San Germanno

At Portobello, Audiencia de Panama, on the 30th day of August in the Year of Grace, 1653

To Atta Olivia Clemens, widow, resident at Senza Pari, vicina di Roma.

Respected Widow,

I am making bold to tell you that my master, el Conde de San Germanno, your blood relative, may have at last been found, at the Convento dell' Agonia in the Audiencia de Quito in the Viceroyalty of Peru. As you may know, that part of the Audiencia is very mountainous, and the convento seems to be particularly remote.

The Church has been paying very close attention

to my master's affairs, reviewing all his business dealings and inspecting his records and correspondence, as the King of Spain and the Pope require them to do. You must know that this has been a most difficult time for those of us who serve him, for we must often weigh the demands and considerations of the Church against the instructions of our master, all the while aware that we, as well as el Conde, are under constant scrutiny. Try as we will, we cannot always achieve accommodation, and for that, we are often given to distress at our inability to do as we must to honorably serve both the Church and our employer.

The reason I have approached you, good widow, is that I know as my master's blood relative you are in a position to be of some use to him during this ordeal. For one thing, you may be able to ask those you know within the Church to confirm or deny whether or not el Conde is actually at the Passionist Convento dell' Agonia, and for what purpose he has been sent there. I am willing to deal with the Church and the Passionists as long as they require, but I would like to know that my efforts are actually relieving my master and aiding in obtaining his release than simply adding to the Church's coffers. I have found the lack of response I have encountered most thwarting, and so I am trying to find the means to get around this bulwark of muteness; to that end I appeal to you for any help you may provide, for I am beginning to worry that I am spending my master's money to no avail.

Not that I would deny the Church any sums she may demand of me on my master's behalf, but I am obliged to put my exertions to his service as well as that of the Church, which I am certain you can understand, having such a manservant as Niklos

Aulirios to serve you. It is fitting that I do this, for it benefits my master and the Church, but I want to be able to account for what I have done in a manner that will satisfy el Conde as well as the Church.

Everything we do here is examined most meticulously, and we must be prepared to submit to such inspection often, without hesitation or any appearance of such. I know it is for the benefit of the Church and the King of Spain, but for me, in this instance, it has become a difficulty, and I ask you to secure what dispensations you can to enable me to continue to search for and defend my master without the constant supervision and arbitrary inspections that now dog all I do. I know that these inquiries are for the protection of our souls, but they tend to interfere with business, as any trader will vouch. Even now, I fear my master may be taken to another place, and my hunt for him may begin all over again because my actions have been so hampered and the information I have managed to garner is not current.

What is most perplexing, I do not know of what he is suspected, for I can find no record of formal accusation. No one has been able, or willing, to tell me more than that he may be at the convento, in what condition or capacity I cannot find out. You, being near the Pope and his court, may be able to learn more than I have been. I know you are a devoted daughter of the Church, and for that reason as much as any, I come to you with my request. I anticipate your reply with eagerness, and will instruct el Conde's ship that brings this, *El Zefiro* to wait at Ostia for two weeks to be able to carry your message back as quickly as possible. I have ordered the capitan to bring you the letter himself. His name is Diego Signo y Almejada, and he will tell you who has seen this, other than you, me, and himself. The capitan is reliable, and he will bring your response to me with all haste.

I am grateful to you, estimable Widow Clemens, for reading my petition, and for your kindness on my master's behalf. I ask you to recommend other avenues I might explore, for I am growing short of possible lines of inquiry in regard to my master. You have always been a stalwart supporter of those of your blood, from your days assisting Cardinal Mazarin in France to your cordial dealings with the staff of the Vatican. Surely your name is among the blessed for all you have done. I pray you will have the success that has thus far eluded me, and I am certain that my master is glad of your assistance.

> Rogerio, manservant
> to el Conde de San Germanno

At Portobello, Audiencia de Panama, September 1st, 1653rd Year of Grace

To the Capitan Diego Signo y Almejada of *El Zefiro*, at Portobello, Audiencia de Panama, bound for Santo Domingo and San Juan, Audiencia de Santo Domingo; then Cadiz; Barcelona of Spain; Ostia, for Roma; Genova; Cadiz; then Caracas, Audiencia de Santo Domingo, and Portobello, Audiencia de Panama, the greetings and full confirmation from Rogerio, manservant to el Conde de San Germanno.

In the continuing absence of el Conde, I authorize this voyage, and provide you with four letters of introduction and credit for your use in purchasing cargo. You have sailed on el Conde's ships long enough to know what markets el Conde strives to serve. I am also providing you with eight hundred gold reals for any purchases that may exceed your letters of introduction; the sum shall also provide pay and bonuses to the crew and any such repairs as may be demanded. The ship's carpenter shall have the authority to order the ship into port if he considers this to be necessary. I have also taken the liberty of arming you with three cannon and a half-dozen musquets to use in case of attack by pirates or Turkish corsairs. Do not waste the weapons or the ammunition, for they are given in case of need, not for a vain show of strength. In addition, I am entrusting into your hands a letter which you yourself are to deliver to the widow Atta Olivia Clemens who lives at Senza Pari, to the north of Roma. Only you are to carry it. You are to inform her who has read it, and under what circumstances, and you are to await her reply. You may stay up to two weeks to secure her answer, so long as you are then ready to depart.

When you reach Cadiz the second time, you are to find out as much as you can about the weather ahead before attempting a crossing. I would rather you wait in port until spring than lose you and the ship to winter storms. It is fitting for you to be prudent.

I remind you that el Conde will not permit any of his ships to carry slaves, and *El Zefiro* is no exception to his rule. Although el Conde may be detained, we must abide by his rule as long as we live by his coin. Remind all your men of the same, and be strict about your maintaining order in this, and all, regards.

Because the Church requires it, Frey Heberto, Dominican, will sail with you to Ostia, where another monk, or monks, will be assigned to you for your return trip. You are to show him all the respect and high regard he is due, and you are to provide him with full access to all you carry, in the name of el Conde de San Germanno.

May God give you safe passage and a swift return,
Rogerio, manservant
to el Conde de San Germanno

At Portobello, Audiencia de Panama, September 1st, 1653rd Year of Grace

To the most sublime Obispo Hector Enrique Ventarron y Cuenco, of San Simeon, Bogota, Audiencia de Santa Fe, the Nativity greetings of the manservant Rogerio, major domo to el Conde de San Germanno, along with his most sincere inquiry in regard to the appropriate manner in which to proceed in what has become an urgent yet delicate conundrum, to wit: the present location of and conditions of detention of my master, and what means are open to me to secure his freedom and restore his reputation once again.

As a faithful servant, I must, as you are aware, seek to alleviate my master's current situation, or, barring that, secure his instructions regarding his affairs in his absence. It would not be fitting for me to undertake to manage his fortune or his business without his specific instructions, particularly since he has no blood relatives in the New World to whom such ventures may be entrusted. So it falls to me to pursue a resolution for him, and to seek to resolve all issues that may have led to his seizure by Church authorities. To do these things, I must be allowed some contact with him, and, having gained that, I will follow his instructions to the letter.

At this time of the year, when our hearts turn to the promise of mercy, I implore you to consider my master's case, and to mitigate his plight, as a show of honor to the birth of Christ, which brought forgiveness into the world.

I ask you to review the law for such cases: it is my understanding that you cannot refuse me this access, according to the edicts of the Pope, for when no blood relatives are available to act on a man's behalf, His Holiness has determined that senior servants or duly appointed deputies may take up the obligations of family members; with that as my guide, I must act to determine his will, for there are many decisions to be made, and it would be improper for me to make them without first consulting with my employer, or I may do his interests more harm than good. It is difficult to presume I know my master's intentions, and therefore I find myself in these straits; I have been unable to secure any help from anyone that would help me to carry out the duties I must undertake if I am to be worthy of my employer's trust.

Most worthy Obispo, I beg you in the name of mercy, to allow me to write to my employer, to know where he has been taken, and to discover his wishes in regard to his case. I have asked for such contact before, and explained my purpose, but my entreaty has been ignored, and thus far all my petitions have met with denials or silence. Yet this leaves me in a most precarious position, for without any exchange with my master, I am in the dark, and may, all unknowing, act against my master's wishes rather than for them. Surely you, who guide the padres and freyes who serve the Church with you, must recognize the need for instruction from those authorized to give it. You have defended the Church and undertaken the teaching of the Gospels to the pagan savages of this land, and your padres and freyes have followed your dictates for the good of their souls as well as the good of those they have brought to the True Faith. So, in the worldly sense, would I do, in order that I may serve my master more fully and in accordance with his wishes. With your release of the knowledge I search for, I may begin to carry out the behests of el Conde, and once again be sure that my dedication is to the same goals that my master holds uppermost in his plans. I ask you to consider my plight and to find it in your heart to grant my request.

With my assurances of my gratitude and my most sincere expressions of appreciation in this trying time, I sign myself

Rogerio, major domo
to el Conde de San Germanno

At Portobello, Audiencia de Panama, on December 23rd, the 1653rd Year of Grace

To the most reverend Prior, Frey Vicente Puentes, Passionist, Convento dell' Agonia, near Popayan, Audiencia de Quito, the greetings of Rogerio de Cadiz, manservant to el Conde de San Germanno, and the consolation of your faith to you and your freyes on the death of Frey Cirilio de San Ysidro; may God comfort you in your sorrow.

I thank you for your prompt response to my letter, addressed to Frey Cirilio and carried by Dalcut de Cartagena. Many another cleric would have returned the letter unopened, and that would not have been useful to the Church or el Conde. I thank you again for your prudence in this regard, for I know it is within your discretion to receive or return all letters to your predecessor. You were most kind to read my missive, and to consider my request. I understand that without the proper dispensation you are powerless to do anything on behalf of my employer. I have been attempting to obtain the needed releases and specific descriptions of what I may be permitted to do for el Conde, and to what extent I may act. I would have pursued such material sooner had someone in the Church been willing to explain what I needed. But such is the way of faith, and I do not question the ways of Heaven.

Although you do not confirm my employer is in your care, you do not deny it either, which has given me reason to hope that you may have some contact with him. If you do, I beg you, in the name of the God all men revere, to tell him that I am doing all that I may to deal with his current state. If he is ailing, I ask you to inform me, that I may send his own medicaments to treat his ills. If he is allowed books, I would be pleased to send him books, so that he may use his time to better his soul with contemplative texts. If he is lacking anything you will permit him to have, be good enough to tell me, so that I may do what I can to supply his wants. Whatever he may endure, if there is something to succor him in his travail, let me know of it, so that I may discharge my obligation to him, and attend to his needs.

As soon as I have the required signatures and seals on the appropriate testaments, I will bring them myself to you, so that you may proceed in the certainty that the Church gives her permission to me to continue my work for my employer. I look forward to the hour when I may express my gratitude to you face-to-face. In the meantime, Dalcut of Cartagena carries a donation of ninety gold reals for your monastery, given in el Conde's name.

I pray God will keep you and guide you in your faith and bring you the peace of the soul. With many expressions of gratitude and with humble expressions of esteem,

> Rogerio de Cadiz, manservant
> to el Conde de San Germanno
At Portobello, Audiencia de Panama, February 10th, 1654th Year of Grace

To the most esteemed hidalgo, Don Calvino Eneas Alba Jorje Yunque y Cabolucha, Presidencia de Popayan, Audiencia de Quito, Viceroyalty of Peru, the greetings of Rogerio, manservant to el Conde de San Germanno, on behalf of his missing master.

Good Hidalgo, I must approach you in regard to a most perplexing matter: more than three years ago the Church detained my master, el Conde de San Germanno, and have given no reason for what they have done. They need not answer any questions in regard to those held in their custody, I know, but I am a man of honor, and I am required by that honor to locate and defend my master against all false accusations. So far I have not been able to confirm his present location, nor do I know anything of his condition, and so I am unable to seek the appropriate legal or clerical processes to end his most unjust sequestration.

For these reasons I come to you in this difficult time to ask you to ascertain where the Passionists have taken el Conde. I appeal to you as a man of law, and as one who knows the burdens imposed upon faithful servants, which I am bound to uphold. I have reason to believe that he is at the Convento dell' Agonia, near your city of Popayan, and so I have come to you to ask you whether or not my master is being detained there, on what charge, and in what state. Surely the freyes will tell you what they will not vouchsafe to me, out of regard for your birth and your position in the world. It is unusual, I know, to come to a civil authority with such a request, but I have found the Church is very slow to answer, and in the meantime, I have many matters of business that need a decision from my master, or I need a transfer of authority from him in order to keep his various ventures proceeding as he would like.

What is the most vexing part of this puzzle is that

my master has done nothing against the Church, and has, in fact, regularly given generously to the Church and supported her good works. There are many who can vouch for him, but thus far there has been no change in the posture of the Church in his regard.

I will provide a messenger to carry letters between us, the same man who has brought you this. His name is Linno van Meer, a mestizo from Caracas. He is discreet and dependable, and you may entrust your answer to him without fear. I have paid his wages and will provide him a handsome bonus on his return, so he will not be a charge upon you. He knows and approves this arrangement, and will abide by its terms.

In gratitude for any assistance you can give me, I sign myself,

                    Rogerio, major domo
                 to el Conde de San Germanno
At Portobello, Audiencia de Panama, April 22nd, 1654th Year of Grace

To Atta Olivia Clemens at Senza Pari near Roma,
    If you are reading this, my ruse has succeeded and John Towerman has actually been able to reach you without hindrance, and in spite of the many obstacles the Church has imposed upon those traveling from the Viceroyalty of Peru and Nueva España. He has been sailing on Dutch ships and has disembarked at Genova, with instructions to make his way to you at Roma overland, and I hope has avoided the most stringent inspections given to travelers from the New World. With this in your hands, I must conclude he has succeeded. He has my instruction to deliver this, completely unread, or to destroy it and to give you a spoken account of how I have tried to locate San Germanno. He is a staunch Protestant, and has

proven dependable and resourceful in the past, which is why I have entrusted him with this mission.

My appeal to the Presidencia of Popayan went unanswered, and thus far I have heard nothing more from the Passionists, either to confirm or deny having him in their care—whatever that may be. No other official, of the Church or the king, has been willing to provide me anything but polite, meaningless letters that acknowledge my inquiry and nothing more, leaving me at a loss to guess in what condition San Germanno now survives. You would know, through your blood bond, if he had died the True Death, but as you have sent no word to me, I must suppose that you assume he is still alive. This gives me as much vexation as hope, but I am glad to have it. These calculated delays and snubs, while infuriating, have steeled my determination to bring Sanct' Germain out of his durance vile.

I have paid out many handsome donations—or, more accurately, bribes; and will continue to do so as long as I must—to try to get enough information to know where my master is being held, all to no avail. I am running out of persons to approach, and I do not know how to continue the search, for no matter what I have attempted to do, I have achieved nothing. I do not lack for monies, and I can continue to make excessive payments for some time to come, but I know that the Church need not part with one iota of news if she decides not to do, in spite of gold and flattery.

Again, I ask you if you can gain some help from the various Vatican and Lateran authorities you know, for I fear I have reached the limit of my various avenues. Without some intervention from high within the Church, I feel I have nowhere left to turn, and that unless I take to the road as a vagabond to search for him, my master will languish somewhere in prison for years to come; without the intervention of a cardinal or the Pope himself, I begin to think that I am stymied. I have a few travelers in my pay to tell me what they hear on their journeys, particularly when they sojourn at monasteries. But the Convento dell' Agonia, where, as I've told you, I have reason to believe San Germanno is being held, does not open its doors to travelers, only to those seriously ill or afflicted in mind.

It is more than five years since he vanished, and I fear that another five could pass before his whereabouts are known. Given his nature, that time could be as intolerable an agony as his days on the cross for Doña Azul were. I do not like to think of the measures to which he may have had to resort to keep himself from thirst and hunger. If I could locate him, I could see he need not survive on the blood of rats or other vermin. The more I try to find him, the harder the task becomes. So, much as I do not want to impose upon you, Olivia, I will do so, and thank you profusely for all the aid you can give me—and that is neither gold nor flattery, but the simple acknowledgment of the blood you and my master share.

If you want to entrust a letter to John Towerman, assume it will be read when he returns to Portobello—everything coming in and out of San Germanno's household is, and picked over for the slightest hints of heresy and intrigue. It is an unexpected pleasure to write to you in such candor, even though it is on so desperate an occasion.

You know how grateful I am, so I will say only thank you for anything you may be able to do on

San Germanno's behalf. It is my sincerest hope that through our combined efforts we may secure his release and bring him safe to Europe once again.

Rogerian

At Portobello, Audiencia de Panama, July 12th, 1654

To the most reverend Obispo Alejo Ignacio Ventisceste y Aisaldo of San Eulogio de Cordova, Augostino, at Antioquia, Audiencia de Santa Fe, the most respectful greetings of Rogerio, major domo to el Conde de San Germanno, currently at La Casa de Eclipse, Maracaibo, Audiencia de Santo Domingo.

I pray that this letter reaches you through the good offices of my messenger, Dalcut de Cartagena, and that you will consider what is asked of you with charity and goodwill in your heart. You Augostinos are known for your compassion, and that is why I have made bold to address you in my travail.

It is nearly six years since my employer was taken by the Passionists to an unknown location for unspecified reasons, and have apparently kept him ever since. I say apparently because no one will confirm or deny that he is in their custody, making further action on my part fruitless. This official silence is most perplexing, for it has left me in the difficult position of having little or no recourse to pursue el Conde's release. The obstinacy of the Passionists astonishes me; there has been no notification of San Germanno's condition given, or any confirmation that he is detained, or even alive, which is why I have come to you for the aid I have been unable to gain from others.

My efforts to gain any information about him have been for naught, and I come to you in the hope that perhaps you might be willing to make inquiries in regard to my master, and then be willing to impart to me all you deem appropriate that I should know. I will bow to your discretion in this, of course, and I will be thankful for any information, no matter how small or inconsequential, you decide to provide, for it would be more than anything I have gained since the day el Conde vanished.

My master commands an extensive trading and shipping business, and without him to make decisions about his ventures, it falls to me to act in his stead, discharging his orders in accordance with the laws of the Viceroyalties of Peru and Nueva España. I have done this to the limits of my abilities and I have made an effort to do all I suppose he would want, but I am still compelled to act without the authority of his mandate, which is one of the things I seek in my desire to find him.

This letter is accompanied by a donation of one hundred gold reals, to be used for the Glory of God and the Triumph of the Faith. I send it on behalf of my master, who has long paid generously to the Church, and would, were he able to do so, provide such a sum himself, as the records throughout the Viceroyalties show.

If you are unable to assist me in my search, I would be most grateful if you would propose some other means I might employ to gain the information I seek. I have few options available to me since the Passionists have decided to reveal nothing in regard to el Conde.

I am going to remain here in Maracaibo for another six months, for I must supervise repairs to three of el Conde's ships that were damaged in the terrible storms of September and are not presently seaworthy, and I have to make sure they are restored to San Germanno's standards. When the ships are once again in service, I will return to Portobello, Audiencia de Panama, probably next autumn if God will but favor our endeavors, and I will hope that Dalcut will find me there with a merciful answer from you.

I am, in all things, a devoted son of the Church and a loyal servant to el Conde de San Germanno,

Rogerio, major domo

May 16th, 1655th Year of Grace

To the most respected and honored jurist, Jose Luis Remo Septimavictoria y Trigobien, Principal of the Magistratura of the Audiencia de Quito, at Quito, the salutation of Rogerio, major domo to el Conde de San Germanno, missing now for seven years, and upon whose behalf I take pen in hand to write to you.

Most worthy Principal, I ask you to read the enclosed copies of letters I have sent these many years in my efforts to locate and secure the release of my master who has been held by the Passionists, but who refuse to acknowledge his situation among them. I know it is their right to do this, but I implore you to urge them to allow me to exchange at least one set of letters with him, so that I can carry out his commands in regard to his businesses. You will see, in my many previous efforts, I have attempted to elucidate my reasons for such contact, but I have not gained one response beyond the fobbing off of my petitions to others who are in no position to grant what I request.

You are my last hope, for I have been unable to secure any information, and I begin to think it may be that my master has turned away from the world and taken Holy Orders. If this is the case, I must have his surety of it, and his official disposal of his titles and property before I can discharge my duties to him. You know that as well as any man in the

New World, and that is why I am importuning you in this way, so that I may proceed to carry out el Conde's commands, if he has any to issue.

The death of Innocent X and the election of Alexander VII to the Papacy may bring about a softening on the position of the Church in such matters, a development I would hope the law would echo, which should make dealing with such a case at this time important to a man advancing in the world.

You have given sound judgment in the past and many have praised your fairness. Let me join their chorus, in gratitude for your help. My plight is not so dire that I fear destitution, but it is severe enough to put me into a most difficult situation if, in my efforts to serve my master, I have, in fact, compromised all he has sought to achieve. He has been a most worthy patron, and I count myself fortunate to act for him, yet I must strive to do his will or I will not be eligible to number myself among those deserving of his favor.

I have done all that I think is sensible, and in accord with what he has done in the past, but after so long, the decisions I have made may now be turned from his goals. I have, for example, commissioned the building of two new ships for his fleet, one to replace the *Nubes de Marzo* that was damaged when it ran aground near San Juan, and one to accommodate the increase in business that has marked the last two years; it should be ready to put to sea in fourteen months, if all goes well. I have also maintained his schedule of ships' routine maintenance, for that is well-established and all the capitans know it, and regard it as part of their duties, for which I need only authorize payment, but to go beyond such obvious things is more than I believe it is appropriate for me to do without consulting el Conde; I trust you will understand my apprehension and do what you can to remedy my problem.

It is most alarming to have such long periods of silence, as a man in your position must know. The demands of the world impose upon us always, and we seek guidance to discharge our duties. Even orders from Madrid come twice a year. Surely you can comprehend my doubts, and if you do that, you will see why I have continued to pursue this matter for so long. To speak frankly, I am losing hope that I will be able to comply with the expectations my master has had of me, which distresses me profoundly.

If you can do nothing, I ask you to suggest someone who may be able to help me. My messenger, Dalcut of Cartagena, will bring your answer back to me as quickly as he can, along with the copies of previous letters for your perusal. You will see that all the copies are notarized, showing that they are full and accurate copies of the letters I sent, and the dates upon which I sent them. Dalcut is a most reliable man whose mission will cost you nothing, for I have paid him for his journey to Quito and back to Portobello already. Your response will make no charge upon you, and it will earn you my gratitude. I pray you, consider all I have done to find my master, and help me to bring him to his own again.

Rogerio, major domo
to el Conde de San Germanno
At Portobello, Audiencia de Panama, June 2nd, 1656th Year of Grace

To the most highly regarded advocate, Gualtiero Onofrio Garcia Hieloisla y Torpescalon of Buenaventura, Audiencia de Panama, the greetings of the man-servant Rogerio of Cadiz on behalf of his master, el Conde de San Germanno.

You have a most distinguished reputation, and for that reason I have decided to lay this problem before you in the remote hope you might for once abandon your posture of taking no case against the Church, and make an exception for my master.

I will admit from the first that I have had no encouragement from the Church to undertake this inquiry into my master's whereabouts, and have been given no information that would lead me to him. Every attempt I have made to find him has been ultimately unsuccessful. I wish you to grasp the extent of the difficulty I have encountered in this regard, so that you will be able to estimate the opposition that you may encounter. I cannot make light of this, nor would I expect that of you. I am including a calendar of events and letters in this case, so you may be apprized of how long I have attempted to gain information and how little success I have had. I would provide you with true copies of all the letters, but those I sent to the Principal of the Magistratura de Quito were never returned, and I am loath to part with my remaining copies if you are not in a position to accept this case.

I have myself twice been questioned by the Passionist Freyes of San Cristobal here in Portobello, and twice I have been released, with no hint of wrongdoing clinging to my name. I have ascertained that you need not fear reprisals from the Church should you be willing to act on el Conde's behalf. I ask that you ponder this case before you decide what you are to do, for I am at a standstill and without some support on my master's behalf, I must give up my search for him, which appalls me.

My courier, Linno van Meer, brings you this message and will wait in Buenaventura for two weeks to carry back your answer. He has been paid and so you will not be out of pocket for sending answer to me. I hope you will not refuse me out of hand, but at least give my predicament the favor of scrutiny before making your final decision.

I sign myself with gratitude,

Rogerio of Cadiz, major domo
to el Conde de San Germanno
At Portobello, Audiencia de Panama, September 17th, 1657th Year of Grace

To Atta Olivia Clemens at Senza Pari, near Roma
Most honored Olivia,

I trust my courier Linno van Meer has got this to you with no interference from the Church; he is a clever fellow and has been most energetic in carrying messages for me, all of which—until now—came to nothing. Until your letter arrived on *La Estrella dell' Aurora,* I had reached an impasse, and was unable to decide how to continue. To order Linno van Meer aboard her for her return voyage was a delight indeed. Your letter brings me joy, for it is the first break in what has been a wall of granite. My efforts have been frustrated at every turn, my petitions denied or ignored, and no matter what I have done, I have, in the end, gained nothing but indifference or enmity. Now I dare to hope that within the year I will know where San Germanno is and in what state he is being kept.

My other messenger, Dalcut de Cartagena, is presently carrying yet another petition to the Presidencia de Quito, although I have little reason to believe it will be read, or if it is, that it will produce anything more than the same courteous nothings that have been the hallmark of all my labors on Sanct' Germain's behalf. When Dalcut returns, I will put him on alert, so that as soon as the Encyclical arrives from the Pope, I can send him out again, this time for something other than disappointment.

I cannot imagine how you have managed to convince Alessandro VII to do this, but however you managed, I thank you from the bottom of my heart, and I know Sanct' Germain will be deeply in your debt, and small wonder: you have spared him from more suffering than he has already endured, and for that alone, I am grateful. I also know that you, as one of his blood, must feel for him; that you have been moved to help him will evoke all his cognizance of the debt he owes you. I look forward to the badgering you will provide him upon his return. How good you are, and how kind. I cannot say enough how deeply obliged I am to you for all you have done, for me and for Sanct' Germain.

Rogerian

Post scriptum: Burn this.

Post post scriptum: If you are having trouble with the work being done on the villa, why remain in Roma? You have other places to go, and you need not supervise all the reconstruction being done. Even if mischief is part of your problem, appoint a deputy and get away for a while. For once, Olivia, step back from difficulties. Only let me know where my letters may find you.

At Portobello, Audiencia de Panama, January 20th, 1658

To the most revered, sublime Obispo Reynaldo Martin Maria Rodriguez y Espinadoble, Trinitarian, of Sagrada Corazon, in Cartagena, Audiencia de Santa Fe, Viceroyalty of Peru, the most humble greetings of Rogerio de Cadiz, major domo to el Conde de San Germanno, on whose behalf I now address you, pursuant to the particulars of the Papal Encyclical *Misericordia et Justus*, issued by Pope Alejandro VII for all New World Bishoprics, which provides for the security of all prisoners held by the Church in the New World.

His Holiness states that anyone held by the Church is entitled to the succor of his relations and servants, and the prompt knowledge of what crimes or heresies he is accused. My employer, el Conde de San Germanno, seems to be in the hands of the Passionists and has been for nine years. I say seems to be because there has been no communication between el Conde and me, and the Passionists have consistently refused to confirm or deny that they have el Conde in their care, although I have reason to believe he is at the Convento dell' Agonia near Popayan in the Audiencia de Quito. With Pope Alejandro's Encyclical, it becomes necessary for the Church to inform me where my master is and of what he stands accused.

I appeal to you to begin the inquiries that will result in discovering where el Conde is presently incarcerated—for I can use no other word for his detention for so long a period—and I will express my thankfulness with this donation, in el Conde's name, of one hundred fifty gold reals, to help in the good work of the new Papal Encyclical. You must have many uses to which to put this money; I pray you will find it to your benefit. As a Trinitarian, you are not part of the long dispute among the Passionists and the Franciscans and Carmelites, and therefore you are more fortunately placed to carry out the Pope's wishes with dispatch.

The donation and this letter is being carried to you by my personal messenger, Dalcut of Cartagena, who travels under escort of six armed men, all of whom will be at your disposal in regard to el Conde. Dalcut will bring any missive from you to me as quickly as the roads will allow, and I will put myself at your disposal at any time you may ask it.

I am fully aware of how diligently you have followed the instruction of Innocent, and therefore I repose all my faith in you. I trust that before the year is quite over, I will have the felicity to behold my employer once again, and that he and I will both praise your justice and fairness. The vindication of el Conde has been my goal for almost a decade, and I thank the Pope and God for this Encyclical. I cannot help but hope that he will shortly be released when it is demonstrated that he has done nothing against the Crown or the Church.

With every assurance of high regard and continuing gratitude, I sign myself,

> Rogerio of Cadiz, major domo
> to el Conde de San Germanno

At Portobello, Audiencia de Panama, July 19th, 1658th Year of Grace

To the very reverend Passionist, Frey Vicente Puentes, Prior, Convento dell' Agonia, near Popayan, Audiencia de Quito, the very humble petition from the manservant Rogerio de Cadiz on behalf of my master, Francisco Ragoczy, el Conde de San Germanno, and through the authorization of the Papal Encyclical *Misericordia et Justus*, for the release of el Conde de San Germanno who is said to be in your care.

Good Prior, I ask you now to confirm or deny the presence of el Conde at the Convento dell' Agonia, and to specify what charges are laid against him, and any judgments you may have reached in regard to those charges.

To help you in your good works, I am sending with this petition the sum of two hundred gold reals, my courier Linno van Meer, and an escort of eight armed men to insure the safe arrival of this letter and the reals. This is not intended to influence you on my master's behalf; the Church has many obligations, and this gold should help in meeting them.

I have included the letter from the Trinitarian Obispo Reynaldo Martin Maria Rodriguez y Espinadoble, of Sagrada Corazon in Cartagena, Audiencia de Santa Fe, one of the first of the New World obispos to receive the Encyclical from Roma, which reiterates the Pope's wishes, confirms the Encyclical, and makes it mandatory for you to reveal all information you have on el Conde de San Germanno, for which I will be profoundly thankful beyond words to express. This compassion of His Holiness is an example to all of the faithful.

Upon receipt of the information requested, I will attend upon my master to escort him back to Portobello and return him to his rights and honors, which have not been accorded him in more than ten years. I am prepared to leave on two days' notice, with appropriate companions for such a journey.

I thank you for all you do to assist my master in this time, and I pray that we will bring this to a conclusion suitable for the Church and el Conde.

Rogerio, major domo
to el Conde de San Germanno

Portobello, Audiencia de Panama, January 9th, 1659th Year of Grace

To Atta Olivia Clemens

Linno van Meer has brought this to you by his usual clandestine ways, and I am confident that he has not encountered any interference from Church authorities. He has many ways to deal with the Church, and thus far, all have been successful.

I write to you with mixed emotions, for although your most wonderful efforts brought about the *Misericordia et Justus* Encyclical, the only information the Passionists provided was that he had been there, but had been sent to the Monasterio del San Fructuoso of the Dominicans at Piura, Audiencia de Lima, and so I must pursue him there. I will need to go to that place if I am to bring about a hasty resolution of this long ordeal. This is to insure that you will know where I am, and where Sanct' Germain has gone.

Your concern for Sanct' Germain is well-taken; I, too, hope that long confinement has not wrought too harshly upon him, for creatures such as you and he do not easily tolerate long imprisonment, particularly if there is restriction of movement as well as isolation from others, for it reduces your sustenance to rats and similar unwholesome provender. When those of your blood are subjected to prolonged periods of such fare, as I need not tell you, there is a price to pay. You and I have seen what such privation can do to Sanct' Germain, and therefore I am attempting to anticipate any demands that he will need to have met promptly. As you can see, I have considered the problem already, and you may be sure that I will arrange what I can to alleviate his most pressing need as quickly as possible, which may not be easy, for I expect to continue under Church scrutiny for some little time to come. Still, no one is wholly subject to his appetites, and vampires are no exception; Sanct' Germain will bear whatever impositions he must, and I am confident that he will find restoration without exposing himself to any additional danger than what he has already endured.

There have been severe storms this winter, and so news from Europe and England has been slow to arrive, and the spring has continued tempestuous, so this will not come to you as quickly as I could like. Sanct' Germain's ships' capitans are under orders not to put to sea until the winter storms are past. Still, a minor delay will seem all of a piece with everything that has happened through the last several years, and I know you will not begrudge Linno van Meer a safe passage to bring this to you, and your response to me.

I look forward to your next letter, which will have to pursue me to the Audiencia de Lima, for I plan to leave in two weeks' time. You can send your letter directly to Piura in the Audiencia de Lima, and I will retrieve it from the magistratura. I know you will understand my decision, and applaud it, for, armed with the Encyclical, I cannot conceive that the Church would refuse to obey the will of the Pope.

This is hardly the first time I have set out to locate Sanct' Germain, but I have not often met with such obduracy as I have encountered in the last ten years. Not even the years he was a slave in Spain, or the time he sent me to you for the duration of the Plague were as troublesome as this decade has been. You have comforted me in my complaints, and kept up my courage when my fears were bleakest. I do not say this for sympathy, but to express my continuing frustration arising from the endless delays. You have endured many of the same foilings at various times, and you know how onerous they can be. I ask you to remember those periods, and to share in my relief that this tribulation is finally ending.

Niklos Aulirios has sometimes had to search for you as I have for Sanct' Germain, and I imagine he has known the despair I have felt; I have occasionally comforted myself when I have been the most despondent with the knowledge that he, too, has been visited by hopelessness. To have it finally come to an end is a delight that Niklos can explain far better than I, and doubtless more eloquently.

I will put this aboard the *Duquessa de Alba*, which is scheduled to leave two days after I depart myself, weather permitting. Linno van Meer will carry your answer to me, and I will send him back to you as soon as he reaches Piura, with whatever news I will have to impart. Let us both hope that it is all to the good.

You have brought about Sanct' Germain's liberation. May you always thrive and enjoy the favor of privilege to which you are so richly entitled.

Rogerian

At Portobello, Audiencia de Panama, January 11th, 1659

To the most admired, exalted Dominican Prior, Frey Leonardo Felipe Oviedo Cubierta y Sabiogolpe of the Monasterio de San Fructuoso at Piura, Audiencia de Lima, Viceroyalty of Peru, the respectful greetings of the manservant Rogerio de Cadiz, and in that capacity, I address you on behalf of my employer, el Conde de San Germanno.

I am informed by the Passionist Prior, Frey Vicente Puentes of the Convento dell' Agonia near Popayan in the Audiencia de Quito, that el Conde has been turned over by his freyes to you and yours. If this is true—and I have good reason to think that it is—I ask you to provide me with a full account of his detention upon my arrival in Piura, in accordance with the reforms of Alejandro VII expressed in his Encyclical, *Misericordia et Justus*. I will introduce myself to you after I present my bona fides at the Magistratura de Piura, and at that time will provide a donation in my master's name of two hundred gold reals for the work of your Order. This is only to show my devotion, and the devotion of my master, to the cause of the True Faith, not to influence you, but to show appreciation for all the Church has done in the New World. Once I have made a formal introduction to you, I will avail myself of the grants expressed by His Holiness in his Encyclical, and ask for the prompt release of el Conde.

Certainly, as a Dominican, you must be concerned with rooting out heresy wherever you find it, but I implore you not to assume that because the Passionists held el Conde for so long it must indicate that he is heretical in his views, but rather to acknowledge that had the Passionists encountered heresy in el Conde, they would have put an end to him; his long survival points to his innocence, not to his guilt, good Prior. If you would be willing to examine all claims against him bearing my remarks in mind, I know God will guide you aright, for in my many years serving el Conde I have never known him to betray his faith in word or deed. Should you desire my testimony, I will give it to the full extent of my capacity, and under the terms of the Pope's Encyclical, which inspired document guarantees that no family or staff may be held as a means to achieve a confession from a suspected heretic or apostate prisoner.

I will travel as quickly as is possible, and my messenger, Dalcut of Cartagena, will present this to you as soon as he reaches Piura. He will be at least ten days ahead of me, giving you ample time to gather the records and make the report I have requested, for he will leave before the heavy storm brewing at sea blows in to Portobello. I, perforce, must attend to el Conde's ships, then I will depart to the south. I pray that when I arrive you will allow me to speak with my master, for as much as I need a report on his last decade, so I must present him a full account of mine. I have attempted to conduct his business affairs in such a way as I believe would serve his interests, but as I have not been permitted to correspond with him, I am aware that it is imperative that I inform him of all that has transpired in his absence. To that end, I ask for an interview with him at as early a time as you can arrange.

In all the time my master was detained by the Passionists I exhausted every possible means of aiding him, and all to no avail, for until the Encyclical commanded it, the Passionists refused to furnish any and all information in his regard; it was as if el Conde had vanished from the earth entirely. Now that he is given into your care, I trust that such difficulties are at an end. I will bring with me authorizations from Trinitarian Obispo Reynaldo Martin Maria Rodriguez y Espinadoble, of Sagrada Corazon in Cartagena, Audiencia de Santa Fe to facilitate the liberation of my master, and to provide you with the necessary material to satisfy the Pope's officers, should any lingering questions remain. I do not ask anything more than what His Holiness Alejandro has provided, nor would I. I have proceeded upon this course with the advice and council of Obispo Rodriguez y Espinadoble, and I repose complete reliance in his wisdom. I pray you will give close attention to his most reverent expostulation.

I am filled with gratitude for the guidance and patronage that has made it possible for me to fulfill my obligations to el Conde, and to be able, at long last, to bring about the resolution I have sought.

> Rogerio, manservant
> to el Conde de San Germanno

At Portobello, Audiencia de Panama, January 14th, 1659th Year of Grace

To the most dependable, upright, and correct advocate, Bartolome Baltezar Bernal Hogaza y Hoja of Portobello, Audiencia de Panama, the salutation of Rogerio de Cadiz, manservant to el Conde de San Germanno.

Most worthy Advocate: in my absence from Portobello, you are charged with continuing my duties in regard to my employer's business. I have included a schedule of voyages, repairs, trading agreements, and policies which are to be upheld while I am gone, along with a history of trading for each one of el Conde's thirty-seven ships, the better to assist you in arranging new cargo. I am supplying you with five hundred gold reals to carry out these necessary duties, which should exceed your needs by almost double. I provide you so much in case there are unexpected expenses—a shipwreck, a storm that damages warehouses or my employer's villa—that must be met without delay. I am certain your judgment will be responsible in such matters.

I will send regular reports back to you as I travel, and I will expect the same from you, which is why I am leaving Dalcut de Cartagena with you to carry our messages back and forth. Dalcut knows the road I will travel, and he will find me if it is necessary for you to reach me at some unplanned point in my journey. When Linno van Meer returns from Europe, I ask you to give any messages he carries to Dalcut to bring to me at once. The six men I have hired to serve as escort have received half their pay and will be given the balance upon our return, which I hope will be swift, and with el Conde once again among us.

It is my intention to travel from Portobello to Buenaventura, then to Quito, to Guayaquil, and from there along the coast road to Piura, using the main roads established by the Crown, not only for the safety they provide, but in order to secure safe lodgings and provender along the way. Too many travelers have met with mishaps on lesser roads, even those that may offer swifter passage, for me to risk so much by departing from the Camino Real. I have decided against traveling by sea, due to the reports of pirates plying the waters from Buenaventura to Callao. My escort should be able to hold off robbers on the roads better than they can defeat pirates on the seas. If the weather is good and we encounter no serious delays, we should be in Piura in six or seven weeks, for we will use our own horses—two for each man—for the entire journey, and not depend on remounts along the way. It may be a bit slower, but it will get us there in safety. We will rest at Quito for three days, and have the horses reshod. I will carry replacement shoes with us, in case one should be cast on the road.

If it should be necessary for us to remain at Quito longer, I will, of course, notify you from our inn, and I will expect to prepare you a report in that place which Dalcut may retrieve from the magistratura there, if he does not arrive before we leave.

Pray for our success, good Advocate, and el Conde will return, his name restored and his innocence established. While I am on this mission, I will repose confidence in your integrity, and I thank you now for your most diligent attention to all the responsibilities delineated in the enclosed material.

With thanks I sign myself

> Rogerio de Cadiz, manservant
> to el Conde de San Germanno

At Portobello, Audiencia de Panama, January 19th, 1659th Year of Grace

*   *   *

To Niklos Aurliros, manservant to Atta Olivia Clemens at Senza Pari near Roma, the most profound condolences of Rogerian.

Your letter did not reach me until I arrived at Quito, which will account for my tardiness in answering your letter of December 21st, 1668. I cannot yet grasp your tragic news, though I have read your letter twice and am unable to comprehend what you impart there; my reason slides away like light from a shadow as I attempt to understand your account. I cannot imagine how you must feel, and I am transfixed by emotions too recondite to set down here. How incomprehensible, to know she is dead. I cannot conceive of Olivia being gone from this world! The True Death! After more than a millennium and a half of life! How this must pain Sanct' Germain, for he must have sensed her loss through the blood bond.

An explosion, a collapsing building, her spine broken—how could it happen? She had said she had had problems with the restorations she had begun, but who could have thought it would lead to this? It is useless to speculate how she might have survived had she gone to one of her other holdings, or abandoned the project for a time.

I am going to save your letter so that I may give it to Sanct' Germain when I finally see him, since he has already perceived the loss of her; your account of the event may help him in some way by easing what his imagination may be telling him.

My messenger will carry this letter to the port of Maracaibo and put it into the hands of the capitan for delivery to you as soon as the ship reaches Ostia. I fear you may not see this before May, but I assure you it will reach you as quickly as possible; my concern for you and for your tribulation is ongoing no matter when you read this, for Olivia was a true linchpin in my life, and in Sanct' Germain's. I am shaken to the bone at this dreadful news. I can think of nothing to say that could offer you relief for your anguish, for so enormous a loss is beyond words—no matter how heartfelt—or sympathy to alleviate. Still, know that I share your grief, although mine is a faint echo compared to yours.

I can write no more; I am too deeply grieved. In the most genuine commiseration,

Rogerian

At Quito, Audiencia de Quito, March 8th, 1659

To the most respected, highly-regarded Dominican Prior Frey Leonardo Felipe Oviedo Cubierta y Sabiogolpe of the Monasterio de San Fructuoso at Piura, Audiencia de Lima, the greetings of the manservant Rogerio de Cadiz who is newly arrived in Piura.

I have presented my bona fides to the magistratura and my escort and I are staying at the Posada de Mil Flores on the Plaza de Santa Ynez. I will present myself to you after noonday devotions tomorrow, and I ask you to be willing to receive me. I bring you another one hundred gold reals to help you in the good work you do.

It is also my hope that I will be permitted to speak with el Conde, and to determine what he requires of me; after so many years, I feel it incumbent upon me to apprise him of all the decisions I have made on his behalf, so that he may assess for himself how well I have upheld my mission. This may not be possible, I do understand, but I am eager to assure myself that he is well. There is some news I must impart to him concerning the death of one of his blood, and I know that it would be more appropriate to tell him face-to-face than to pass a letter to him.

I am prepared to remain here as long as it is necessary to bring about el Conde's unconditional release. To that end, I will make it a point to secure the services of an advocate in order to speed the process that must be undertaken. I am fully aware that el Conde will not be vindicated in a matter of days, nor in a week. However long it takes, I will pursue el Conde's complete exoneration of all hint of wrongdoing, as I must as his manservant. I have been in his service half his life, and I cannot abandon him. No doubt you will appreciate my position and my devotion, for the dedication of monks has long been an example to me.

You are reputed to be a most sapient, diligent monk, and that inspires me with hope, for I know that you will review el Conde's case with wisdom and tranquil evaluation, and will undertake to decide the matter fairly, which is no more than either my master or I would want, for any fair assessment of the case will readily make his innocence apparent. I will stand ready to assist my master in any way you may require. It is fitting that I should do so, as you are certainly aware. I have great faith in your sagacity, as I am sure my master does.

Anticipating our dealings together, I sign myself,
                    Rogerio of Cadiz, major domo
                    to el Conde de San Germanno
At Piura, Audiencia de Lima, March 9th, 1659th Year of Grace

To the most worthy advocate, Bartolome Baltezar Bernal Hogaza y Hoja of Portobello, Audiencia de Panama, the greetings of Rogerio of Cadiz, from the Posada de Mil Flores at Piura, Audiencia de Lima.

I have had my first interview with Frey Leonardo Felipe Oviedo Cubierta y Sabiogolpe, Prior at the Monasterio de San Fructuoso; I had hoped for a more congenial first meeting, but as it came about, I was asked many questions and given precious little information. The Papal Encyclical was some help, but it has not yet brought about the direct contact the Pope has endorsed, nor have any churchmen been moved to follow the dictates the Pope has outlined in *Misericordia et Justus.* This has caused me some apprehension, for I had thought that the Papal Encyclical might bring about a higher degree of accessibility to el Conde at once. I am disinclined to abide in patience, but it appears that I must.

Because I am waiting for another invitation to come to the monasterio, I feel I must inform you that I am likely to be here longer than first anticipated; I am reluctant to speculate on how long that could be, and to that end I have decided to obtain the advice of an advocate, so that I might have the benefit of council in regard to the law. I had assumed I would need this at the time of el Conde's trial—if there is to be one—but I think it would be wisest to retain legal assistance now. I have inquired about advocates in this city, but I must tell you that the few here are disinclined to accept a client not wholly in favor of the Church. There is good reason to view this turn with alarm, for it bodes ill for el Conde, in that it appears that many have already turned their backs on him and will not pursue justice on his behalf. I am afraid I may have to proceed on my own for the time being, which makes me uneasy, but not nearly so uneasy as retaining reluctant council, for I cannot believe that a hesitant advocate would achieve much of use.

I have received your letter along with the sad news

from Roma. I am grateful to you for dispatching Dalcut so promptly, for it was most important that I have that notification before I spoke to el Conde. I have also reviewed your report about storm damage to *Los Lobos del Yermo*, and I concur—it is impractical to try to repair her at San Juan. It will be some time before shipwrights can be sent to her, and she is safe enough to sail to Maracaibo, where she can be taken care of properly by el Conde's own men, who should be dispatched promptly, with enough money to pay for their labor, their lodging, and any lumber and other supplies to complete the work. You may authorize any and all to be paid as they are incurred, and if there is any difficulty in arranging this, send word to me promptly.

As I have remarked, it may be some time before el Conde is freed. I will continue to inform you of all developments as they occur, as I trust you will inform me. Dalcut will continue to carry messages back and forth, but if you think Linno van Meer should replace him from time to time, that would suit me very well.

I appreciate your continuing efforts on el Conde's behalf, as I know he will when he is once again at liberty.

Rogerio of Cadiz, manservant
to el Conde de San Germanno

At Piura, Audiencia de Lima, March 12th, 1659th Year of Grace

To the newly appointed, most excellent Obispo Joaquin Ramon Jesus Antonio Altomarea y Timonmano, Augustino, of Santa Isabel of Portugal, at Cajamarca, Audiencia de Lima, the greetings of the manservant Rogerio of Cadiz, presently at Piura.

Most reverend Obispo, I appeal to you on behalf of my master, el Conde de San Germanno, who has been held by the Church for more than a decade, and in spite of the exhortations of His Holiness Alejandro VII in *Misericordia et Justus*, still remains imprisoned, currently by the Dominicans here in San Fructuoso at Piura. I have made repeated attempts for the last several months to gain access to el Conde, in accordance with the terms set down by His Holiness, and I have thus far been met with excuses and delays. Now I am told that plans are being made to transfer el Conde to the charge of the Franciscans in your city, at the Monasterio de los Angeles del Navidad. If this is indeed going to occur, I ask you— indeed, I beseech you—to permit me to speak with him before he is once again held in isolation.

For more than ten years I have looked after his affairs, and during that time I have done many things which I have hoped were in his interests, but which I have not, in fact, discussed with him. I am concerned, for if I have not acquitted my charge as he would wish, it behooves me to set right any errors I may have made. So far I have not been permitted to do so much as pass a letter to el Conde, and so there are matters he and I have been unable to discuss even so remotely as an exchange of notes would allow. Also, for the sake of his blood relations, I would like to be able to report on his present condition, in order to reassure his noble relatives that he has taken no injury from his long isolation. Recently, one of those to whom he is bound by blood died, and it is my task to inform him of this most lamentable event. I know that others would be much relieved if I am able to inform them that el Conde has suffered no lasting harm during his long incarceration.

With the Papal Encyclical to guide you, I appeal to you, Obispo Altomarea y Timonmano, to allow me to accompany my master during his transfer. I have been unable to secure such an assurance from Frey Leonardo Felipe Oviedo Cubierta y Sabiogolpe, the Prior of San Fructuoso where el Conde is now being held, which has resulted in my appeal to you.

This comes by the good offices of my messenger, Dalcut of Cartagena, who will wait upon you until you have a response to send back to me; he will not impose upon you, for I have paid him for his work and his accommodations during his journey. I am authorizing him to bring you one hundred gold reals to show the sincerity of my plea and to help you Augustinos in your work about the world. If you cannot bring yourself to allow me so much access to el Conde, perhaps you will permit me to have at least an interview or two with him before the Franciscans take him in. Surely the Pope would countenance that degree of contact, and you would not be subject to any review for allowing what the Papal Encyclical requires.

To reiterate: I ask you to consider my position as well as that of my master, and to be willing to address both his situation and mine. I am sworn to serve el Conde; to do so, I must know what he requires of me. After so many years, I am troubled that I may have failed in my duty. Only a discussion with el Conde will provide me with the information I must have. It is not beyond your power to grant this, and so I ask it of you as I prepare to travel to Cajamarca in the hope of gaining audience with el Conde.

With my thanks for your consideration, I sign myself

> Rogerio de Cadiz, manservant
> to el Conde de San Germanno

At Piura, Audiencia de Lima, September 21st, 1659th Year of Grace

*   *   *

To the Franciscan Prior, Frey Camilo Beltran Horatio Bolsa y Salvaje of the Monastario de los Angeles del Navidad, Cajamarca, Audiencia de Lima, the greetings of the manservant Rogerio de Cadiz, whose master, el Conde de San Germanno, has recently been transferred to your care.

I am newly arrived in Cajamarca and have presented myself at the magistratura, and to the Augustino Obispo Joaquin Ramon Jesus Antonio Altomarea y Timonmano of Santa Isabel of Portugal. It is now my intention to come to your monastery, good Prior, in the hope that you will honor the mandate of the Papal Encyclical *Misericordia et Justus*, and permit me to have words with my employer. I am fully aware that your Order is more inclined to be aware of the needs imposed by the world, as your Founder exemplified.

There are many reasons I would appreciate an interview with el Conde, not the least of which is to inform him of what has transpired among his various concerns in the last decade, that he may have an opportunity to prepare himself for the changes that will confront him when he returns to the world, his innocence vindicated and his reputation restored.

Certainly, you will have to make your investigation of him and his activities, and therefore I ask you to be thorough in your inquiries. Sadly, many of those who might have given useful testimony in regard to my master can no longer do so. The Corregidor of the Audiencia de Lima, Don Ezequias Pannefrio y Modestez, who was familiar with el Conde's works, died last year, and his successor never met my master, so he cannot offer you anything that might throw light upon all el Conde did while in the Audiencia de Lima, some years since.

For however long you require for your process, I

will remain here in Cajamara, and I will follow your acts as closely as one in my position may, for to do less would not be honorable. I have an obligation to el Conde, and I will not seek to avoid it. If there is anything you will permit me to do in service to my master, you have only to tell me of it and it is done. I say this to you so you will comprehend my intentions, good Prior. I have never abandoned my master before, and I will not do so now. I will devote my time to his interests and his freedom until both are achieved. Your answers and summons may find me at la Posada del Potro in the Calle de las Cinco Lunas; I plan to remain here as long as necessary.

With abiding faith in your compassion and sagacity, I sign myself

> Rogerio de Cadiz, manservant
> to el Conde de San Germanno

At Cajamarca, Audiencia de Lima, Viceroyalty of Peru, April 2nd, 1660th Year of Grace

To the most patient, persevering advocate Bartolome Baltezar Bernal Hogaza y Hoja of Portobello, Audiencia de Panama, the joyous greetings of Rogerio, manservant to Francisco Ragoczy, el Conde de San Germanno, who today, at very long last, is a free man with a restored name.

After more than fifteen years, it is finally done. It has cost a fortune in time and donations, but all of it was worth the price now that el Conde is finally released, all charges against him—whatever they were—dismissed, and his possessions returned to him without any liens against them by Church or Crown. It is truly a triumph.

El Conde himself has endured much; at least the Franciscans permitted him access to their gardens and cloisters at night so that he could prepare medi-

caments for their infirmary, unlike the Passionists
and Dominicans, who kept him in a cell for as long
as they had him. You will not be astonished to learn
that el Conde no longer wishes to place himself in
the danger he feels the New World has for him, and
for that reason, he has decided to return to Europe.
He has ordered us to hire an escort and travel in easy
stages to Maracaibo, Audiencia de Santo Domingo,
Viceroyalty of Nueva España, and take ship there,
whichever of his may be eastward bound when we
arrive. I ask you to send your reports to his factor
there, Eugenio Joao Sao Reinaldo at el Conde's warehouses at the harbor.

I am deeply appreciative for all you have done,
particularly in arranging for Dalcut de Cartagena's
proper burial when the fever killed him last year,
and for maintaining all el Conde's records so well.
Because of your good work, I know it will be much
easier for him to reestablish himself in the world
again. To express his thanks, San Germanno is sending an authorization for you to remain in his villa
until the end of your life. He has also granted you a
pension of sixty gold reals a year for as long as you
live, and a memorial to your heirs of three hundred
gold reals upon your death. He forgives you the
monies you have so artfully purloined from his coffers through your subtle manipulations of figures,
not only because you have done your work well,
but because, compared to what has been paid to the
Church, your theft was insignificant.

As you can see, this comes with many letters to be
sent on, which task I leave to you, for I know that
you may tend to the work far more efficiently in
Portobello than I am able to here in Cajamarca, and
many of the letters are distinctly to your advantage.

I estimate we will depart from Maracaibo in August or September, after the most severe summer storms are over, and before the winter storms can blow in. Before we sail, el Conde will prepare schedules and give you instructions for reaching him, and arrange for your successor upon your retirement or death, which will spare you having to find someone to take on your various responsibilities when you can no longer fulfill them.

In utmost gratitude for your faithful service, I sign myself,

Rogerio de Cadiz, manservant
to el Conde de San Germanno

At Cajamarca, Audiencia de Lima, Viceroyalty of Peru, July 22nd, 1666th Year of Grace.

THE DEMONIC

WHEN is it too late for the damned?
    Strictly speaking, probably never.

With proper repentance, the possibility of true salvation always exists, no matter what one's birthright, training, or line of work happens to be.

It's never too late to say one is sorry.

Never.

THE DEVIL YOU KNOW

by Nina Kiriki Hoffman

Nina Kiriki Hoffman has been writing for more than twenty years, and has sold over two hundred stories, three short story collections, novels (*The Thread That Binds the Bones*, *The Silent Strength of Stones*, *A Red Heart of Memories*, *Past the Size of Dreaming*, and *A Fistful of Sky*), several middle school books, and a *Star Trek* book. Her young adult novel *A Stir of Bones* was published by Viking in September. She has cats.

WHEN Dominic Cross was nine, he watched a monster his father had summoned from the netherworld escape its ensorcelled circle, kill both his parents, and devour them.

Then it turned to him.

Paralyzed with fear and anguish, he could not move.

His father had called this monster to demonstrate wizardly control of other beings to him. "We'll start the demonstration with a small being," his father had said.

What manifested within the magical container his father had constructed was not small. It was huge and horrible, dripping with glistening light, its teeth as long and silvery as sword blades, its many eyes lit from within by red fire.

It was too large for the circle. One of its tails scythed sideways, destroyed the confinement by sweeping away the lines his father had laid down so carefully on the cellar floor.

His father held up hands with fingers spread and chanted the articles of confinement, flashing fire toward the monster. Words and fire ran off it. It rushed forward, its jaw gaping wide, and bit Dominic's father in half, then gulped him down. Dominic's mother, who had been tending the brazier in the corner, screamed, and the monster turned. She, too, vanished down its gullet before Dominic could catch his breath.

The monster paused. It slid its forked snake-tongue out between its teeth and licked its lips. "Aah," it murmured, its voice strangely soft and melodic. "Wizard meat. Finest meal in this world. What a party they shall have in my belly."

Then it turned and stared at Dominic.

Run, he told his feet. *Hide.*

Wait, said something else in him. *Mother and Father are gone now, and I have nothing.*

He couldn't understand it. It had happened too fast.

He shivered. He couldn't run. The monster's gaze held him still.

"Wizard spawn," it whispered. "Tender and juicy, luscious and lovely. So full of open doors, the promise of powers still sleeping, a toothsome treat." Its head lowered toward him.

The shivers stopped. This was right. He had spent his whole life with his parents, traveling around the young United States—barely more than a hundred years old! So fresh and wild! Not like the old country, his father always said—as they searched for new knowledge and powerful places, teachers who would share, new things to see. With his parents, he had gone to states and territories where Europeans had settled, and other places where older and stranger people lived. He had no home, no other relatives, no friends. Mother and Father, gone in an instant. Nothing was left for him here.

Better he should die now.

Its teeth loomed above him, taller than he was, its mouth a cavern behind the forest of its teeth, its breath bloodsweet and honey-tainted. Its flickering tongue darted out, brushed over his face in a strange, dry caress. He closed his eyes. *All the powers that be, protect me in the life to come.*

"Such a taste," the monster said. "Such a bright young taste. And yet, I am no longer hungry. To eat you now would be to waste you. Besides, I have a better idea." Something warm and scaly snaked around Dominic's shoulders. Something whippy wrapped around his legs. The limbs pulled him tight against a hot soft surface.

Dominic opened his eyes. The monster had reared up until its spiked head brushed the ceiling. It had many limbs, some ending in tentacles, some in hands, some multitipped as a cat-o'-nine-tails, some single-tipped like a dowsing rod. Two of its limbs clutched Dominic against its stomach, which was furred and hot as a furnace. Dominic laid his ear against it. *Mother. Father. Are you in there? Are you really dead? Mother?*

He heard gurglings and grumblings, but no answers.

"Yess," murmured the monster in its honey-toned

voice. "Yes. I shall adopt you. With a child on this side of the veil, I will be able to cross over anytime I please, once I have trained you to summon me. Yesss," it whispered, one of its hands stroking Dominic's hair.

They stayed in the cellar for two weeks. Sometimes the monster sent Dominic out to find things, but it tethered his spirit so that he couldn't run away. When he was with the monster, it loosened its tether on him. It let him cry and scream and curse it. It laughed at him.

Early on, the boy rolled up into a ball, stricken through and through with terror and pain and sadness. It wrapped him in many arms and held him against its warmth. At first he struck it and kicked it, but it held him even so. He exhausted himself fighting it. He could not escape it, and it refused to eat him. Gradually its warmth seeped into him. He could no longer cling to his pain. He let the dark memories go, and fell asleep.

Sometimes the monster stroked him with a hand or a tendril or a whip, traced his back, or smoothed his hair. At first he did nothing, terrified of it. Then he tried to squirm away, and sometimes it let him. Then he grew to long for the warmth of its touch, and he sat still when it reached out.

It fed him stew that it brought from a rip in the wall between its world and this one, and he never asked what was in the stew; it fed him, and afterward he felt well.

The monster taught him wizardlore. When he didn't learn fast enough for it, it touched him with some of its less-human limbs. Sometimes after a touch like that, he fell asleep, and then the monster walked through his dreams. When he woke up, he knew that he had learned new things, but he wasn't sure what they were.

Sometimes his mind slid toward memories of his mother and father, then slipped away again. He had a flicker, an instant of an image, a half-second's recall before forgetting. Then he would be upset, though he could not remember why.

The monster would distract him with food or a task or a new technique to summon, stroke, and direct power.

One day the monster said, "You know the calling chants and the chalklore. You will summon me every solstice and tell me what you've learned. Won't you, my son?" One of its more human hands patted his back, and he stared up into its red eyes, thrilled against his will that such a powerful being trusted him to do such an important job.

"I will," Dominic said. He couldn't have said anything else, living under the welter of compulsions the monster had laid on him.

Still, he said it because he wanted to.

"I have one last gift for you." One of its limbs, the one tipped with a black fang, reached out and scribed the summoning runes and circles on the palm of Dominic's left hand. Blood welled up in the black lines left behind by the tooth's touch. The faint poison pain of it was sweet and excruciating. "Only speak to this and I shall come."

It flicked its snake's tongue against his lips in a monster's kiss. "You are my beautiful boy," it whispered. "I will see you soon. If you want to see me sooner, you have but to call."

It slipped through the hole in the barrier between this world and its own, and the hole sealed up behind it.

Dominic sat in the cellar, alone and bereft. Half a day passed before he rose and climbed up into the wider world.

He sleepwalked for a while. He slept under wagons and bridges and in barns, drank from rain barrels and streams, filched food from people's vegetable gardens at night, ran from dogs and men riding horses. He avoided face-to-face meetings. He could tell when someone watched him, and he found that he had an art to cover himself with shadow so that their gaze passed over him.

One day he woke, his hands half-buried in a trash heap, the taste of moldy bread in his mouth. He stared down at himself. He was filthy and skinny. Bones bumped out the sides of his wrists, and his arms were like sticks. He had newspapers tied around his feet.

He stood so long studying himself that someone came out of the back of the restaurant to dump more trash and saw him. "Get away from there, you human varmint!" the man cried, and he ran.

Looking behind him at one man, he ran into the arms of another. "Oh, you poor child," said this man. "What happened to you? How did you come to be in such a state?"

Dominic had been so long alone he had forgotten how to converse. He looked up into the man's eyes. Something inside him relaxed.

"Let me take you home to my Margery," said the man. "We've got some clothes that our boy Seth outgrew. We can give you a bath and a warm meal, at least."

The man took his hand, and Dominic did not pull away.

*   *   *

He stayed with Bill and Margery a year. In all that time he never spoke to them, but he listened to them, sat quiet in the evenings when they read from the Bible, and did whatever tasks they asked of him. He picked flowers and gave them to Margery on her birthday, and built a birdhouse in the woodshop to give to Bill.

Most of his real life happened at night, when he left the house from his bedroom window and snuck out of town to his secret place by the creek, where he called back his wizardlore—what his father had taught him, and what the monster had taught him; sometimes he forgot which was which. He practiced everything he had learned, built his skills and power.

His day life and his night life ran side by side, wholly separate.

At the beginning of the summer, compelled by orders laid on him, he summoned the monster.

It was much larger than he remembered, and it made him bring it a child to eat. He chose one from a farm family of eleven children, the one who was always running away. He could not watch when the monster ate it. Something that had thawed during the time he lived with Bill and Margery froze inside him.

The monster made him tell it everything that had happened to him, everything he had learned. Then it taught him more powerful wizardlore. He thrust away knowledge of the dead and devoured child, and hungered for the lessons the monster gave him. His stomach twisted. He said a spell to quiet it.

He forgot.

He learned.

The monster embraced him.

After the monster left, he thought about what it

was. He couldn't quite remember why he hated it even as he loved it. He knew there was some reason why he must resist the monster.

He knew he couldn't fight it alone.

The first person he recruited was a wild child who had lived with her uncle out in the country. The uncle had called her a witch brat and kept her chained in the barn until one of the neighbors dropped by to borrow an ax and saw the child, then complained to people in town about it. The sheriff went out to investigate and brought the child back. He turned her over to the Christian Aid Society at Bill and Margery's church, and they brought the little girl home.

She was small, perhaps six years old, with tangled dark hair. She wore a black dress, black stockings, and scuffed black high-button boots. Her fingernails were gnawed bloody. She did not speak.

Fires started near her. Draperies went up in smoke. Carpets smoldered. Furniture caught flame. Bill and Margery put out the fires and prayed for her.

Dominic took her to his secret place that night. "What is your name?" he asked her.

She growled at him.

He stroked thinking sleep into her and found that, after all, she had a voice, thoughts, memories. Her first name was Sally. Her middle name was Trouble, everyone said so. Her parents had loved her, but they died of yellow fever when she was four. She had lived with a succession of relatives; this last uncle told her that if she set fire to anything in the barn he would kill her, and she believed him. She didn't know how to control the fires, but when they started, she managed to put them out before they burned much, and hide the evidence. Her uncle gave her food and water every day and emptied her slop pail. In some ways it had been a better place than some she had been.

Dominic woke her up. "I'll teach you to control your burning," he told her. "I'll be your older brother and take care of you."

She was astonished that anyone could help her. She was amazed that anyone would want to be her relative.

He taught her wizardlore, and she learned. He pulled her into his night life and civilized her in their day life so that Bill and Margery felt good about taking in the two orphans. She followed Dominic everywhere, when she could keep up with him, and when Margery didn't sit her down and make her work on samplers.

Among his other wizard work, Dominic practiced techniques to bind someone else's will, to tether another's spirit; they came easily, part of what he had learned from the monster at solstice. He tested them on Sally, who wasn't interested in resisting him. He worked until he could control her as though she were a puppet, make her send her fire power wherever he willed it.

She laughed.

Sometimes during the day he tightened his hold on her, made her pour tea and serve cookies or pull weeds, just to see if it were possible. She relaxed into his control; she poured without spilling, handed plates around without dropping anything, never pulled a vegetable by mistake, only the weeds. Afterward, she always laughed.

Dominic found a drifter sleeping in an alley beside a tavern. The man had a green glow over him. Dominic squatted by the man's head and waited for him to wake up.

It took two hours. Dominic spent the time weaving controls over the man.

When at last the man opened his eyes, he cried out and scooted back against the tavern wall. "What are you?" he cried.

Dominic glanced behind him, saw nothing, turned back to the man with his eyebrows up.

"Don't tell me it's the DTs," said the man. "I ain't got the shakes bad enough for it to be the DTs. What are you, boy, that you got that scaly skin on you, and those yaller eyes?"

Dominic rose and looked down at the man, then glanced at his hands, their backs brown from working in Margery's garden. He knew from Margery's mirror that his eyes were silver. Perhaps the man would be no use to him after all.

The man sat up and rubbed his eyes, looked at Dominic again. "Oh, nemmine, I was looking at your shadow."

Dominic glanced behind him again. He had no shadow, since they were already in a shadow between buildings.

"What you want, boy?" the man asked.

"Help," said Dominic.

"Now, that is something I am purely not qualified to give to anybody. Can't even help myself." His voice dropped to a mutter. "All the time visions, all the time sights that make my eyes sore, nobody else sees 'em, can't hardly drown 'em in sudden death, but you got to try. Sometimes they get quiet. Sometimes I can sleep."

"Maybe I could help you," Dominic said.

"Help me? What's a boy with such big teeth know about help?"

Dominic frowned.

"Nemmine, nemmine, must sound like I'm talking crazy again, it's an occupational hazard, since I guess I *am* half crazy. Or more, to hear my Nelly talk of it. Why you think you could help me, boy?"

Dominic squatted again. "Maybe I could help you control your visions, and then you could help me."

"Boy says he could help me," muttered the man. "What's a boy know, especially such a scrawny little one? On the other hand, look at that shadow. Not a shadow that's out to help anybody, but it's got power in it. Makes my head spin, and I ain't had a drink yet today." He straightened, pushed himself up against the wall until he stood. "Well, boy, let's see what you've got."

When they both stood, the man towered over him, loose-limbed and swaying in raggedy clothes and battered boots. Dominic drew in a breath, then reached up with his thumbs and wrote symbols for choice in the air before the man's eyes. Power heated his thumbs.

He dropped his hands and stared into the man's eyes.

"Hoo-whee." The man blinked, rubbed his eyes, stared back. "Now you look like a ordinary child. What'd you do?"

"Gave you a choice which eyes to see with. Choose the others again."

The man blinked three times, then jerked his head back. "Whoa! Now you got a bunch more eyes, all red, and about six extra arms or maybe legs, hard to tell what's on the end of them, only it's not feet nor hands. I ask you again, sonny, what the heck are you?"

"My father's son, I guess," Dominic said. His stomach turned over as a wave of darkness swept through him.

The man blinked. He shook his head. "It's just a little child," he muttered. "What kind of help you looking for?"

"I have to fight a monster."

The man shook his head and backed away. "Sorry, sonny. I appreciate your help, but I'm not the feller you need for a job like that." He edged down the alley, then ran.

Dominic held out his hands. He could tug on the reins and bring the man back to him.

He twitched his fingers and let the reins drop.

When winter's heart came, Dominic strapped on snowshoes and went to his secret place alone. He had a tool in Sally, but he was not ready to use her yet. Besides, he needed more.

He summoned the monster. It sat on the snow, turning it to steam and running water. "My beautiful boy," it said. "How you've grown." It swept a tendril around his edges. "How you've learned. You've been practicing. And look. You brought me a gift." One of its arms snaked out behind Dominic, retracted with Sally in its grip. She screamed.

Dominic's mind went blank.

The monster's mouth gaped wide.

"No!" Dominic cried. What was she doing here? Why hadn't he put sleep on her? He should have known she would follow him. Why hadn't he known?

The monster bit down. Sally's scream drowned. She disappeared inside the monster.

"No," whispered Dominic.

"What a fine fiery meal," said the monster. "Exquisite taste."

Tears froze on Dominic's face. He shoved the memory of Sally away from him.

The monster spent all night teaching him advanced techniques for controlling other creatures. Before it departed at dawn, it embraced him.

Dominic went home one last time to gather a few things, then left Bill and Margery's house. He walked out into a snowstorm, not caring if he survived it.

Apparently being a monster's child made one impervious to cold. When he was hungry, he ate whatever he could find. Pine needles and tree bark fed him; snow fed him. Apparently, being a monster's child meant—

He stayed far from people. A month, two months he lived in a forest. Then spring came.

He had only a little while to prepare before he summoned the monster again.

Prepare what? Prepare how?

He sketched symbols in front of his eyes with his thumbs, then gathered his things and walked, looking everywhere.

He wandered until he came to a road, and then he followed the road east until he came to a town. Twilight had fallen. Spring peepers called from a nearby stream. Lights glowed behind curtained windows. He walked down the town's single muddy street between frame houses, searching. Nowhere did he see the spark of power he was looking for.

He walked until he came to a larger town, and this time he found several sparks, none of them very bright. He slept under someone's porch during the day and prowled the streets at night, learning the ways and habits of the sparkling ones. Not enough time to develop them before he called the monster again, he decided, but he could lay light controls on them now, and activate more intense training after the summer meeting, in preparation for the winter meeting.

For the summer meeting, he brought the corpse of a child to the place he had prepared, far out of town. The child had been buried that morning; he waited until after dark to retrieve it.

The monster was not interested in dead meat, and sent him to find it something better. His legs carried him back to town, while rage raced like lightning through him. He walked with his eyes closed down Main Street, feeling the compulsion to find a live person, resisting as best he could.

Someone grasped his arm. "Honey? You all right, there?"

He opened his eyes and looked up into the face of one of the saloon girls, her hair pale, her lips dark, her eyes kind.

"Looked like you was sleepwalking," she said. "Don't you know that's dangerous? A half-growed boy like you, some drunk cowboy could ride right up the street and trample you down without even seeing you in the dark. What? What's that you're doing to me, baby?"

He turned and walked away from her. She followed.

He searched everywhere. He found shining lights, people with powers, most of them unaware of their own talents. He woke their powers and trained the people in the use of them. The monster taught him more with every meeting about the uses and nature of power, and he used his education. He kept his found people in his control, at first clumsily, so that they resisted and suffered, and later, as he improved his own skills, in a control so silken and light some never knew it. He could walk past a house at night and touch lightly on the sleeping mind of one of his people, know everything important that person had done that day, nudge a dream slightly sideways so that the person would learn something important the following day.

Years passed. Twice a year, he went into the country, far from anywhere someone could stumble across by accident, and met with the monster, gave it a meal, turned away while it ate, and stayed to learn what the monster chose to teach him.

The rest of the time he pursued his passion: finding the talented, adding them to his collection.

At the turn of the century he bought a mansion in New York. Those of his people with the fewest ties to outside and the greatest powers, he took home with him. In the cellar of the mansion he built a glassworks and an alchemy lab, and in the upper room of one of the towers, he laid his summoning ground. In between he had a library and living room and kitchen, bedrooms and classrooms, assorted parlors and a solarium.

As he worked with the monster, he learned more and more about controlling lesser powers from other worlds. He could summon them and make them do his bidding.

In 1932, he took an apprentice.

One day many years later, his apprentice said, "What are we doing?"

"What do you mean?" Dominic studied the boy. Back when he had first taken the apprentice, Dominic had performed a spell that had slowed aging in them both. Dominic had been fifty at the time, and the boy had been fourteen. Now the boy looked almost sixteen.

"Why do you do what you do? Why do we search

out any signs of people with power and go and capture them?''

"I'm building."

"Building what?" Dominic had traded the boy's heart for their immortality, which had proved a mercy in many ways; not much about their work troubled the boy, though Dominic was often haunted by his own dreams, particularly the ones he couldn't remember. At the time of the immortality spell, he had also gifted the boy with endless curiosity; usually he liked the boy's questions. "You work so hard, Master. Why?"

For a second, the faces of the forbidden flashed through Dominic's mind: his parents. The runaway farm child. Sally. The saloon girl. An orphan. A condemned man. A sheriff. A drunk. A tubercular woman. A madman. A host of others. As his skills grew, he had learned to select carefully, plan ahead, find the ones no one cared about, the ones who might be seeking death already; he spent half a year finding the next one, and then he tried to save all his favorites by sending them into a sleep so deep they wouldn't disturb him while he talked to his own master.

Someone had to die so he could learn.

What more did he need to learn?

Someone had to die because he didn't know how to stop his master. In everything he had learned, he had never found the words or signs or work that could contain or control or defeat the monster. Of course, it would not give him that knowledge; it was too wise. He hadn't found the knowledge anywhere else, either, and oh, he had searched, and had his people search.

"Be quiet, now," he told his apprentice.

*   *   *

He could make his apprentice be quiet, but he could not still the echo of the question in his mind. What was he doing?

Perhaps the next talent he captured would hold the key that would unlock the monster's hold on him. That was it: that was his mission. He plunged himself into the search even more energetically.

Then he stumbled across a nest of powers all training each other, and they defied him.

If they could defy him after he had had more than a century of his master's training, perhaps they could defy the master as well. He enlisted his strongest talents and went to fight this new collection of powers.

One of them kissed him.

He lost all his training and much of his memory at the touch of her lips. He fell back into his four-year-old self, the one he had been before his father began teaching him wizardlore, the one who had held his mother's hand as they walked through the forest and felt utterly safe. It was a mother's kiss she gave him, the kiss that said I love you. Everything will be fine.

Though he had seen his mother devoured, though he knew nothing was ever fine, he believed this kiss long enough to be wholly defeated.

Dominic woke and wondered where he was and what had just happened. He turned his head, saw that he lay on a couch in a room he could not remember. A wall of glass doors half hidden behind drapes showed a view of blue sky. There were other couches in the room, which was quite large but looked like something in someone's house rather than in a public building. Somewhere nearby people spoke to each other, and he smelled eggs and bacon frying and coffee brewing. He put a hand to his forehead.

"Dominic?" A large brown-skinned woman in a floor-length green dress, her hair long and wavy and silver about her shoulders, leaned over him. Her sky-chip blue eyes were kind. "How are you?"

"What happened?"

"I kissed a curse out of you," she said.

He touched his lips and stared up at this stranger. His apprentice approached and studied him.

He reached for the cords that bound his apprentice to him. They were gone. He frowned.

"Master," said his apprentice.

"Galen." He almost never called his apprentice by name, but somehow now it seemed necessary.

"Are you all right?"

Dominic sat up slowly. He reached for his network, the connections he maintained with all his talents, those who lived in his house, and those he kept track of.

Nothing.

He opened his left hand and stared at his palm. The signs of summoning were still there, etched in black and red like a tattoo.

"What is that?" his apprentice asked.

"My utmost curse." He held his hand up to the silver-haired woman. She took his hand in both of hers and studied what was written on his palm. She glanced behind her, then, and one of the others—one of the many others—how had he come to be in a house full of strangers?—came to them, a young man, his eyes the same vivid blue as hers.

"Have you seen this before?" the woman asked the man, showing him Dominic's palm.

The man stared only a second before making an avert sign. "An unbound summoning of a great dark," he said.

"Do you know how to bind it?" Dominic struggled to his feet.

"Who would call such a thing?"

"It was a mistake."

"How did you survive it?"

For a long moment Dominic said nothing. He had never spoken about the monster to anyone. He remembered how well muteness had served him in Bill and Margery's house, the last place he had felt safe, until the woman kissed him into confusion last night.

"My father," Dominic said. He coughed. "When I was a child, my father taught me. He was going to show me how to summon something simple." He swallowed. He glanced at his apprentice, whom he had taught to summon simple things, and even a few complicated things, but nothing like the monster. When he taught his talents, he was very strict about their getting every detail absolutely right. "I don't know what he did wrong, but this thing came instead. It—" He frowned. He closed his eyes. Could he remember? Could he let himself remember? Could he say it aloud? She had kissed a curse out of him, and he found that it was the curse of silence. Finally he could say what had happened. "It ate my parents. Then it adopted me."

No one spoke.

Slowly he opened his eyes. All three of them stared at him, wide-eyed.

"Twice a year," he said, and his body began to shake. "Twice a year, I must call it. And it—" He shook so hard he had to sit down again. "—demands a price. I cannot stop myself from paying it. I make others pay it with their lives. T–twice a year—"

He put his hands over his face. His left hand was hot against his cheek. His eyes burned. All their faces—

He lowered his left hand, held it out to the woman. "Can you kiss this away?"

She lifted his hand, placed her other palm against his. His marked hand burned.

She changed. Not to normal vision, but to his second sight. He lowered his right hand from his face and stared at her, saw that she was something other than she appeared, something as huge as his monster father, something that existed partly in this world and partly in others.

Was he asking one monster to replace another? The worst wounds came from ignorance, didn't they? His father's ignorance in summoning. His own ignorance, not to watch his back trail so that he hadn't seen Sally behind him in time to save her. Closing his eyes to his next choice so that the one he hurt was the one who wanted to help him.

"Do you willingly renounce all that this has brought you?" asked the woman. He heard her voice in this world, heard its echo across others.

He thought of the monster's embrace, its praise when he learned well, the small comforts he had clung to because he had to believe that something about all this was right. He thought of all he knew and all he could do, how everything he had done had turned him into who he was now. He thought of the times he had tried to kill himself. It had proved impossible.

Maybe this way would work.

"I do," he whispered. Perhaps she was a bigger monster. At least she was a different monster.

She pressed her lips to his palm.

It burned. He writhed and shook and twisted,

gasped and gulped as pain seared through him. It burned and cleansed. He kept his hand as still as he could, kept it tight against her lips.

She kissed a circle around his palm, and each kiss was like being drowned in fire. Then she kissed the center.

Perhaps this was death.

He surrendered himself to it.

A hundred years later he opened his eyes and looked up into her face. His double vision was gone. Most of his senses had vanished, dulling the world down to normal sight and sound and touch and smell. All he saw was a human face above him, its eyes searching his.

"Thank you," he whispered.

THE RECALL OF CTHULHU

by Tom Dupree

Tom Dupree has been a newsman, adman, critic, and editor.
His work has been featured in a number of science fiction,
fantasy, and horror anthologies, including DAW Books' *Historical Hauntings*. He lives in New York City with his wife,
Linda.

ONE drives nervously through certain rural country in north central Massachusetts, far from the
bustling metropolis, without knowing precisely why.
The crisp New England air becomes heavy and fetid.
The motorist who might be soothed by the verdant
grandeur of lush emerald hills is instead assaulted
by brambles and unkempt forest grasping over the
roadway.

The rare signs of human habitation are also unnerving: broken, pitted wood fences long unrepaired;
foul rusting yokes upon which large, lean black birds
rest at odd angles and stare at passersby with disquieting intensity; wilting plants of indeterminant genus
that push from denuded gray land once slit by a
plow but thence shunned by its owner.

When this dank region is spoken of at all, it is
chiefly by returning travelers in muffled tones of

dread and relief. One finds that the clammy hand of night can reach into the protective cocoon of an automobile. No timbre save hissing static may be retrieved from a radio. Tape and disk mechanisms are unable to emit the sounds encoded on them and sometimes slow down or speed up unaccountably. Various pilgrims have reported slow guttural resonance like the groaning song of the leviathans of the deep; others have heard distressing atonal piping that vaults upward on its alien scale to attain a painful pitch beyond hearing. The unluckiest have experienced mechanical problems, made most ominous by the imminent approach of nightfall.

The portable telephones which have so infested our culture are here quite useless—either the land takes its guests too far away from the digital world for communication to reach, or else there is some force, climatological or self-determined, which conspires to isolate this area from the orbit of rational discourse and reason. The visitor tends to cling to the false shelter of the automobile and wish himself far away in a warm bed, if only the damned machine will successfully transport him. Never has anyone who has voyaged upon these dark lanes evinced the slightest desire to return.

The inhabitants of this forsaken clime are a solemn and oddly distanced lot, gazing without expression from well-trodden pasture or from the porches of tiny colonial-style houses which are not quite plumb, oddly misshapen in a way that provokes revulsion rather than empathy. Their dwellings are spaced miles apart, and no wonder, for they do not seem to particularly relish the company of humankind. There is no wave toward a passing vehicle, no smile, no acknowledgment. Only heads slowly turning to follow the progress of a car will betray the fact that

the native watchers are indeed alive. The encroacher
wishes to escape their forbidding community no
more ardently than the citizens of Dunwich wish to
see him gone.

It was in the cloying gloom of late afternoon that
one of them, an ancient dairyman named Abner
Brockman, followed the latest vehicle with his vacant
and sallow gaze until the sound of its passing gave
way to the stillness that always pervaded the stricken
countryside at this time of the day. He turned back
to his herd, a feeble collection of desultory animals
that nosed their way through a dirt-pocked pasture
nearly picked clean. The scent of mold and decay
was on the air, and Brockman instinctively looked
upward apprehensively in the direction of the table-
like rock of Sentinel Hill. He was unable to make out
the summit in the diminishing light, but he could
somehow feel the presence of the barren hillock
where no tree, shrub, or blade of grass would ever
grow.

The first whippoorwill of evening raised its
lonely moan, and Brockman pulled his jacket tight
against his neck. These birds frightened and un-
nerved the residents of Dunwich, where local superstition held that whippoorwills were creatures
that wait for the souls of the dying, and that their
cries are timed to the wretched victim's last breath.
It was still early and the bird was joined by no
others, but that did not prevent a shiver from cours-
ing through Brockman's body as the dull silence
descended again.

The metallic clang of a cowbell bit the air as old
Sarah, Brockman's doddering prize Guernsey, pad-
ded toward the fence. Something was bothering her.
Her tail swatted furiously and she picked up speed.
Now the other cows joined in, bleating pathetically

and fighting to escape the middle of the field—not in one direction but toward all sides in a stampede from the center. Whatever the disturbance was, it emanated from a bald patch that the half-ton animals were laboring to flee. Brockman moved closer.

Suddenly the ground heaved with a sharp jolt, as if an explosion had been set off beneath. The cattle leaped away with even greater force. As Brockman stared in amazement, a tight plume of dirt sprayed into the air like water from a fountain and left a small hole in the pasture, *through which something was struggling to emerge.*

A cloven hoof pawed its way out of the hole and was joined by another. The hooves strained to widen the aperture, and a bovine nose appeared, snorting with a prodigious effort. Rooted to the spot, Brockman watched as the fawn-colored head of a full-grown Guernsey pulled into the light. How had the beast fallen into the earth? he wondered. And how was it attaining the strength to correct its condition? The rest of the herd had run as far away from the bizarre display as pasture fencing would allow, many of them headed in the direction of Sentinel Hill, which it had always before been their nature to shun.

The forward half of the cow was now free, and it used its hooves as leverage against the plane of the pasture. With a moist pop the rear half emerged, and Abner Brockman's grip on sanity loosed to the point of dissolution. For he was accustomed to the creatures of a natural order; what he now beheld was an atrocity from somewhere outside the known laws of biology, from beyond the three dimensions which deluded men of science into believing they had any inkling of the soul-shattering mysteries that long predated the emergence of Homo sapiens on the planet.

About halfway down its body, the creature simply failed to be a cow any more. It was covered with matted black fur, through which crawled dozens of wormy gray tentacles, each waving and undulating independently to create a horrible writhing skirt below which no legs protruded. At the end of each tentacle was a reddish sucker, opening and closing with a hideous sodden sound. Where the tail might have been on a normal beast was a longer, thicker trunk or feeler that swayed and pushed against the ground. A greenish-yellow substance with the consistency of syrup oozed from the fur surrounding the tentacles; its moldy ichor attacked Brockman as surely as if he had been struck by a fist, and he felt the ache of nausea rise in his belly as the rank odor hung heavily on the still air.

As Brockman watched in stupefaction, sets of eye-balls asserted themselves among the fur and disappeared, only to reemerge at another spot. They were constantly winking into existence and receding, all over the creature's rear half. Then a slit appeared in the midsection and opened slightly to reveal a set of canine teeth, above which a larger set of reddened eyes appeared and set, then a nose. The dark fur over the obscene countenance lightened while Brockman watched and resolved into a half face, elongating impossibly along the side of the beast until it was better than a yard wide, a preposterous imitation of the human form. It was still barely recognizable as the cruelly distorted face of a young man, topped by crinkly albino hair, whose eyes were now jutting wide with exertion as it attempted to speak.

The mouth moved slowly and a deep bass rumble

issued forth from it, a noise that at first sounded like
an animal growl. But as the cavity opened and
closed, a ghastly green tongue occasionally protruded to help produce a variety of humming, clicking, and sibilant sounds, and somehow Brockman
understood that there was an intelligence operating
this blasphemy. The cow's head that remained on the
damned pseudo-beast raised its snout skyward, and
matched the unearthly noises coming from its torso.
In unison, the twin vocal boxes spewed what
sounded at first like gibberish, but then resolved into
strange croaking words:

"*Ygnaiih . . . N'gai . . . Y'bthnk . . . Bugg-shoggog . . .
my mother . . . YOG-SOTHOTH!*"

That was enough for Abner Brockman. He fell to
his knees, blubbering nonsensically, drool rolling
out of the sides of his mouth, then pitched forward
into a cowpie. His hair follicles were already beginning to lose their color, and his reason was forever
lost with them *as the abomination moved wetly
toward him.*

F'tagn Whateley slithered closer to the fallen man
and his extensions drooped in frustration. He had
tried everything he could think of to make a connection. He had taken on the frame of the creatures with
which this human had surrounded himself. He had
made the vibrations of welcome, had even used the
human tongue—and eyes! F'tagn could smell success
as the man watched and tried to comprehend, and
he had undulated with excitement. But it was always
the same. Was he so horrible? His life surely was.
Some Great Old One he was making.

F'tagn couldn't help that he was a half-breed. It
wasn't his fault that mapped upon his handsome glu-
tinous frame was part of a human face, elongated in

a fetching way, to be sure, but still there. He was a twin, born several human generations ago of Old One and earthly woman in an arcane ritual atop Sentinel Hill that was supposed to seal the eventual fate of humankind. But that still made F'tagn a pup in the multifaceted eyes of the rest of his pop's crew. He hadn't even been around for one single aeon. And it was so hard to fit in. Most of the other Old Ones turned their tentacles away whenever F'tagn oozed by, repulsed by the human part of him. They could sense it, smell it. After all, the rest of them were from some grand unnamable place beyond angled space. F'tagn was from Massachusetts.

Eternal life could be so unfair.

Pop might have thought of this before he had relations with old albino Lavinia Whateley that randy night so long ago. In the phrase of the demons of Nyarlathotep, what possessed him? Several of the night-gaunts that hung around the great stone city of R'lyeh, now sunken in the ocean, would chitter conspiratorially at the sight of F'tagn, and it was plain that his Great Old Man had done a bit of bragging at some point. Everybody was curious about the physical details: how'd you do it, hoss? A couple of shoggoths had gone out and experimented with farm animals in the vast Midwestern regions, but when the smoke cleared, all that was left were mutilated cows and frustrated shoggoths.

But however he'd managed it, F'tagn was living proof that Pop was an amorous pioneer. F'tagn and his twin brother Wilbur. The lucky bastard—actually, they were both bastards—Wilbur had favored their mother. He could pass for human in Dunwich, and he grew up among people. They may have distrusted him, even feared him, because Whateleys tended to keep to themselves, and that kind of behavior attracts gossip, especially in New England. But at least Wilbur got to be out there in the world. In contrast, F'tagn had been boarded up in the second story of his grandpa's house for most of the time he was a Young One. That experience would create psychological problems in most any kid, but F'tagn had inherited something that nobody had expected, certainly not his dad. He had been conceived as a leader of the new generation. But F'tagn was proud of his human side, and he yearned to communicate with his half-kind.

It didn't help that Wilbur had seemed as intent on bringing forth the reign of the Great Old Ones as fervently as any true immigrant from the stars. Wonderful. He got the gene of human appearance, and what did he do with it? He devoted his life to the destruction of the world order and the domination of conquerors from the depths of time and space. Not to mention the fact that Wilbur hadn't bothered to hide his disdain for their mother, insane and decrepit though she might have been. Toward the end, before Wilbur even overstepped his bounds and got his just deserts, Lavinia had grown afraid of him. F'tagn felt for her. But every time he tried to reach out like a good son, his mom would run screaming from the house.

Like most humans who were zealous enough or nuts enough to look into the apocalypse issue, Wilbur had gotten a lot of it wrong. The drill was that great Cthulhu, the Oldest of Old Ones, was dreaming in the ocean, in his house in sunken R'lyeh, waiting for some clever folks to unearth certain forbidden books and spit out just the right incantations. That would open the cosmic gates and bring back the original rulers of the planet, the Great Old Ones. The entire posse would come roaring in to devastate the world and, of course, tear out the humans—including the incantors, which would make necromancy a pretty self-limiting career path.

Of course, this was all horseshit.

To call the Old Ones back, no mumbo-jumbo was needed. They had never left in the first place. Insanity and nightmare were their calling cards the world over, and they'd developed plenty of insidious ways to mess with human beings. And Cthulhu could pop in whenever he wanted, thank you very much. He was dreaming in R'lyeh, sure, but that was only because he was *exhausted*. In this aeon alone, he'd worked on the Black Plague, about three dozen major wars, and the Holocaust—and those little numbers had happened without Wilbur's or anyone else's help. Why eradicate the human race when it was much more fun to play with them, to instill terror and suffering that would really last? The Old Ones learned their lesson when they snuffed out the dinosaurs. So dumb. The old-timers told F'tagn that it had been very, very boring for several aeons afterward.

But that didn't prevent people like Wilbur from finding the old dusty tomes and trying to make sense of the ornate gobbledygook inside. The trouble was, these books only had small pieces of the picture and, more often than not, completely distorted ones. The one they called the *Necronomicon* in particular was fairly fashionable among the hooded-robe set, but it would embarrass them like crazy if they ever got a faithful translation. Like somebody just starting to learn a foreign language, these weekend wizards would say the most hilarious things. You wanted to finish their sentences for them and put them out of their misery. Wilbur himself spent more than one night up at the old stone altar on Sentinel Hill making this ludicrous pained face, clamping his hands to his temples like an idiot and screaming "YOG-SOTHOTH!" Which to Old Ones simply means, "How ya doing?" or, to a tentacled creature like himself, "How they hanging?" F'tagn had slipped into his native tongue when he was talking to the man lying before him; he realized he should have continued speaking in human, but the concentrated effort it required had just been too great.

This obsession of F'tagn's with human connection, which most of the Old Ones considered a debilitating flaw, meant that he had few friends. He didn't consider it a big loss: they lived in a dimension of their own, oddly shaped angles and all. These fuddy-duddies were so non-Euclidian! But he did get out socially. For example, there was the monster who had become close to a Boston painter named Richard Upton Pickman, even posed for him in his gallery. That was fascinating. F'tagn hung around it for a while, peppered it with questions about the relationship, but it became clear that there had been no real communication, that he was dealing with a beast who simply enjoyed seeing himself in pictures. It was a matter of ego, not empathy. Plus there was the upsetting fact that the model had been rendered while in the process of devouring a human being. No matter how many times he heard somebody say that they were just animals, F'tagn could never develop a taste for human flesh.

In general, F'tagn was shunned and mocked as a disappointment to his father, whom he hadn't seen in decades. No doubt, Pop was out haunting some other poor lonely hamlet, making a hundred eyes at another disturbed human waif. He had a swaggering new reputation to uphold, after all. But F'tagn got the definite idea that Pop had wanted to use his cross-dimensional ardor to improve his own standing, to suck up to Cthulhu. It would be the ultimate desecration, creating a new race of conquerors from the very wombs of their prey. And kicking it off with twins, to boot! But the splitting of the seed from beyond had unexpected effects—as perhaps might have been expected if anyone had bothered to reflect on it in the first place. Wilbur got the looks. F'tagn got the heart. And the Whateleys would go down in history as the single most dysfunctional family on earth—or under it.

F'tagn *was* the first of a new line of Old Ones. Just not the kind Pop had wanted.

F'tagn was so sorry. Sorry that his own kind made dinner out of people. That his very countenance was enough to cause a simple farmer to go mad. That Old Ones carried such dimensionist bigotry along with them every century of their lives. The world was a big place—big enough so that one day, just maybe, if they tried very hard, two species might walk hand in feeler, together at last in peace and harmony. Well, any change begins with a single act. And F'tagn Whateley was going to be the being who got the ball rolling.

A sharp clap of thunder disturbed F'tagn's reverie and he looked down at the poor dairyman before him. Thankfully, he had lost consciousness. It was tough to make out his features in the deepening gloom. F'tagn brushed his face gently with a tentacle, an action that would probably have returned Abner Brockman to sleep had he witnessed it. The silence that had ruled the late afternoon gave way to the excited cries of a flock of whippoorwills, and F'tagn looked up to the sky. The hellish birds had massed above the barren Devil's Hop Yard on the ridge, circling in frenzy. Then, on an invisible signal, they poured down the hill toward Dunwich.

F'tagn knew what that meant. They were trolling for the souls of those who were about to die.

Old Ones must be gathering, he realized, for a night of carnage.

He shambled down the hill as quickly as he could, and headed for the town square.

One of the many advantages Old Ones had over humans was that they could go among them unnoticed, moving at will *between* the dimensional spaces. You could never fool an animal, not even one as dumb and sweet as a cow, and more than one victim-to-be had made the mistake of ignoring a barking dog or hissing cat which sensed the mind-shattering presence of an Other. Besides, the way most of F'tagn's cousins looked, it would be impossible to sneak in anywhere without the protective coat of invisibility. He doubted that even Pop could have scored the way he had without sparing his paramour the family's good looks. So most OOs began their fun with auditory and olfactory components. They'd bang on walls and doors, and leave their spoor in the middle of a room—it didn't take long to develop a smell of decay so acute that it could fell a starving hyena. Another popular gag was to leave tentacular tracks in the dirt or snow and watch some superstitious outdoorsman babble with fear as he tried to explain. F'tagn didn't approve, but this was all fairly harmless stuff.

But Old Ones couldn't hide from each other. And when he arrived in town, F'tagn saw immediately why Dunwich had attracted so many whippoorwills. Though the locals may not have realized it yet, their fair township had just become host to a veritable

Double-O convention. For some reason, lots and lots of things were here.

The square was a riot of slithering, crawling, scuttling, shambling beings of every description imaginable, and some that probably weren't. The fishboys out of Innsmouth were here, the pyramid people of frozen Antarctica, the three-lobed burning eye, the goat with a thousand young, the jelly things, the fungous orbs from Vermont, the shining trapezohedron creatures, the blasphemous bee buzzers, the haunters of the Monolith, and many more. Even Pickman's model had bestirred itself to wander up from Boston for the occasion.

Of course. The occasion. All became clear.

Hallowmass.

It was the closest thing to a holy moment—had they dared to describe it as such—on the Old Ones' eternal calendar, the night when, as one, they reaffirmed their dominion over their weak, timid enemies in a gruesome orgy of gluttony and debauchery. They always fasted before the big day to make sure they were supremely hungry. F'tagn had once described the celebration to a scale-crusted frog-man as "the spring break from hell," but there was no response from the humorless batrachian.

This year, for Hallowmass, they had selected F'tagn's home town, right under his nose. Why did it not surprise him that he hadn't been invited?

The grisly conveneers massed against a tiny schoolhouse, its windows warm with golden firelight. Judging from the agitation of the whippoorwills, now piping as loudly as they could, there were quite a few people inside—no doubt terrified by the cacophony of noises outside and a nose-burning aroma beyond description, so pungent that it threatened to beat down the door all by itself.

F'tagn could hear wails through the walls, and was dismayed to make out the cries of children among them.

The front flank moved toward the door, as much in unison as their varying methods of locomotion would allow. F'tagn knew what would follow. The famished mob would take corporeal form and visit an unspeakable fate upon those inside—keeping them alive as long as they possibly could. Dunwich would become an abattoir, and augment its reputation as a haunted, doomed spot for years to come.

F'tagn screwed together his courage and slithered past the leading edge, his back to the door. The creatures halted, puzzled. Most of them had never met F'tagn before, and their antennae, feelers, and eye-stalks sent them mixed signals. The stench of human was definitely upon this one, but he looked as much like an Old One as did the most horrific of the Hallowmass revelers.

Panting with hunger and anticipation, a monkey-crab feinted toward F'tagn with his pincers and scampered back, but he held fast. The crowd moved inexorably closer, and F'tagn readied his most threatening infra-bass roar. He had no chance against so many, but maybe they would think twice about harming one of their own. If that was, in fact, how they regarded him.

Three pink, gelatinous rats, each the size of a large cat, ran in to attack. F'tagn let loose his howl and swiped at them with a tentacle, and they leaped back toward the crowd. But it was already so close that there was no room to retreat. As the front rank re-coiled from F'tagn's aria of aggression, they were pitched over by the body mass pressing in, and the rats took the full weight. Tiny bones cracked and the hellish rodents squealed in mortal pain. But what really turned the tide was the delicious iron smell of blood.

This was too much for the carnivores in the mob, which was just about everybody. Those closest to the rats literally fell on them and began dining, but they had to compete with a host of maddened rivals made delirious by the scent. One scratching, slicing fight led to another, and soon interdimensional blood was flowing all over the square as the Hallowmass convention proceeded to feed upon itself. It was the most horrible sight F'tagn had ever seen—but they had completely forgotten about the people in the building.

Upstairs, the whippoorwills had no idea what to do. Prepared to capture human souls from the schoolhouse, they were thrown into pandemonium. Without direction or purpose, they flew around at random, keening their annoying piping sounds and smashing into each other at full speed—only to become main courses themselves as they descended upon the grasping mob.

Within a few minutes, the crowd had lessened by more than half, and it was evident where the excess had gone. Happy, finally-sated Old Ones exchanged pleasantries, made signs of mutual respect in the limited number of physical ways that they could manage, and promised to meet again next year. Only a few malcontents—like Pickman's model, who had, not unexpectedly, survived—complained about the lack of human on the menu; many more raved over the exciting, unexpected way that the meal had been served. It was clear that this event would be one of those legendary stories told to jealous Old Ones who had had the misfortune to be elsewhere, for eons to come.

F'tagn leaned back against the door, inside which

the schoolroom had gone completely silent, what with all the piping and clawing and chewing. Maybe he hadn't communicated with his human relatives. But he had saved them from a fate they would be better off not knowing about. F'tagn was happy. He'd started something between Old Ones and humans. Maybe even gone a small way toward affecting the Old One diet! He was just starting to plan what to do next, when . . .

. . . F'tagn Whateley disappeared from the spot, and from Dunwich, forever.

A long time must have passed, for F'tagn was groggy when he awoke in a great city of granite and marble, of monoliths and sepulchres. And water. Lots of water in this city. There was only one place it could be.

R'lyeh. Cthulhu's undersea crib.

F'tagn started to get up, but his human-face torso was chained to a stone tablet and each tentacle was restrained. He had to shut all his eyes when he pulled against the chain.

The Hallowmass episode had gotten back to the boss somehow. How could it not? He sighed. Pop's experiment with earthly union had produced a mutant. And evidently it hadn't amused the big guy—F'tagn was responsible for too many dead and digested Old Ones. Not to mention disturbing a long Cthulhuian dream.

The leader had spoken. He'd pulled the plug. F'tagn was out of commission.

Well, so be it. Maybe R'lyeh was the right place for him now. Maybe he might even get to meet the great thing. Maybe talk to him. Maybe the next time Cthulhu woke up and rubbed his many eyes, they could reason together. Plan a new future for the dimension that gave F'tagn birth.

After all, stranger things had happened. Way, *way* stranger.

And besides, F'tagn had aeons to think about it.

REDEEMED

by Allen C. Kupfer

Allen C. Kupfer teaches literature and film study at Nassau Community College. An expert on a wide variety of subjects ranging from the life of Jonathan Swift to the spaghetti western, his previously published works include the western *Double Crossfire* and short stories in such anthologies as *Realms of Magic* and *Oceans of Magic*.

*T*HEY enter. The doors open. Perhaps it won't be long now. But why do they linger outside? They do not want me to hear.

"Father Bartolomeo, our subject is within. There is no question but that the man is possessed. Thank God you arrived quickly."

But I do hear. I can hear.

"The subject's name is Robert Concetta. We found him strangling his wife. Father Medina is inside with him."

The door opens. Hurry, please! I cannot tolerate this much longer. The agony increases by the second. The servant of God named Bartolomeo enters holding a silver cross and a black bag. They stare at Concetta. They stare at Concetta.

"Monsignor Laughlin, the subject seems subdued

at the moment. He sits tied to the chair almost peacefully."

"So I see, Father. There has been a change in him."

The priest faces this way, looks not at me but at him.

"Father Medina, has anything occurred that you should tell us about?"

Yes. Yes, indeed. You should know about this.

Medina's open eyes drip blood. The eyes sting.

"Jesus Christ!" *Medina cries.* "Damn it! Help me."

"The demon has entered the body of Father Medina," *Bartolomeo says.* "We must act immediately."

Bartolomeo opens his bag and removes a book. He reads from it. The words are Latin and strangely familiar.

"Christ!" *Medina wails.* "Stop, Father!"

Yes, the words burn. With each recitation of the words "Corpus Christi" a jolt of pain shoots through me.

"Anoint him," *Bartolomeo orders, and Monsignor Laughlin sprinkles holy water. Each drop sears the skin and red welts form on the face. The incantations, the prayers, continue loudly, but they seem distant, as if said from miles away. As the water seeps its way under the eyelids, the pupils widen and allow horrifying visions. Light . . . more light than I have ever seen. It is terrifying.*

"Stop it, stop it!" *Medina pleads.* "I can't stand it."

Laughlin answers, "Bear it, man! Your faith will help you."

With a sudden jolt, Medina's hands circle Laughlin's throat. Bartolomeo presses his crucifix onto Medina's forehead. The body trembles violently, the pain surges through him, and finally the hands relax their grip on the throat. Medina falls to the ground, barely conscious.

From the floor I see the two priests withdraw from the room, taking Concetta with them. Concetta may go. He is so . . . average. Medina, on the other hand, is not. Medina is a priest. The exorcist will put more effort into saving Medina.

They have gone. I hear the door locked from without. As if a door could hold me! As if anything could hold me if I did not want to be held.

They will be back soon. When they return, they will have renewed strength and more efficient weaponry. They will attack with full strength. They will rescue one of their own, as worthless as he is.

I await their return. I have waited eternities. I welcome their return.

I recall no birth, no creation. I simply was. And from the dawn of my consciousness eons ago I have dwelled in the realm of chaos and evil. The blind poet Milton centuries ago wrote of Satan and his followers. I was among them. I, too, was cast out of heaven to dwell in the darkness, to organize chaos into a force of evil. I have been a part of all evils in this world. I have caused heartbreak, misery, destruction, cataclysm. I have infected humankind since the beginning. I have thrived on man's confusion, gloried in his misfortune, delighted in his calamity.

On occasion, the forces of God have tried to stop me. These men—clerics of various religions—have at times made me uncomfortable, sometimes to the point where I had to flee; but I am indestructible. I am no man. God himself decreed that this should be so. I am above man. I am superior. And I cannot be destroyed by any man as long as my purpose and my drive are within me.

Purpose. For eternities I gave no thought to purpose. I did what I did because it was my nature to do so. I never attempted to contemplate my purpose. Passion dominated my soul, not reason. What need did I have of reason? I have been the maker of human misery.

But I have lately contemplated my existence. What is my purpose? What will be my reward? Even the humans question the purpose of their lives, and many search for it

*until their deaths. They seek the reward of God's presence
after their lives have ended. Many achieve it; more do not.
I have seen to that. But why? Is it my lot in the universe
simply to live in opposition to God? Why? After all this
time . . . I question why.*

*I once saw myself as a righteous revolutionary. And for
ages I have fought the war against the Holy Angels and
God himself, reveling in my victories.*

*Today, though, I feel lost and alone. There was once a
brotherhood of sorts in the Darkness; that brotherhood
means nothing to me now. It is a false alliance. It is not
in the nature of any citizen of hell to be any other citizen's
"brother." It is a sham.*

*I must admit I still feel great satisfaction in bringing a
pathetic human "sinner" down. That is why I have over-
thrown Medina's being. Concetta was basically an average
man. That is why I abandoned his body. Medina, on the
contrary, is a wretch, the kind of human scum easily taken
down. A priest he may be, but I—and God too, I must
assume—know him for what he really is: a faithless hypo-
crite, a thief, and a child molester. His soul all but wel-
comed me, although he doesn't realize it. True to my
demonic sensibilities, it gives me great pleasure to possess him.*

*At least I thought it was true to my demonic sensibil-
ities.*

*But am I not describing a sense of justice? Will not the
sinner be punished? Isn't that as God stated it should be?
And does that not make me a servant of God of sorts?*

So what is my purpose? To serve God?

*I have been living in darkness, a darkness I could never
have imagined. A darkness of the intellect. I have come to
my senses. And out of the darkness I have come, as is
said, to see the light.*

*I see that my purpose in existence is actually God's
purpose. So I have no real purpose for my deeds. With the*

*loss of purpose, I have lost my drive. Without them, I have
less than the mere mortals.*

That is why I await you, exorcist. I await you.

The priests return. They are joined by two others,
dressed in their priestly attire. From this corner of the
room I notice that they encircle Bartolomeo as he reads
from his prayerbook.One splashes me with holy water. It
stings terribly.

"Help me," *emanates from Medina's throat.*

The monsignor responds, "Have faith, Nicholas. We
will save you."

Bartolomeo continues with his monotonous prayer. The
two new priests approach Medina, and each holds one of
his arms in order to restrain him. I can feel the clammy
wetness of the palms of their hands as well.

"What the hell are you going to do to me?" *Medina
shrieks.* "Don't hurt me."

Hurt me, I think to myself. Hurt me.

"We renounce thee, Satan!" *says Bartolomeo.*

"I'm scared, Laughlin," *Medina says.*

I renounce thee, Satan.

Suddenly the room is full of incense. Medina's head is
drenched with holy water in what I suppose is a reen-
actment of baptism. The body shakes furiously. I shake
furiously.

Medina vomits, then cries, "You sons of bitches,
you're goddamn hurting me!! You're killing me!!"

You're saving me, I think.

Laughlin whispers something to Bartolomeo. The exorcist thinks for a moment, then says in agreement, "You're
right. We cannot put Father Medina through this."

The other two priests release Medina's arms. They will
withdraw again. They will stop the exorcism.

That CANNOT happen.

I withdraw from Medina. His eyes turn up into his

head, he shudders, he drops unconscious to the ground. Perhaps this experience will change him, will . . . reform him. Perhaps not. It is no concern of mine.

The priests stare at me in horror. I am abominable to them. They look at me in awe. They are confused, it seems.

"TAKE ME," *I roar at them.*

They continue to stare incredulously.

"RAVAGE ME," *I cry. I move toward them.*

One of the priests hurls a crucifix at me. It touches my hide and sticks to me like a magnet. I have made myself flesh, and the crucifix burns into my hide. I roar in joyous pain.

"In Jesus' name, I order you back to the darkness of hell," *Bartolomeo says.*

"IMPRISON ME," *I bellow.*

Bartolomeo's eyes study me, seemingly puzzled at the words.

"The demon is taunting us," *Laughlin says.*

But Bartolomeo does not respond to him. He is trying to recall.

I expand my presence so that I fill half the room. The priests cower.

"It is attacking!" *one of the other clerics cries. They move toward the door to escape. All but Bartolomeo, who remains unmoved.*

I am reaching him. If I speak directly—if I simply relate my desire to the priest, I will incur the wrath of the Accursed One. He CAN destroy me. Therefore, I must be indirect.

Loudly, I say, "Break . . . blow . . . burn . . ."

Bartolomeo's eyes widen. He knows. I have reached him.

"Father, we must leave," *Laughlin says.* "Your safety must come first."

"No," *he answers.* "I know what must be done." *He points to Medina, who is still unconscious on the floor.* "Take him and get out."

"I will not leave you alone in here with that . . ."

"Get out," Bartolomeo repeats emphatically. "I know what must be done."

The others leave. I am alone with Bartolomeo. He studies me. He is a brave man. Already I can feel myself deteriorating. I am decomposing. I am ceasing to be what I am. It is agonizing. Pain racks my being. My physical self is bleeding. Pustules form on my hide and break open. Putrid pus drips from my pores.

Does the Prince of Darkness know what I do now? Is he trying to destroy me?

Hurry, priest, HURRY!

I utter rushed words, though I say them carefully so that they will clearly be understood. "BATTER MY HEART . . ."

Bartolomeo responds ". . . three-personed God."

I lower my body to him. He reaches into his black bag and withdraws a handful of small white wafers.

His hand touches his forehead, then his chest, then each shoulder.

I crouch lower. As I do, the now-brittle flesh on my back cracks open. Filth pours out.

Bartolomeo looks at me with momentary uncertainty.

THIS IS NO TIME FOR DOUBT. THIS IS NO TIME FOR HESITATION. HURRY! SOON I WILL BE LOST!

I cry out in agony.

The priest presses a Holy Host onto my head between what earthly artists have always depicted as horns. The intense heat of the Host spreads throughout my head and into my eyes. Then he presses one into my chest. It, too, burns. Quickly, he places one on each of my shoulders.

I have the cross upon me. I scream out in pain, in awe, in agony . . . in ecstasy!

The other priests hear. They open the door in fear for Bartolomeo's life.

I am still conscious. I still exist. I still throb in pain. I am immobile.

My eyes drip not tears but some foul liquid. Yet they are tears.

"God is miraculous," *Bartolomeo tells the others.* "We have not exorcized a demon. We have **saved** him."

Pain. Not torment. Pain. The ecstatic pain of the martyrs. Now I know.

"Father, how do you know?" *Laughlin asks, neither fully understanding nor believing.*

Bartolomeo explains. "He was quoting from John Donne's 'Holy Sonnet Fourteen.' "

"Why would it do that? What does it mean?"

"It is a sonnet . . . a prayer, more precisely . . . spoken by a sinner begging for violent action to be taken against him in order to prevent him from sinning any further."

Bartolomeo. Thank you.

" 'Batter my heart, three-personed God' . . . it begins," *Bartolomeo continues.*

"It ends with the lines 'Take me to you, imprison me, for I/Except you enthrall me, never shall be free;/Nor ever chaste, except you ravage me."

Bartolomeo speaks still. The others listen, not sure whether to believe. I approach a type of death. I cannot move. I dissipate. I become less corporeal. The pain is torturous.

But a light I have never experienced before is . . . is it within me? I am dying.

I do so gladly. I shall be made anew.

What is this?

I am not who I was.

I am . . .

Tanya Huff

The Finest in Fantasy

To Order Call: 1-800-788-6262

DAW 21

MICHELLE WEST

The *Sun Sword* Novels

"Intriguing" — *Locus*
"Compelling" — *Romantic Times*

and don't miss:

The Sacred Hunt

To Order Call: 1-800-788-6262

DAW 41

Tad Williams

THE WAR OF THE FLOWERS

"A masterpiece of fairytale worldbuilding."
—*Locus*

"Williams's imagination is boundless."
—*Publishers Weekly*
(Starred Review)

"A great introduction to an accomplished
and ambitious fantasist."
—*San Francisco Chronicle*

"An addictive world ... masterfully plays
with the tropes and traditions of
generations of fantasy writers."
—*Salon*

"A very elaborate and fully realized setting
for adventure, intrigue, and more
than an occasional chill."
—*Science Fiction Chronicle*

0-7564-0135-6

To Order Call: 1-800-788-6262

DAW 45

Curt Benjamin

Seven Brothers

"Rousing fantasy adventure."
—*Publishers Weekly*

Llesho, the youngest prince of Thebin, was only seven
when the Harn invaded, deposing and murdering his
family and selling the boy into slavery. On Pearl Island,
he was trained as a diver—until a vision changed his life
completely. The spirit of his long-dead teacher revealed
the truth about Llesho's family—his brothers were alive,
but enslaved, living in distant lands. Now, to free his
brothers, and himself, Llesho must become a gladiator.
And he must go face to face with sorcerers...and gods.

Book One:
THE PRINCE OF SHADOWS   0-7564-0054-6
Book Two:
THE PRINCE OF DREAMS   0-7564-0114-3
Book Three:
THE GATES OF HEAVEN   0-7564-0156-9
(hardcover)

To Order Call: 1-800-788-6262

DAW 4

Jude Fisher
Sorcery Rising

*"This tale of magic, mystery, intrigue and feud works well,
and the characters are so convincing (including a strong
and appealing female lead) that I can't wait to read the
next installment."* —The London Times

Katla Aransen, master knife-maker from the island
nation of Eyra, has come to her first Allfair, the great
gathering of the nations of Elda. Proud to the point of
arrogance, rebelliously willful and strong-minded, yet
naive about religious fanaticism, Katla secretly climbs
the bitterly contested holy mount that stands above the
plain of the Allfair. Unfortunately, her "sacrilege" is witnessed by elders of the Istrian nation, who swear to
catch this blasphemous young woman and put her to
death. And before the Allfair is over, forces will be set in
motion which will threaten every country, every people,
and perhaps change the entire face of Elda forever.

0-7564-0083-X

To Order Call: 1-800-788-6262

Kristen Britain

GREEN RIDER

As Karigan G'ladheon, on the run from school, makes her way through the deep forest, a galloping horse plunges out of the brush, its rider impaled by two black arrows. With his dying breath, he tells her he is a Green Rider, one of the king's special messengers. Giving her his green coat with its symbolic brooch of office, he makes Karigan swear to deliver the message he was carrying. Pursued by unknown assassins, following a path only the horse seems to know, Karigan finds herself thrust into in a world of danger and complex magic....   0-88677-858-1

FIRST RIDER'S CALL

With evil forces once again at large in the kingdom and with the messenger service depleted and weakened, can Karigan reach through the walls of time to get help from the First Rider, a woman dead for a millennium?   0-7564-0209-3

To Order Call: 1-800-788-6262